The Office of Desire

Also by Martha Moody

Best Friends

THE OFFICE

of *Desire*

MARTHA MOODY

Riverhead Books

a member of Penguin Group (USA) Inc.

New York   2007

RIVERHEAD BOOKS
Published by the Penguin Group
Penguin Group (USA) Inc., 375 Hudson Street, New York, New York 10014, USA • Penguin Group
(Canada), 90 Eglinton Avenue East, Suite 700, Toronto, Ontario M4P 2Y3, Canada (a division of Pearson
Penguin Canada Inc.) • Penguin Books Ltd, 80 Strand, London WC2R 0RL, England • Penguin Ireland,
25 St Stephen's Green, Dublin 2, Ireland (a division of Penguin Books Ltd) • Penguin Group (Australia),
250 Camberwell Road, Camberwell, Victoria 3124, Australia (a division of Pearson Australia Group
Pty Ltd) • Penguin Books India Pvt Ltd, 11 Community Centre, Panchsheel Park, New Delhi–110 017,
India • Penguin Group (NZ), 67 Apollo Drive, Rosedale, North Shore 0745, Auckland, New Zealand
(a division of Pearson New Zealand Ltd) • Penguin Books (South Africa) (Pty) Ltd, 24 Sturdee Avenue,
Rosebank, Johannesburg 2196, South Africa

Penguin Books Ltd, Registered Offices:
80 Strand, London WC2R 0RL, England

Lyrics from "Lovesong," by Robert J. Smith, Simon Gallup, Laurence Tolhurst, Paul S. Thompson,
and Roger O'Donnell, copyright © 1990 Fiction Songs (PRS), are used by permission.

Library of Congress Cataloging-in-Publication Data

Moody, Martha.
    The office of desire / Martha Moody.
        p.   cm.
    ISBN 978-1-59448-949-5
    1. Medical offices—Fiction.   2. Interpersonal relations—Fiction.   3. Ohio—Fiction.   I. Title.
PS3563.O553O45   2007   2007017249
813'.54—dc22

Printed in the United States of America
10 9 8 7 6 5 4 3 2 1

Book design by Meighan Cavanaugh

In memory of my father,

John Gardner (Jack) Moody

1917–1994

The Office of Desire

Whenever I'm alone with you,

You make me feel like I am home again . . .

You make me feel like I am whole again.

—The Cure, "Lovesong"

CAROLINE

Brice once said that if you understood our office, you understood the world. I thought that was extreme, the sort of thing you'd expect from a guy who'd show up some mornings and say, "My mother was drinking my blood again last night." But now that our office is gone I see things differently. I might even agree with him, on certain evenings when my leg aches and the howlers are going at it and I can't for the life of me settle back to sleep.

At the height of his raving—that is, after things had gone south with Jesse—Brice said our office was a hive of greed and lust and tenderness, held aloft by ("Who's that guy that holds up the world? Ajax?") the twin arms of pain and power.

See what I mean? Too much. The sort of thing I used to think driving home from a sad movie or when I was alone at a football game and everyone but me seemed to have friends. But that was Brice. I miss him. I miss everyone, but especially Brice.

Now that I'm in another life. Another country.

There were three employees: Alicia the nurse, Brice the money guy and manager, and me, Caroline, the "über-receptionist," as the doctors always called me. Brice referred to us as the office ABCs. It was unusual for a busy two-doctor internal medicine practice to have only three employees, but since we sent our claim tickets to a billing service for collections and used the hospital lab for most of our testing, three employees in our office were plenty. We worked together, and each of us was flexible. I answered the phones and set up referrals and did scheduling, and Alicia took the patients to the exam rooms and phoned patients back to answer questions, while Brice did payroll and dealt with insurance preauthorizations and problems and filled in whenever Alicia or I needed help.

We were happy. I remember back in '97 when I flew to Atlanta for my high school boyfriend's wedding. Alicia and Brice thought I was crazy. "She thinks he's going to look up the aisle and say, 'Caroline, is it really you? Let's run away,' " Alicia said.

"Maybe she's planning to go with them on their honeymoon," Brice said, "hand in hand in hand."

Our office was a frame one-story across the street from the Midburg Mall. A converted house near a mall in a medium-size Ohio city—you can't get more ordinary than that. Brice used to say that General Foods should test-screen their products in our waiting room. One of our elderly patients remembered when the place was a sixties ranch house (the basement still had that rectangle), before the homeowners improved it by adding a family room that jutted into the backyard. Zoning changed when the mall was built, and the house was snapped up by a dentist, who shelled out the place and reconfigured it with a lobby and a staff area and exam rooms, tacking on a second addition (an X-ray suite) in the front. In a satellite photo, our office building would have looked like a capital T. The upper bar of the T, perpendicular to the road, held the exam rooms, while the stem of the T contained the lobby and the business office. Patients walked from the parking lot in back around to the front door.

When our docs bought the place they added doors to the exam rooms (dental offices don't need them), changed part of the X-ray suite into Dr. Strub's private office (Dr. Markowitz took the former dentist's office, in the back), split the crown and root canal room into an exam room, break room, and bathroom, put in dusk blue industrial carpeting, and repainted the mint green walls cream. Dr. Strub's then-wife picked out the lobby furniture and art. The chairs were upholstered in floral prints and the paintings were fuzzy gardens and bright seascapes. Around Christmas, because of the mall traffic, you couldn't turn left out of our parking lot, but our patients knew to turn right and circle the block. We were worth the trouble, they said.

A few years ago, the only disagreement between staff and bosses was what we thought of our basement, where we kept our records. Alicia and Brice and I said the basement was damp and horrible—a *Night of the Living Dead* basement, as Brice put it. The docs said, What are you talking about? We put in that portable dehumidifier and it's fine. Of course, they didn't have to go down there. At the bottom of the steps the metal cabinets that held the charts sat on a remnant of the dusk blue carpet from upstairs, which masked the gray-painted cement floor. On this side of the basement, there was wood paneling on the walls. The far side of the basement was unfinished and not closed off, so that you looked straight from chart racks into dimness. Its only decoration was a white pegboard hung with an assortment of tools: a hammer, a wrench, a pair of pliers, and, most impressively, a wicked-looking ax with a huge handle, the implement Brice used two or three times each winter to chip ice off our back entrance steps, because our roof dumped water directly on the landing, and salt alone didn't work.

Brice spent his last days in the unfinished part of this basement, although none of us knew it at the time.

"Do you think I'm a normal person, Caroline?" Brice asked me once a few years before, something plaintive in his voice. I studied him in surprise. He was attractive, slight, with thick dark curly hair, blue eyes, and pale, lightly freckled skin. An Irish look, I thought. Skin that was sensitive to sunburn and rashes.

It was lunchtime, and we were sitting in the linoleum-floored break room eating sandwiches we'd packed from home. Alicia wasn't with us that day, probably because she had some son-of-hers business going on (teacher conference, orthodontist visit). For some reason Brice and I were were talking about how the docs always said "healthy" instead of "normal." A priest might call someone normal, or a psychiatrist, but not our Drs. Markowitz and Strub.

"As normal as I am," I said, whacking my fake leg (I lost the real one to cancer at age seventeen) against the table leg, because both of us were unattached (although he had his mother) and work-obsessed and what some people might refer to as odd. I spent my free time reading books and hanging out with whatever boyfriend I had at the moment; Brice spent his watching movies.

Brice said, "Well, *that* makes me feel better."

My leg isn't wooden, by the way. Modern prostheses aren't. It's made of metal and plastic and has a heft to it, like a real leg. It could hurt you.

I'm not much of an observer. I see the big picture, sure—life, death, survival—but, other than the physical characteristics of certain men (Evan, for example, I can still describe down to his toenails), I miss a lot of detail. There are things about other people of which I am totally unaware. I was astonished, for example, when Alicia said that she was worried about the sort of weird philosophers her son was reading for the debate team. You're afraid of ideas? I thought. You're afraid of what Jesse *reads*? But of course she was, and maybe rightly as it turned out.

I remember the first shipment we got of individually wrapped alcohol pads that were clearly generic, that said ALCOHOL PAD in big black letters. It was the winter of 2002–2003, just after Dr. Strub's divorce became final, when he was spending a spooky amount of time in the office, staying late at his desk to eat Chinese delivery food straight from the carton. It was when all of a sudden everyone in the government was talking about Saddam Hussein and Iraq and UN weapons inspectors, a time when normally Dr. Markowitz would be reminding Dr. Strub about the foolishness of rash action and the inconvenient but essential value of free speech, when Dr. Strub would be railing about 9/11 and American values and his villainess of choice, Hillary Clinton. That winter, though, Dr. Markowitz trod gently, about politics and everything else—he didn't have the heart, he told me, to torment his partner with Bushisms.

A lot happened in the news, actually, in the time our office fell apart. There was the Iraq invasion ("At least that's over," I remember Dr. Markowitz saying the day after the TV showed people knocking down Saddam Hussein's statue); there were photos of cheerful young women who resembled the daughters of our patients pointing at naked Iraqi men in Abu Ghraib prison; there were—for philosophical reasons, apparently—planes and trains and buses blown up in Russia and Spain and (of course) Israel; there was John Kerry running against George Bush for the presidency. A lot went on, but I'm not sure we even noticed it. Our own traumas were too big to let the world's traumas in. In that way, I suppose, we were lucky. Oblivion could be a sort of blessing.

"Cost savings thirty-five cents per hundred," Brice said cheerfully that winter, flicking an alcohol pad packet across my desk, while Alicia, behind me, made a comment about generic beer getting her as drunk as Bud. "Is that enough to care about?" I said to Brice, and Brice said, "But of course!" in his airy, John Malkovich–inspired way. Not long after this, Brice unpacked a new batch of envelopes I was supposed to stamp with the return address myself—a ridiculous waste of time, but Brice said Dr. Strub insisted that this way was fifty-five percent cheaper. It was also about this time that I noticed Dr. Strub saying Alicia's name in a new way: A-leee-sha, as if he wanted the name in his mouth as long as possible. And Alicia had started showing up with her hair loose instead of in a ponytail, wearing white uniform dresses and white nylons instead of scrubs, with a new pair of shoes that had a Mary Jane strap. Then Dr. Markowitz was standing at the entrance to the staff area staring into space, before striding quickly toward Brice's office. "Have you noticed Will and Alicia?" I heard him say as he shut the door.

"She's such a slut!" Brice said later that day about Alicia. He sounded anguished. "That's what kills me: I never thought she could be such a slut." I was surprised, because it was almost as if Alicia had betrayed him, when for years he'd talked about his friend Iris with whom he went to movies and flea markets, referring to her at times as "my girlfriend," although she looked like one of those Louise Brooks lesbians to me.

Was it paradise, that office? It wouldn't have looked that way, with the stained trail of carpet leading from the front door into the first chairs of our lobby, and the dent made by the doorknob in the wall in exam room 3. But thinking about the old days there now makes me want to weep. We took turns dealing with scary Mr. Esposito, our patient in waste management whose company's name kept bobbing up like a dead fish in the local paper. There was never any fighting about who brought back the patients, or whether Brice and I were competent to check a blood pressure (technically, we didn't have the training for it), or who was wasteful and overexuberant in unwinding the exam table paper. Concordance—there's a word. We ABCs formed a sort of concordance, and I suppose it's no surprise that the thing that first discorded us was lust.

~

It must have been the February of that winter. There'd been snow that morning and the day's patients were arriving in the waiting room in boots and puffy coats. I was alone in the break room finishing my turkey and cheese sandwich, and I knew that Brice was just outside the break room door lying in wait for Alicia.

When patients came into our waiting room, the wall hiding the business office was to their right, and through a sliding window in that wall they could see me. Alicia sat with her back to mine, her desk facing the outside wall. Brice's office, an old bathroom, jutted out from the wall to Alicia's left, and his door opened into a vestibule facing the back door, where all of us came in. The break room was on the opposite side of the building, between two exam rooms, so where Brice was standing now was way out of his area.

Alicia burst through the break room door, Brice trailing her. "So, what are you and Dr. Strub up to?" Brice said, stuffing his hands in his pants pockets in a fake casual way as Alicia stopped and dipped quickly to open the small refrigerator, her brown hair fanning her shoulders.

"Up to?" Alicia echoed. Our break room was tiny, smaller even than Brice's office. We had a round table with three chairs, no windows, and a clock from a pharmaceutical company hanging on the wall. The doctors ate lunch, when they ate it, in their private offices at the ends of the hall.

"Is there a relationship besides a professional one?"

Alicia's right hand hovered above several yogurts. She frowned, said, "Coffee—I need the energy," and pulled out a container. "Of course there is," she said, standing and looking straight at Brice. Brice was short, and they were almost eye to eye. "We're friends."

Brice's gaze went distant; he pursed his lips and nodded like a bobble-head doll.

"Is friendship illegal now?" Alicia asked, snapping off the yogurt's lid. "For two single people, friendship is forbidden?" She glanced my way and made a bothered face.

Brice said, "This is your job, you know."

"I've been here six years and I've never gotten less than a superior evaluation. I've gotten a merit raise every year."

"Why would you want to jeopardize that record?"

They were talking so seriously. They were saying "superior" and "merit" and "jeopardize," as if our evaluations weren't tables Dr. Strub had Xeroxed from some management textbook and completed with check marks each January. The three of us always got superiors. Anything different, we would have had to punish Dr. Strub. Anything different, we would have been devastated.

I popped the last piece of sandwich in my mouth, stuffed my garbage in my lunch bag, and stood up to leave. I'd spent seven minutes eating, although I'd declare I'd taken a break for half an hour. Did I ever feel taken advantage of, hurrying back to work on my own time? No, I never did. "I should warn you," Brice was saying, "Dr. Markowitz came to my office this morning to ask about you and Dr. Strub."

"So?" Alicia looked at Brice, pulled a plastic spoon out of the pocket of her white dress, and started stirring her yogurt.

"He's worried it could affect your job performance. I told him it didn't, but—"

"Jesus Christ." The plastic spoon that Al was using broke, and she stuck her fingers in the yogurt tub to pull out the pieces.

Brice made a face and looked away. "You're not going to eat that now, are you?" he said.

"Excuse me?" I said, waving my hand back and forth to part them, but neither seemed to hear me.

"Sure I am," Alicia said, tossing the shards of spoon dangerously close to Brice and into the trash. She licked her fingers. "I'm hungry."

Brice gave a little shiver. "I don't know why I'm talking to you about matters of discretion."

"Excuse me?" I said again. Alicia and Brice were blocking the door. "Let me out?"

"Oh, is how I eat my yogurt a moral issue?"

All the years Alicia and Brice had worked together, they were fine. They'd laughed hundreds of times about Brice's $2,000 paper cut (he'd passed out at the sight of his own blood, which led to an ambulance and the ER). They'd psychoanalyzed his nutty mother almost daily, and when he talked on the phone with his worthless plumber (typical of his mother not to deal with this, although she was at home all day), Alicia stood beside Brice and made sure he insisted on a replacement tank, actually grabbing the phone and introducing herself as Brice's angry sister. Brice brought Alicia Kit Kat bars that he slipped into the top drawer of her desk (he brought me Reese's Peanut Butter Cups), and every birthday gave Alicia silly earrings (little cows, dangling bikinis, spooky Mayan faces), and called her Our Alluring Alicia to the old-man patients. But all the goodwill between them disappeared with that cup of yogurt. I saw it happen.

"I'm trying to warn you," Brice said. "I'm trying to be your friend."

"Friend?" Alicia said. "Is that allowed?"

"Let me out, guys," I said, pushing my way through.

HAP MARKOWITZ

Dr. Will Strub—my medical partner, my longtime friend—said, "Alicia and I didn't *plan* this, Hap." Will and I had both known Alicia for years. Which one of us hired her? What year? Neither of us remembered. Maybe we did her interview together. A good, fun girl, someone with ambition, someone whose parents and siblings were missing teeth but who saved up to buy herself and her son braces. Someone who had learned not to say "ain't" or "he don't." Once Will had told his patient Ed Kimble, who drove his own hauler, that he should ask her out. Ed never did, and even if he had, I'm sure she would've said no. Will underestimated her: she wasn't going to be interested in some trucker.

She was very attentive to her kid. She came to us from the hospital—took a pay cut—because working in our office she could have every night and weekend free for Jesse. By the time she started working for us she already had him reading online encyclopedias and writing reports for school with titles like "The Tragedy of Our War in Vietnam." He was nine. Once I remember him after office hours sitting in Caroline's front-desk chair explaining Bernoulli's principle— which I probably did learn, once—while his mother stocked the exam rooms. The only times Alicia requested off were days she needed to go talk to some teacher. "How's Mama Hen?" Will would say. "How's the baby rooster? He spelling 'borborygmi' yet?"

It started back in October, Will told me that February, on one of those blue-sky, orange-leaf days that always show up on wall calendars.

He'd finished his charts ("Hap-ster," he liked to tell me, "this documentation shit is hell") and was waiting for the mall traffic to die down, just wandering up and down the hall outside his office, trying to keep his promise not to call up Mr. Chin's for food. His divorce was almost final, everything over but the signing. All of a sudden Will noticed a splotch on the beige counter in exam room 3—he must have turned a note over before the ink was dry—and he rubbed at it with a paper towel but nothing changed. It was late, after seven, and Alicia was standing beside her desk with her jean jacket on over her scrubs, ready to leave. She was often the staff person who left last, the person who kept things in order.

"Is there some spot remover somewhere?" Will said. "Comet or something?"

"There's some spray stuff under the sinks," Alicia said. "What do you need it for?" Will told her, and she followed his finger down the hall into the room. "It should be in here," she said, bending over the cabinet under the sink, and apparently the spray stuff wasn't visible right away, and she kept moving things around to search, Will a couple of feet behind her, and it was just that, he said, that beautiful ass in the air, and kaboom, he was besotted. Besotted, he said. Insane. Her ass was like some flower, gorgeous and globular and clefted. He traced its shape with his hands in the air for me, his face so avidly lascivious I had to look away.

He didn't rush things, oh no. It took a month until he got inside her. Back when he was studly—remember?—that's how he did things. Some time for things to build. Some mornings he stood staring in the closet, thinking about which shirts Alicia had admired. Some evenings they both stayed on late, until Will said, "I've got to go," and watched her hide her disappointment. Doing Pap smears, all he was aware of was the smell of her beside him. Hadn't I noticed how before Alicia had sometimes been moody in the office, but the last few months she acted happy all the time?

There was a reason guys our age liked younger women, Will said. We were in our primes, and they were reaching theirs. You didn't realize, Will said, what loss of collagen did to an older woman's skin. Young flesh had a distinct quality. Young flesh was alive. There was no sin in noticing this. "Even you'd admit it," Will said.

Will had married Harriet, he said now, because it was the path of least resistance. At the time all the other unmarried residents were marrying, and Janis and I had just celebrated our second anniversary. But Will and Harriet's marriage was never right. As the years passed, even Harriet saw how ill-matched she and Will were, until her self-described instinct for spiritual clarity (!) led her to her very own charlatan, the frozen food heir who did shamanistic healing (she thought he was sublime, he found her practical). Will wanted at least one of his daughters to go into medicine, but when Sarah got mired in premed, Will realized that the best thing he could do is tell her, Sarah, do what you want. She ended up as a massage therapist, and Chloe, her big sister, taught mentally challenged kids in an elementary school near Dallas. They were happy now, Will said. They followed their dreams. Why shouldn't he follow his?

∼

Frankly, I thought Will was in the wrong career, but it was too late. Being a doctor for Will was like wearing a shirt that didn't quite fit: it covered him, he could button the neck, but the armholes were too small and he couldn't move in it. He should have been a coach (he played third base into college). He should have been a motivational speaker. He should have written books about making people happy.

A really good doctor, Will and I agreed, was a worrywart, a grouch, the sort of person who didn't notice his wife wearing a red night-gown. That might have been Will's dad, that might be me (it *was* me), but that was never Will. He had no idea why his patients tolerated him. Well, he did. People were his thing. He knew to phone people when their cholesterol was good to say, "Hey, Joe, you sure we didn't mix up your blood sample with a sixteen-year-old's?" He knew to call an eighty-seven-year-old Baby Snookums, the name her big brother gave her. He knew to ask after all the kids, especially the one in jail. There was nothing magic, Will said, about being a popular doctor. A lot of it was simple baloney. "I leave the tough cases to you," Will would say, doing that gesture where he pointed at me with both thumbs.

When Will did it, somehow, that gesture was okay. In a movie it would be excruciating.

It always amazed me, the way Will accepted his happy place in the world. I was a good student, but Dr. Carver, our anatomy professor, terrified me, while Will was all "Hey, Dr. C." and "Think I'll make it this year?" and "Golly, I hate head and neck." In med school, Will called me Brainiac. *Hey, Brainiac, is this cranial nerve five or just some vessel?* Will's father was a doctor, a friend of Dr. Carver's golf partner. Carver was a lousy golfer, Will said. If Carver insulted Will's dissection technique, Will could make a crack about his putting.

"Don't you worry Will's using you?" Katie Wong, my microscope partner in histology, asked me, and I said no because I was ashamed of the real answer. Of course he was using me. I used him back. He ele-vated my position in the world, making people like the dean's secretary beep at me and wave, making Dr. Carver say things like "Hap, you keeping Will here on the straight and narrow?" In the Waiting Room, the bar the med students congregated at on Fridays, I walked in and sniffed my way to Will's Old Spice and placed myself roughly in his shadow, and I never had to drink alone.

~

Clearly, by the time I mentioned Will and Alicia to Brice, their classic doctor-screwing-nurse relationship had been going on for several months. Maybe I should have been angry with Will. Maybe I should have felt betrayed. But in a way I felt relieved for him, and eager to accept that true love could be messy. I had several patient couples, including two gay ones, well suited to each other, devoted, affable, as happy as patients of mine could be, whose relationships I gathered had begun under some cloud. During a prior marriage, in a classroom between student and teacher, behind a restroom in a park. These patients trusted me with their incontinence and breast exams and hemorrhoids, but if I had asked any of them point-blank for the details of their first meetings, they would have stammered and blushed and not spit out much of the story. Why? What difference would the truth make, especially now, especially to me? There was an endearingly ridiculous human tendency to sanitize, to dust around the edges of reality like straightening a room before the company showed up. For example, no teenage girl whose pregnancy I'd diagnosed admitted to having sex more than one time. I never argued about this. "One time is enough," I said to my pregnant ones, nodding.

"I know what you think," Will said that winter day in my office. "But we love each other, we do." I nodded, but Will bit his lips and looked around, as if he hadn't quite convinced himself. I could imagine what he thought I was thinking: *Is it love or lust?* Alicia was a lovely young woman, with shiny hair and a nipped-in waist and a peach-shaped bottom. Both her upper and lower eyelashes were unusually obvious (I asked Janis once if it was possible she dyed them, but Janis said it was probably mascara), and her eyes were narrow, so the effect was slightly caterpillarish, which doesn't sound attractive but it was. She wore a birthstone representing her son on a long gold chain around her neck, and when she bent forward the little guy swung wildly between her breasts.

"Look, Will, I don't care what your relationship with Alicia is," I said that day in January. "All I'm saying is that if you two are serious, maybe Alicia should take a job somewhere else."

"We're fine," Will said. "We have our personal lives, and we have this office, and when we're here we're very, very professional."

"Just think about it."

"Oh, Hap." Will shook his head cajolingly. "You're worried about sexual harassment, aren't you? That's a nonissue. This is consensual. Alicia's been married two times. She's mature."

Alicia, mature. She was certainly *ripe,* but that wasn't the same thing. I said, "What if you split up?"

"We can cross that bridge. Look, Hap"—and Will gave me the boyish, callow look that had never changed in the twenty-five years I'd known him—"don't sweat your socks off, okay?"

He needed me to argue, I realized. He wanted me to resist him about Alicia, so that the two of them, together, would have the chance to prove me wrong. I did what I could. I said, "My socks are feeling pretty clammy."

CAROLINE

We were an internal medicine office—medicine for adults, as some national marketing campaign at the time trumpeted—and with all our older, chronically ill patients, we had a lot of deaths. I think of the demise of our office as a death itself, and I can say exactly which kind: it was a three-month death.

A three-month death was one in which the diagnosis and the end fell within a single season, where people hid from their acquaintances behind hymnals and racks of clothing to avoid having to explain what they were going through.

I knew right off when a recent three-month widow or surviving son was standing at my window. Their face would be drawn and dazed, and they wouldn't respond when I first asked if I could help. A sudden death could be comforted by saying that the dead person didn't know, a protracted death by the acknowledgment that it was a blessing. A three-month death was different: the person knew and it was not a blessing. At some point there had to be a moment—waking up gasping for breath at three a.m., legs that on a certain afternoon would not move at all—when a person thought, *My God! This thing's not slowing down!*

Shock and awe, the state of everyone involved in a three-month death.

Actually, there were fifteen months between the day in May when Dr. Strub and Al got married and the office's closing down, which, if you think about it, is three months for each of us who worked there. It's ironic, because although lust has improved and permeated my life in countless ways, this particular lust, even at the time and especially looking back, seems to me like the worst thing in the world.

HAP MARKOWITZ

"To clammy socks!" Will said that day in May, lifting his glass and meeting my eye. We were at a dinner the night before the wedding, and everyone there knew about my comment of three months before, and how wrong I obviously was. Alicia, beside Will, was wearing a maroon suit thick with embroidery, an outfit that, Janis later observed, resembled a full-body chastity belt. I lifted my glass to the both of them and smiled.

"Oh, they *worked* together," an elderly female relative of Alicia's said across the table.

"They're still going to work together," a younger female relative said loudly and slowly. "Alicia is the nurse in Will's office."

"Get to see each other," the old lady said, nodding. "Nice."

"Hap didn't think we could do it." Alicia smoothed her skirt on her lap as she sat down. Since their engagement six weeks before, she hadn't called me Dr. Markowitz once, even in front of patients, although she still called Will "Dr. Strub" at work. "Hap thought we were just an affair."

Brice's eyes met mine across the table, and I smiled into his glower. "I just can't figure out about Iris," I heard him say to Caroline, regarding—I assumed—some potential date he had lined up for the wedding.

Caroline said, "It was short notice for a wedding."

"But that's Iris." Brice sounded miserable. "She's a short-notice kind of girl."

Originally Alicia and Will were to be married in the fall, but they moved the date up to May, on the weekend after Alicia's son competed in the national championship tournament for high school debate. Alicia's son, Jesse, had gone from a chubby preteen to a tall and handsome young man. He dressed like a Young Republican—he looked more like Will's relative than Alicia's—and he sat quietly next to Will with his eyebrows raised, listening in on conversations like an anthropologist making mental notes.

"Well, Brice, maybe you're next," I said. "On the marriage plan, I mean." Stupid thing to say. I glanced at Janis and widened my eyes in self-disparagement; under the table, she patted my hand.

"As if," Brice answered.

Caroline said, "Your true love doesn't know yet what she's missing"—which both Janis and I noted, when we talked about it later, was a motherly thing to say. Caroline indeed looked motherly, with her large breasts and soft lap and knowing sort of smile, although everyone in the office, Brice included, knew about her proclivities, which involved a virtual smorgasbord of men. In fact, Janis and I driving home wondered if she'd ditched her date for the wedding in order to accompany Brice. Caroline had always brought dates for our office Christmas dinners, the latest an apparent bodybuilder who must have been ten years younger than she was.

"Alicia's family seemed excited," Janis said as we climbed into bed. "Marrying a doctor." Janis was wearing a flowered flannel gown that didn't really hide her bony chest. I wrapped my arms around her waist, pushed myself into her back. We always slept nested.

Alicia's family, especially the females, had been friendly in an overeager way. Will's people, especially his two daughters, were cool and remote, a family of Afghan hounds forced to tolerate an invasion of poodles.

"Ah, marrying a doctor," I said. "There's a dream come true." Janis and I chuckled. She lifted her head and realigned it on her pillow, and we were both almost asleep when the phone rang. It was one of Will's patients in the ER with a clot in his leg, and yes, I had to go to the hospital to admit him. Will would probably not go in until morning, but putting things off wasn't my way. Risking anything was not my way. Still, when I moved, Janis's body resisted my leaving like a magnet, and beneath my feet the wooden floor was surprisingly cold.

CAROLINE

Dr. Markowitz could sometimes use help with his grooming. Looking at the big picture, he was fine (he never looked sloppy), but the details escaped him. I can't think of how many times I told him about a spot on his shirt or tie or a bit of food stuck to his face. I never blamed this on his wife. She spent her visual energy on her house and her garden; she didn't seem to notice her own looks, much less her husband's.

Once Dr. Markowitz was standing beside my desk at noon, looking over his list of patients for the afternoon. "Tubman, Jenkins, Cathcart—there's trouble," he said.

I looked up at him and grinned. "And you have Mickey Roush three patients later." She was a notorious hypochondriac, whom Alicia called Make-me-a-Grouch.

Dr. Markowitz made a comical snarl. I noticed something on his right cheek. "You have something on your face—there," and I pointed to my left cheek, because mirroring worked best with him.

He would always dab the thing off with his finger, look at it, and tell me what it was and how it got there. I found this humiliatingly predictable, so to save him I said, "It's a sesame seed."

Alarm filled his face, his finger flew. "Oh dear," he said sadly, peering at the speck, "breakfast bagel."

We exploded into laughter. Exploded.

That was right after Al and Dr. Strub got married. Right after.

I think of that moment often, especially now. I never saw Dr. Markowitz laugh like that again. His mouth open revealing his fillings, the crinkles at the side of his eyes. A thousand times I must have hoped that we would laugh like that again. We never did.

CAROLINE

"Oh," I'd say to the patients, "you have an office visit today with Alicia's new husband."

A few said, "Who's Alicia?" but most of them looked startled.

"Yes, they're married now. Isn't that wild?"

To which I'd get a variety of answers:

"I didn't know they were dating."

"I thought he was married already."

"I hope that doesn't mean he'll be on vacation all the time."

"Isn't that wonderful!"

"Yes, it is wonderful," I said. "Someone for everyone."

Brice was in a state. His friend Iris had up and moved to Iowa City. "Iowa City!" he raved. "Who the hell moves to Iowa City?"

"Some of your comments didn't help," I pointed out.

He almost stamped his foot. "But she *was* hairy!" he said. "She could have at least shaved some parts!"

Dr. Strub had asked Brice to get the word out that he and Alicia were married. He wanted Brice to hang the JUST MARRIED sign that had been on the back of their car in the waiting room below my window. I found it interesting that Dr. Strub didn't ask me to do this. He may have known that I knew too much. I knew, for example, that Alicia had told Vicki Burns from the health food store at the mall how during office hours one Thursday Dr. Strub had bent her over the exam room 4 table and taken her from behind.

"*In case people didn't know we were dating,* he told me," Brice said about the sign. "Dating, my foot. Screwing their furry rabbit brains out."

There was no way I was going let Brice hang that stupid sign. Our waiting room was neat and tidy. My life might be a little messy, my house might not be perfect, but that waiting room I kept in order.

"We'll get my billing up," Dr. Strub had told Brice, his pride hurt that Dr. Markowitz had bested him in office visit numbers during the month before Dr. Strub's wedding. "Alicia's found a coding course for me to take."

From cock teasing to coding courses: I guessed marriage was as good a way as any of quenching your desires. Your uncontrollable urges uncontrollable? Your libido interfering with your life? Tame that urge with marriage! Married, Alicia seemed to have lost her seductive power. Dr. Strub no longer showed up at her desk between patients. Her waist looked thicker, although she left a pink plastic tube from a tampon on the counter beside the employee washroom sink.

"Did you see that horrible pink thing?" Brice said. "What's that about? Do you think she's trying to torture us more?"

HAP MARKOWITZ

Two-thirds of my patients were on antidepressants. I used to worry I was overprescribing them, but Will's patients were on them too. It startled and comforted me to realize this, because Will's patients were loud in their laughter and hearty in their comings and goings. I didn't know if the antidepressants worked better for his patients, or if his patients simply started at a happier baseline. Maybe he drew out their happiness, while I evoked the misery in mine. All sad sacks, this way to Dr. Markowitz! Special misery-loves-company treatment for sad sacks!

I didn't even like antidepressants. They threatened to make people chirpy. For someone with a tragic view of life—we were born, we managed, we died—there was little that provoked more scorn than chirpiness. Still, I knew that everyone didn't feel as I did, and at the pressure of wives and daughters and occasionally the patient himself, I succumbed and took out my prescription pad to write "Prozac" or "Zoloft" or "Celexa." I wasn't sure that their effect wasn't placebic: when the patient reached for the script, he already looked happier.

Years ago Caroline, after one of her vacations with a man-friend, had a gift for me, a refrigerator magnet that said YES, THE SKY MAY BE FALLING. I wanted to hug her. "Thank you," I said. That was what I treasured about our receptionist: her exquisite sense of calibration, her *knowing* (YES, THE SKY MAY BE FALLING), although she spoke disparagingly of herself and downplayed any compliments. "He's a little Eeyore today," I overheard her say to Brice about me one day. That was exactly right. I was never "a lot Eeyore," I was never Eeyore, period, but "a little Eeyore" suited me. That's why I would never take a happy pill. I didn't want to lose my Eeyore edge.

~

Janis and I met at the university library when I was in med school and she was in college. She wore, even then, flowered skirts and sensible sandals, her hair pushed from her face by a headband, and through the years she never changed, in my eyes, one iota, but for some reason one morning after Will's wedding I saw her as she must look to someone else: like a frumpy high school teacher in a movie, the one with a secret crush on the principal, the one who'll surprise even herself by dancing wildly on a table when the hero and his band break into song. Except for Janis there would be no table, no students shrieking "You go, Mrs. Markowitz!"—no release. Our kitchen hung with copper-bottomed pots scrubbed to a gleaming asepsis; our backyard was a museum gardening (her garden club had asked her many times to speak about her plants, but, out of shyness, she always said no); our morning bed was made and heaped with pillows by the time I got out of the shower. Janis's weakness was colorful body lotions scented with various foodstuffs. Cucumber, coconut, strawberry. I always knew what to buy her.

Years before, we'd talked about fertility treatments. We'd talked about Janis going for a graduate degree (she wasn't sure what; maybe architecture?), about her helping out in the office, about her volunteering for the medical guild program that provided tutors for the deprived children of Midburg's central city.

"I guess there's nothing I want to do that much," she said.

I was out of the house at least sixty hours a week—more when I had a bad weekend on call—and when I got home the house was always silent, Janis transplanting iris corms or sitting at the kitchen table drinking tea. The clink of Janis's cup on the saucer—that might be the only sound I'd hear. At times, through the years, I wondered if she'd be better off taking a lover. "Are you satisfied?" I said once, years ago.

She lifted and lowered her hands in the graceful way I imagined a geisha might. "I'm like an aloe," she said. "I don't need much."

We never pursued a fertility workup or treatment. Janis had regular periods and a sister with two daughters. It was probably my sperm count, or its motility; I doubted there was anything wrong with her. Her gynecologist said as much to me once—a casual comment in the doctors' lounge at the hospital ("Maybe you should get tested")—and I never pursued it, I never picked up the phone and said to my favorite urologist, "Manny, think you could see me?" even though Manny, out of respect and affection (yes), not to mention appreciation of my large referral base, would probably have seen me that very day. But I never phoned him. Janis never asked me to, and I realized after Will's wedding that she rarely asked for anything—she was indeed (I deferred to her knowledge of plants) exactly like an aloe.

I must have stifled her. I must have let her down. In my attachment to my practice and my patients I had made myself a walking duty, not a complete person and certainly not a husband. I couldn't think about this much: no time. Still, somewhere in my mind there was a nagging awareness, like a sore foot that was only bearable if you kept walking. I hoped the thing was actually healing. I hoped I wasn't doing it more damage.

CAROLINE

For a while we hadn't heard that much about Alicia's son, Jesse, but after Alicia's honeymoon her attention snapped like a measuring tape back to him. Until the school year ended, each morning she dropped him off at high school, then drove to work separately from Dr. Strub. In the summer, before he went off to debate camp, Jesse dropped off and picked up Alicia so he could have the car.

"Jesse!" I stood up and leaned out the window one afternoon when he was waiting for this mother. "Come over here and let us see you."

When he was six or seven, Jesse used to barge into Brice's office and hop on his chair (he liked it because it turned and rolled), but now he approached the waiting room window like a patient.

"Debate camp!" I said. "Wow." Jesse was seventeen but looked older—attractive, tall and thin with a hank of dark brown hair flopping over his forehead. Brice, who knew old movies, said he looked like a young Clark Gable. "I hope you knock the other campers dead."

"Yeah, well, I hope so."

"He hopes so!" Brice said from behind me, startling me because I thought he was in his tiny office. "He hopes so! That sounds like a man who knows his mind!"

"Your mother's really proud of you," I said. "We hear about you all the time."

Jesse's gaze dropped, and there might have been some embarrassment in his grin, which made me feel a twinge of guilt since I knew that Brice and I were going to tease him. After Alicia and Dr. Strub's wedding, that was what Brice and I did to people. It was as if Alicia had walked away from our game of Parcheesi, so Brice and I had switched to checkers, a game she couldn't join. We told paranoid Miss Eagleton—assuring her the tale was a lie—about thieves at the mall who hid under parked cars and attacked people's ankles. We told Mrs. Jacobs we loved her blue hair, and Mr. Jenkins that suspenders like his were newly au courant. I doubted if Jesse would realize we were ragging him. He was an earnest sort.

"You know who Jesse reminds me of these days?" Brice said, touching my shoulder. "Jimmy Carter."

"Oh, don't be silly, Brice," I said, turning to give him a stern look. "Jesse's too young to know Jimmy Carter."

"Thirty-ninth president," Jesse said. "Lost to Ronald Reagan over the Iranian hostages."

"You *are* intelligent!" Brice said. "I knew it." He waved a finger in the air. "And your stepdad thinks you're very smart too!"

"You'll be applying to colleges next year, right?" I said.

"Yale," Brice said. "Princeton."

"Oxford," I said. "The Sorbonne. What is the Sorbonne, anyway? You always hear about it, but you . . ." I looked up at Jesse behind the window and he had a new, distant stare, and I realized that he knew full well that we were ragging him, that he already had us classified and pinned like bugs on a specimen board. I pictured him typing up the labels: genus *Losera,* species *patheticus,* nonmating pair. I felt ashamed. Why in the world was I picking on a high schooler? Jesse would clerk one day for a judge, be the newest eager beaver in the think tank, show up on the cover of *Newsweek* whispering in the president's ear. He was a young man of ambition, while Brice and I had given up.

I didn't like what Brice and I had become since Al got together with Dr. Strub. I didn't want to be a person who's always whittling and be-littling. "I think it's great that you're a debate whiz," I said to Jesse. "I bet we'll see you in the newspaper someday."

"Uh, okay." Jesse snorted and dipped his head. "Thank you."

"Aren't you the suck-up," Brice said later, emerging from his office once Alicia and Jesse had left.

"Come on, Brice." I glanced out to the waiting room to be sure all the patients were gone. "He's seventeen and look what he's done."

"What's he done? Stood up in front of people and argued?"

Brice used to love Jesse. He let him sit in his chair, he gave him pen-cils to put in the electric sharpener. For Brice to attack Jesse now let me know he still felt hurt by Alicia. We never talked about it, but Brice and I would both have told you that Alicia had betrayed us.

"He works hard. Alicia says he's always on the Internet doing research." Brice's face went strange. "Better than what *you're* looking up on the Internet," I said.

"Movies, that's it. I look up movies."

"*There's* a useful way to spend your time."

"Old movies," Brice said. "Classics."

The pathos in Brice's voice hit me at that moment. "Old movies. Classics"—as if those words were his best defense. Brice researched movies on the Internet and sat in the basement of his mother's house and rewatched *Vertigo* or *Easy Rider* for the thirty-ninth time. He could tell you in which movie and scene Janet Leigh's blouse was missing a button or a grip's foot and ankle were visible. That was Brice's life beyond our office.

"Do you think I'm normal?" Brice had asked me, years before. Less normal than I was, I thought now. The thought was somehow uncomfortable; it made me notice when I swallowed. At the same time the thought was consoling, like the melt from a lozenge trickling down my throat.

HAP MARKOWITZ

I never complained much, and sometimes I thought that if I did I'd have more friends. A lot of human interaction is bellyaching followed by soothing, and it was rare indeed that anyone got the chance to soothe me. Janis, occasionally. So I missed, in a way, the normal tit for tat of human conversation. I was always a doctor, listening and silently forming my impression about what I'd heard.

The office revolved around Will. Everyone knew it. There was nothing charming or ingratiating about me. My patients were tense and serious. "Did you see this?" they'd say, handing me newspaper clippings about drug side effects and interactions. Will's patients were easy to console, to urge, to boss around. My patients were pricklier. I liked to think they were more intelligent. Caroline always said that when a prospective patient called in she could tell by the tone of their voice if they'd ask for Will or me. I could have pressed her for details, but I was afraid to know.

I thought of Caroline as the hobbling center of our office, although she never actually hobbled. In fact, it was amazing how fluid her gait was, as if she'd had the prosthesis since she was a baby. She always wore trousers to work, and most of our patients didn't know she'd had an amputation. She made it through her cancer surgery and subsequent chemo, she told me once, with dope, heavy metal, and margaritas, and this got her kicked out of her parents' house, which she believed was the perfect outcome. There had been money in her family, apparently—her grandfather had owned a tool-and-die company—but her parents frittered it away. She never mentioned them. She'd sued successfully to get the malpractice settlement money (delayed diagnosis—her family doc kept saying the lump in her leg was a bruise) transferred from her parents to herself, and with it she bought a brick two-story with a front porch and an attached garage, a cozy yet elegant place. Janis and I were once there for a cookout.

I heard her talking to Brice at some point about alcohol, which she had no interest in at all. The day her oncologist said, "Caroline, you're cured," she walked out of her office and made the decision for clarity. The shrugging way she said this reminded me of a yogi or a Buddhist, someone with a Longer View. I loved Caroline, always. Being around her was like stepping out into the fresh, ionized air after a storm. If Janis ever died, I'd think, maybe I'd end up with her—although she probably would be taken by then, by one of the men she brought to our office Christmas dinners, men I perhaps self-protectively thought of as unsuitable: too needy, or too callous, too *young*. By and large, I had to admit, they were all good-looking, pleasant men. Perhaps on a graded scale of attractiveness they would each rank higher than Caroline, although Caroline, in my opinion, had a deep and subtle appeal, like a Bach fugue for the organ or a tweeded jacket that on close inspection was flecked with bits of color.

CAROLINE

Alicia talked about her married life all the time. Will's kitchen that looked nice enough until you opened the cupboards, which were a nightmare. The recipes she made that didn't take much time. The dry cleaner that would wash and press ten shirts for five dollars. The nightly sex Will wanted, even when the both of them were tired.

It couldn't have been easy for her, as Dr. Strub's new wife, dealing with some of the patients in our office. Even Brice noticed when Mrs. Runcible, in for a blood pressure check, looked at Alicia as if her name had been in the paper for drunk driving.

"I didn't know you and Dr. Strub were dating," Mrs. Runcible said from the patient chair by Alicia's desk.

"Excuse me?" Alicia said, removing the stethoscope from her ears. "One forty-five over ninety-six."

"Ninety-six?" Mrs. Runcible said, extending her free arm. "Check the other side. There must be quite an age difference." She hesitated and, when Alicia didn't answer, added, "Between you and the doctor."

"Seventeen years," Alicia said, although I knew that for ten months a year it was eighteen.

"He has grown children, doesn't he? From his original wife."

I turned my head to see Alicia with her finger to her lips, shushing Mrs. Runcible as she checked the pressure in her other arm. "A little worse," Alicia said. "One forty-eight over one hundred."

"I can't believe that," Mrs. Runcible said. "I'm taking all my medicine and I feel perfect. I'll have your husband take it when he comes in."

"Certainly," Alicia said pleasantly. "Have Dr. Strub check it."

Touché, Al, I thought. Good for you.

Although there were other times Alicia seemed less sympathetic. "What's up with her? She looks terrible," she said once when the second Mrs. Lockaby had left, even after Mrs. Lockaby had congratulated her on her marriage and asked about her son. The second Mrs. Lockaby, we both knew, had been the center of a scandal fifteen years before, when Dr. Lockaby, the gastroenterologist, left his sons and wife for her when she got pregnant, staying with her even after she miscarried.

Alicia said, "Fifteen years from now, I want to look like I was worth a scandal. Why doesn't she get a skin peel? Why doesn't she do cardio?"

"You thought about supper?" I heard Dr. Strub ask her in the back hall. "How about that red chicken stuff I like?"

"I'd have to stop by the store for that," Alicia said. "I thought we could do spaghetti."

"Oh, okay," I heard her say a moment later, and I figured Dr. Strub had either touched her somewhere or pouted. "I'll pick things up."

"Good girl," Dr. Strub said, and I did wonder, brushing past them toward the lobby to fetch the next patient, if "good girl" was really a phrase a wife should be pleased to hear.

HAP MARKOWITZ

Will said, "She probably has some underlying irritable bowel. She got turista too, but she was in the bathroom a lot even before that." He stared at the wall behind me, and the voice that came out of him next was softer, almost frightened. "I hope we didn't make a mistake. She tries hard." A puff of dust seemed to release inside my chest, like the tomb of something had been opened. I coughed. Four months before he had been singing the praises of Al's collagen. Now this.

"And then we've got Jesse's summer debate camp. Guess how much." Will took a seat. And before I could answer: "Five thousand for five weeks. Plus the plane fare. But he thinks if he has a great senior year he can get a debate scholarship for college."

I didn't say anything. I'd always liked Alicia's son. He was one of those smart kids who couldn't wait to tell you what he'd read, and then, at about age ten, he went silent, just the way I did, and later it seemed to me that when we looked at each other there was a kind of understanding.

"I'm not begrudging him. He's a great kid." Will gave an almost spastic shake of his head. "But Al's got this exalted view of our income. I went over the May numbers with Brice and we're down again."

Of course we were down. Will had his week off for his honeymoon and Medicare had cut their reimbursements. You had to make a decision: live with less or change the way you practice. I'd live with less. I didn't want to see more than twenty patients per day or bill higher codes for each patient or start charging for copying charts and dictating letters. Will knew my opinion on this. "It wouldn't kill you to bump your codes a bit," he said—an old plea. "You're so *thorough,*" he added, and I recognized his subtext: all I'd have to do to up my billing is change the office visit coding number on a form. While Will would have had to ask more questions, write down more answers, do breast and rectal and neuro exams he hadn't often had to do. I wouldn't have been exaggerating to say that he sounded bitter.

Our partnership was a funny thing. In many ways we were incompatible. But if a medical partnership was indeed, as Will's father said when we first started, a marriage without sex, ours was one of those puzzlingly solid unions that eventually the neighbors simply shrugged at. Will could have been the glitzy blonde while I was the dull professor. Will could have been the husband with the earring and the Harley while I was the wife who clipped coupons and did crosswords.

Will made me Hap. My full name is Horatio Albert Markowitz. I was named for Hyman, my mother's dead-by-drowning brother, and my father's deceased grandmother, Anna. My mother, who loved English mystery novels, thought Horatio and Albert were dignified names. At least Horatio is better than Hyman. In third grade a male music teacher took to calling me "H.A.," but in med school Will changed that name to Hap. My mother—of blessed memory, as religious Jews speak of the dead—never liked my new nickname. It was foolish, she said, the name of a Disney dwarf. For me, the name Hap redefined me, made me comfortable in the world. When I met Janis she commented on it. "Hap? That's a good succinct name." Maybe I fell in love with her at that moment. Years later, she still talked about it: "He was quiet with those soulful eyes, and I loved his name." Hap. The word was like a talisman I took off to lay upon my chest of drawers each night, the thing I first put on in the morning.

It mattered to me—always—that Will was happy. He could be happy, I could be not unhappy, and if that was the state for each of us, we were fine. This marriage of his to Alicia had me worried. Will went into it with too much hope. He didn't think what a wife eighteen years his junior might expect in exchange for her youth. I worried that Alicia was feeling cheated. I wondered if she sat in the car listening to Will talking financials and thought: *I got married for this?* Even people in the medical field, people who should know better, believed that doctors made oodles of money. This wasn't true anymore. The year before, one of the hospital pharmacists who did a lot of overtime made more than either Will or me.

"Did you two do a prenup?" I asked that day in June. Janis had surprised me by wondering about this.

Will stood up, started pacing. "This wasn't a business decision, it was an eros thing." He seemed to reconsider what he'd said, jutted out his chin. "We got married for the good of the office."

Harriet walking out on Will had hurt him, no matter how much he denied it. For a few months Mr. Chin's had brought General Tsao's chicken to the office every evening for Will's dinner, and every morning in the break room Will fixed a breakfast of microwave oatmeal in an increasingly encrusted mug. I knew something was going on between Will and Alicia when she started to wash that mug out. I said, "You could have kept living in sin as far as I'm concerned."

"I'm a moral person. Al's a moral person. We were ready."

I wasn't sure where morals fit into this. I knew there had been things going on in our exam rooms that I would rather not imagine, but Will and Alicia were, as he kept reminding me, adults, and as far as I could gather from Caroline and Brice (although to some extent I'm sure they protected Alicia), Will and Alicia, even at their most hormone-addled, continued to perform their jobs.

"We couldn't not get married," Will said, turning to me with a blank face that was his version of panic. I knew that look so well—I had seen it when Dr. Reynolds announced that three students would have to retake biochemistry, and when Will's mother phoned him to tell him that his father had had a stroke—and it was a look that gave me pain. Rare to see such vulnerability in a man, and I was the person who recognized it in Will, who could set him down and soothe him and run him through his options. Why did I stick with him as a partner? He gave me my name, and he made me feel useful. "You're so logical, man," Will used to say when we were in med school. "You put everything in perspective." And later: "Buds, you saved me." Gratitude was always seductive, especially gratitude that bald.

But that day there was something different in Will's panic, an undertow less pleading than ferocious, as if this time around he was daring me to help him out.

"I'm going to get my billing up," he said. "This coding course in Chicago . . ."

He wanted me to take the coding course too. He wanted me to say we were in this together. But I couldn't face this at that moment—I couldn't, to be honest, give up my position on the pier to sit down in the boat beside him—and instead I heard myself ask a question that was surely an attack: "Alicia's not pregnant, is she?"

"She's on the pill." He swallowed, and the panicked look was gone, replaced by something almost tender, ruminative. "You know, maybe in the grand scheme of things I was meant to be a dad to Jesse. We play video games down in the basement, he beats me. . . . You know, I never had a son."

This got to me. For a moment, I wanted a stepson myself.

"But these younger women, whoo-boy"—Will was chuckling—"you think you're riding them, and then you realize they're riding you." Uncomfortable, I shifted in my seat. Will stood up. "But it's a heckuva ride." He headed toward the door. "I'm going to go document, Hap-Buds. See you later." I didn't even get out the word "goodbye" before he was gone.

Will could ditch me, I thought as he headed out the door. He could get a different partner. He wasn't patient, wasn't thoughtful, wasn't always logical. He could act out of anger and whim. Alicia could be getting to him, pulling him from me. She could take him away completely.

I'd raise my codes, I realized. I'd up my billing. If I had to, I'd take the damn course.

CAROLINE

Alicia called me a slut once, Brice told me. About a year before. Because I always had a boyfriend, and not one I was hoping to marry. Because I slept around the way a guy did.

"She said that?" I said. "What a wise woman."

I sat a little firmer in my seat, turned my attention to the computer screen. Brice hovered behind me a moment, then disappeared into his office. I was angry. Alicia had an angle in every relationship she had. I doubted that she ever would have blabbed at the health food store about her exam room sex with Dr. Strub if she didn't think that spreading this knowledge would give her an advantage. She knew a man of Dr. Strub's age could look foolish chasing a younger woman, but once he'd caught and married one he'd look macho.

I wasn't going to talk about my love life or my current lover. His name was Evan and he was a young man, twenty-four to my thirty-eight. He fondled my breasts like two puppies, called them Sam and Georgette. Sometimes I let Evan come between them; other times he came inside me, then fell asleep with his face buried in my chest. He was very breast-o-centric. Me, I loved Evan's upper arms. Before each visit he'd put on a muscle shirt, and we both adored the moment when he slipped off his sweater to reveal his rippling shoulders and the tufts of hair under his arms.

"Buff" is a word I learned because of Evan, and "ripped" and "definition," as in "Evan has such definition in his upper arms." In the grocery store I used to finger the green peppers, their rises and hollows reminding me of him.

We met at a bar, and I was only there because my female neighbor wanted to meet men and asked me to accompany her for safety. Evan was just some lunk drinking beer, I was just some middle-aged woman sitting there with a Sprite and a flirtatious friend. Still, something drew us together. He came to my house (I could get around there even with my leg off, and he lived in the basement at his parents') and when we woke up the next morning we didn't look at each other and go "Eek!" and scurry apart. We looked at each other and said, "How do you get arms like that?" and "Man, your boobs are awesome," and chatted about our jobs and movies and which sections of the paper we found worthwhile. I'm proud of our behavior that next morning. We could have used the time like an exit ramp, but instead we made it a tunnel heading further in. We didn't have much in common, and his family would disapprove of me (too old and fat) and my friends of him (too young and stupid), but to each other we were slightly luminous beings.

The bulges in Evan's arms puffed out when he was about fourteen. He lifted weights, and his job was physical (loading trucks). He ate a lot of protein. He had a muscular dad. The causes were all uninteresting, but the effect on me was close to miraculous. Desire is a dog impossible to train.

~

One day at lunch Brice and I started talking about his libido. Alicia didn't eat with us now; she had a yogurt and a sandwich at her desk. Brice had gone so far as to mention removing the third chair from the break room table. "I don't think I'm normal," Brice said that day.

"You always say that."

"But today I mean it," he said.

He had no desires. He could recognize when a woman was attractive but he didn't imagine her naked or watch to see if her breasts bounced or keep sneaking glances at her butt. Guys did this, he knew—he saw it all the time. He'd even noticed Dr. Markowitz eyeing the helpful granddaughters of certain patients. But Brice had no interest. Period.

For a whole year, Brice said, he thought he was gay but mentally denying it, like Kevin Kline in *In & Out*. He joined the Y and changed in the locker room. Really, he said, men were repulsive. Like God and his angels designed them as a joke. At least women's private parts were private.

"Men aren't repulsive," I said, sounding hurt and puzzled.

Brice laughed. "Well, you," he said. He knew about me and men. One unexpected—to me, at least—side effect of chemo was that it made me sterile. You could think of this as sad, but think again: no periods, no sick kids, and all the messy, unprotected sex I ever wanted. I didn't worry much about AIDS or herpes or chlamydia, although I did try to pick my men with some measure of discretion, and made them use condoms for at least the first month, until I knew they could be trusted. Despite my concerns right after surgery, my half-a-legness was never a problem. There were even gimp aficionados—there was even gimp porn—although I didn't like to think of myself in quite that something-for-everyone way.

"It's weird," Brice said. "I'm not without feelings, I just don't have extreme ones. Like when people say their feelings got the best of them? There's no best of me."

I believe that people are born to yearn. There's yearning in our substance, in our DNA. That's why all good stories are essentially love stories, even tales people don't immediately think of as being about love. What is the white whale to Ahab but a love object? What is Jay Gatsby to Nick Carraway, or the river to Huck? "Love object"—the thing that pulls you toward it, the not-you you're convinced will make you whole.

For as much as people harrumph about controlling their destiny, even more they ache to be made helpless. The damnedest people fall for the damnedest objects, and often for the damnedest reasons.

"Oh, Brice," I said. He was telling me he wasn't human, and yet I knew he was. "You're upset about Alicia," I said. "That's something."

"That's not passion."

"No, but it shows you care."

"Caroline, I can see you're trying to be nice, I appreciate it, but . . ."

"Why does her being with Dr. Strub bother you so much?" I asked.

"It's trailer park! It's big hair and painted toenails! I thought Alicia wanted to better herself, not nail some stupid doc so he'd marry her!"

"You sound pretty passionate now."

"I'm not passionate, I'm angry."

"But why are you this angry?"

Brice made a peeved face.

"I'm not kidding!" I said. "You saying her rear is looking fat and married? You know that old Kinks song? *Girl, you've really got me going, you've got me so I don't sleep at night.*"

"I don't need songs quoted at me, thank you."

"But it's a love song!" I said. "Or at least an obsession song. See? You're more normal than you think."

That summer, lots of bumper stickers said CHOOSE LIFE and I knew this message was supposed to be antiabortion, but I thought of it as exactly what it said. Mrs. Gibson's granddaughter was getting married in Florida, but Mrs. Gibson was worried about the flights. "Are you kidding?" I told her. "How many more times do you think you'll be at a grandkid's wedding?" Someone told Franny Harris about an online dating service. "Worth a try," I said. Grant Oakley didn't want to treat his diabetes, what with the pills costing so much, and anyway he'd rather die than end up with a foot cut off like his grandma. "Trust me,"

I said—and for this I stood up and walked around the wall and into the waiting room, where I rolled up the left leg of my pants—"it's not the end of the world."

I liked that line of Henry James's: *Live all you can; it's a mistake not to.*

Through the years, my favorite patients were the ones who'd made it through something: cancer, heart attacks, strokes—exactly what didn't matter. Something humbling and scary. Something that could make a person realize, in a visceral sense, that life goes on no matter. Simply getting older didn't teach that. An eighty-year-old who'd never been sick could whine worse than a toddler. I used to think that half the people in our practice could use a dose of sickness. I sometimes pictured a shower of disaster raining on a person as they walked out our office door. "Have a good day!" I said, but I was thinking—in a nice way—Get cancer!

That day in the break room, I thought I'd helped Brice. I believed that I'd awakened something in him, made him see himself in a new way. Late that afternoon when I passed his office he was sitting there looking at nothing, head cocked, mouth pursed, like a Boy Scout blowing on a flame.

CAROLINE

The summer after Dr. Strub and Alicia got married was a brutal one, so hot you walked outside and felt your pores expand, so hot the mailman carried a handkerchief to keep himself from dripping on his letters, so hot the kids working the fast-food drive-ups kept their windows closed until you waved your money. I never minded that sort of heat. Dr. Strub loved it. He stood between Al's desk and mine and talked about when he was in med school, summer of '78, how at dusk he'd head to Phillips Ledges with a nurse he was seeing from the ER, and they would stretch out on the cool and mossy rocks. Seeing his eyes glaze and his mouth drop open, I understood that that summer had been heaven for him, and I knew he recalled activities beyond lolling that had taken place on those boulders.

There are some men you look at and understand are physical, and Dr. Strub was one of those men. Women generally found him attractive—he was tall and thin and had his hair—but he never appealed to me. I could enjoy a stupid man who understood his limitations (Evan), but Dr. Strub had no awareness he was limited at all. I found him generally comical, so the sympathy I felt for him that summer surprised me. I could see, the way he cast looks in her direction and reached out, awkwardly, to pat the back of her hair, that he wanted Alicia to make him feel young once more, to dart into a shallow cave and giggle as he toyed with the zipper of her pants.

Which Alicia was not having, not anymore. She sat scowling at her desk, arms and legs crossed, rustling papers, shaking her shoulders to make her husband drop his hand. "What's up in your world, cupcake?" Brice would say. "Nothing," she'd answer. "Procedures." I kept my face buried in the computer screen, acting as if where I slotted George Mazurki really mattered. Or I was in the basement pulling charts, while Alicia upstairs let the phone ring, ring, ring. She missed Jesse, who had left for debate camp that week.

I said to Alicia, "Why don't you and Dr. Strub have lunch together, at least?" Because she said outside of work they never saw each other anymore, she was always tired and went to bed early and he stayed up late.

Alicia said: "Why should he eat lunch with me? He can eat in his office and dictate."

She'd developed a grudge about Dr. Markowitz. "He doesn't like me," she said, more than once. "You watch him." She thought he should see more patients, bill for higher codes, go out into the community and give speeches to rustle up new patients.

One day in July, Dr. Markowitz showed up with Midwest Cardiology's employee handbook. "I thought you girls and Brice could look this over," he said to Alicia and me. "Maybe we can use it as a template."

Some things weren't getting done. A whole stack of refills hadn't been called in one Friday, and one Tuesday Alicia forgot to tell me she'd added two patients for emergency visits, both of whom blew up at me when I couldn't verify their appointments.

I said, "Brice, you know you're in the soup when they start talking employee handbook." I was standing leaning against his door, head tilted, trying to keep my eyes off his hands. For some reason I'd started looking forward each morning to Brice's thin pressed white shirts with their cuff-linked cuffs. I liked looking at his hands, long and thin-fingered, the knuckles sprinkled with dark hairs. I'd first noticed those hands in the break room—how Brice moved them, fingers together, as he talked, how they hesitated and darted like two fishes. Maybe the heat was affecting me too; that or the way Dr. Strub kept bringing up his summer of love. Maybe Brice wasn't, as I'd always assumed, gay and closeted even to himself. Maybe the right woman could arouse him.

"You know who you look like?" he said, a quizzical look on his face. "Patricia Neal in *Hud*."

"Really?" I said, flustered. "Is that okay?"

"Better than okay. Solid."

"Oh. Good. You find her attractive?"

"In an objective sense," he said.

"In an objective sense"—what did that mean? I went through the rest of the day restless, vaguely troubled, not noticing Rabbi Kerchner at the window until he said to the person behind him, "And I thought she liked me!"

That summer, I saw Al and Dr. Strub at an outdoor concert. Al was wearing a polo shirt tucked into belted shorts that grazed her knees. She looked like a lady golf pro. Poor Dr. Strub, I thought.

The next day I took a pile of charts to Dr. Markowitz's office and reported what I'd seen. I put a certain zest into the words "lady golf pro," but Dr. Markowitz only smiled faintly and raised his eyebrows. I turned to the door, disappointed. It was overoptimistic, but I'd been hoping for the laugh.

HAP MARKOWITZ

Will stood at my office door. "I've got a billing suggestion, nothing major." It was between callbacks after office hours. Every evening I had five or six callbacks, a service Will's patients didn't seem to demand.

Will said, "I went golfing with Larry Rizzo Wednesday and I realized something: we've got to start thinking like the family practitioners. FPs don't do anything they can't bill for."

"Okay," I said, stretching out the second syllable in a dubious way. "Such as . . ."

"Well, ear syringing." His answer was quick. He'd been thinking about it.

"I think of ear syringing as a service." Flushing out earwax so someone could hear again: patients loved it.

"But why should it be a free service? It takes time, it takes resources."

I considered myself a one-stop doctor. We discussed your breathing, your bowel movements, your blood sugar, your anxiety about your daughter, and then you said: Doc, think you can clean out my ears? "Sure," I'd answer. But in the modern American view of life as a business, my "sure" was throwing money away. And God knew there was no higher God than money.

Still, Will wasn't totally wrong. It was usually Alicia who did the actual wax removal, and—including the setup of the plastic gown like women wear at the beautician's, the emesis basin filled with warm water, the fluid drawn up in the syringe—it probably took three minutes. Beyond that, the occasional patient got dizzy, which required their staying in the exam room several minutes more. Cleaning out ears was not without cost. Still, how many ear syringings did I average in a week? One? Two? It was hardly worth an argument. So I said to

Will, unable to resist a sigh as I spoke, that, of course, we could do it his way.

Alicia had become a real monster, the Lady Macbeth of our office ("Those weren't my refills to call in! I don't call in refills!"); and although recently I'd read some actor's interpretation of the play as being about Lady Macbeth's love for her husband, I still thought that what drove Lady Macbeth—and Alicia—was love not for a person but for power. You could see it in the way Alicia strode to the entrance of the lobby, lifting her chin and calling the next patient. I'd heard her on the phone making dinner reservations. "This is *Mrs.* Strub," she said.

I told myself to stop thinking like this. I told myself to remember the old, brassy Alicia, who wrote out her potato salad recipe on a decorated card for me to take home to Janis, who referred to Mrs. Nugent (ten children, fourteen pregnancies) as a walking uterus. Alicia, I reminded myself, was no more than a young woman who had stumbled into a marriage she must suspect was less than the staggering stroke of luck she'd thought it would be. Why in the world did Will keep her working in our office? She made noises that she'd like to stay home (". . . hard to schedule a time for the remodelers"; "Jesse's not going to be around much longer, and . . ."), but Will, when I mentioned replacing her, gave me his blank look. One lunch, I found Alicia alone at her desk hunched over a yogurt. "Why don't you go to the break room?" I said. "Get away?"

"I'm happy here," she said.

I had to remember Alicia's face as she ate that yogurt. I didn't want to think of someone I worked with as Lady Macbeth. Like any exaggeration, it opened a door to pain and trouble. I might not be able to close the door completely, but I didn't want to always feel a draft.

"Great," Will said about the ear flushing. "We'll have Caroline start scheduling syringe appointments right away."

Scheduling? Appointments? I frowned. "So we can collect for a second office visit," Will said.

"Oh, come on." My upper lip was actually curling. "Gaming the system," K.C. the ER doc used to say, calling me in the middle of the night to see a patient whose family doc, from his bed at home, had decided needed my immediate attention.

"Hap," Will said, "just do this. Please. It'll help me with Alicia."

He had to defend me to her, I realized. I was a point of contention between them.

Later, Janis and I thought up things I could have said. "Aren't you and I the business partners?"

Or: "I don't think office policy should be based on your wife's desires."

Or: "Why don't you let her quit working? All she does is make the office miserable."

But Will and Alicia were *married*. Foolish or not, irritating or not, I had to respect their position. "Okay, then," I said instead. "I'll do it."

CAROLINE

Alicia felt like she had tiny weights—minute, the size of hearing aid batteries—implanted beneath the skin of her face. Under her eyes, at the corners of her mouth, at the angles of her jaw, and you wouldn't think weights that size would bother her, but they were there day and night: when she showered, when she checked a pulse, when she rolled into her pillow at night, and after a while even smiling seemed like work because those weights pulled her face down. It was spooky to look at herself in the mirror and see a normal

Alicia, she said, when inside she felt tugged and misshapen, her shoulders aching like she was in the lead cape that you wear at the dentist's.

Will did her bloodwork and that was okay, and she was on the pill with regular periods so she wasn't pregnant (my first thought), and then she started thinking she must be depressed like everyone else in the world, and then she started imagining herself on Prozac or Zoloft like Mrs. Edgington (yuck) or Ms. Kestrel (career woman lunatic) or Mrs. Lui (frustrated housewife whose husband looked like a guinea pig). Forget that, she thought, and she signed up at Moore's Fitness, because they promised a new you, but the next two weeks it was just the old Alicia, only sorer. Dr. Strub told her she should walk but it was too hot to walk, and what about him? He barely even walked across a parking lot.

She'd been listening to a program on WFJC as she drove home, and what Dr. Dobson the psychologist said, basically, was that loss of respect was often the first sign of trouble in a marriage. Al was way beyond loss of respect. Will's scrotum looked to her like some stretched-out sock, and she could hardly stand to look at his veiny you-know-what.

But this was the man she had married, the guy she was supposed to grow old with (and she didn't think that with her first two husbands, but this time she'd decided it was for keeps). It would probably just be her *watching* him get old. She couldn't stand it. She felt like she was walking down an endless hall with no end and no side doors, and if this was life why keep on living?

She talked like this almost daily, her back to mine in our small office, only stopping when she heard me on the phone or calling the name of a patient through my window. I kept my eyes up, looking out for one of the doctors to greet as they came down the back hall, calling out the patient's name before they reached my ledge, hoping that Alicia, blubbering on behind me, would hear my voice and catch the cue to stop. The occasional patient heard something. I exchanged, with too many people, sad and colluding smiles. "Poor Dr. Strub," we could be saying.

Via e-mail from his debate camp in Texas, Jesse told Alicia she should see a psychiatrist.

"My own son!" she said. "He's seventeen! What does he know?"

Oh, sure, there were probably people besides Jesse who thought she was depressed. "Depressed," the diagnosis of the decade, one word for alcoholic priests and mothers with too many children and old people with dead friends and students who were confused about their futures. "Depressed": like you're sitting in a hole. Alicia wasn't going to be depressed. Depraved, resentful, disappointed—she could buy those things. Not depressed.

I'm sure Brice heard every word of this. He could have heard every word, had he wanted to. It was a thin wall separating his hamster cage of an office from Alicia's desk. We talked about it. He was aware, he said, of a steady buzz of complaint from her, the odd word sticking out: "lazybones," "misery," "insubordination." "I heard her talk about Strub's you-know-what," he said, rolling his eyes. "God."

"How about a hobby?" I asked Alicia.

"Do *you* have a hobby? What's *your* hobby?"

Interesting she had to ask, considering how much I knew about her.

"I read. And"—I'd been hearing her truth for weeks; I decided on a dose of my own—"if I go too long without sex I don't feel right. So I guess sex is a hobby."

There was a silence. I turned to look at her. She had turned totally around in her chair and was staring at me in ferocious exultation, as if I were proof that the sort of things she feared indeed existed. Moral superiority can be a real tonic. For an instant she probably forgot all about the weights in her face.

"You and my husband," she said at last, with a snort. "At least he's married. Aren't you worried about chlamydia?"

"Doxycycline." I shrugged, naming the antibiotic.

"Herpes?"

"Zovirax." I might not have been as careful as I should be, but I wasn't reckless, and it made me mad to be lumped in with her idiot husband.

Her brow was furrowed, her mouth twisted; she was precariously close to giggling. "What about AIDS?"

"For crying out loud, Al, I'm not sleeping with someone new every week."

A timid knock on the window. Alicia looked up and her mouth dropped open; once again I had made her day.

"Mrs. Gilloughly," I said, sliding open the window.

"I have a one o'clock appointment. I'm sorry"—her eyes slipped wildly between us, like someone surprised by a patch of black ice—"I didn't mean to interrupt your girl talk."

~

"I've got to get my mother in here," Brice said the next day.

He and I were the only ones left in the office. I had my purse out and my keys in my hand. I was supposed to meet Evan for a quick bite before a baseball game. After almost a year together, we now went places—movies, restaurants, miniature golfing—before we came back to my house.

"Your mother?" I said. "Are you sure?"

For years Brice had been trying to keep his mother out of our office. But finally his big sister, Lynda, had gotten to him. "It's Hail-Mary-

Mother-of-God," she told him on the phone, calling their mother by her latest abusive name. "Did you know she was in Wenzler's office five times last week?" Wenzler was Brice's mother's doctor.

"What for?" Brice asked his sister.

"Oh, ears ringing, skin crawling, achiness. The usual."

"Maybe it's her allergies," Brice said.

"Yeah, right. She's allergic to life."

Brice said, "She's got the Xanax."

"Yeah, but she doesn't take the Xanax, although I'm sure she tells Wenzler she does. He tells her to increase it."

"Of course the quack told my mother to increase her nerve pills," Brice said to me. "He gave me antibiotics for an ear infection without coming within ten feet of my ears. Lynda said, 'You've got to do something about her.' And I said, 'If you'll notice, I'm doing the ultimate thing. I'm living with her.' "

"What did Lynda say then?"

"She said: Dr. Wenzler refused to see her this morning."

"You're kidding," I said. "Wenzler refused to see your mother?" She must truly have moved from annoying to impossible.

"We need another OJ trial to keep her occupied," Brice said to his sister. "That was a good summer."

"For God's sake, Brice," Lynda said, "this isn't a joke. Can't you get her in at your office?"

"The dreaded question," I said.

Brice said, "I told her: I see her at home, I don't need to see her here too. She'd have to drive six miles. Wenzler's closer, and he doesn't have mall traffic."

"What did Lynda say?"

"She said to stop being selfish."

I winced. Brice's sister was a formidable enemy.

"You have to admire my mother, in a way," Brice said. "She's big, like Norma Desmond or Margo Channing. She can't imagine that anyone in the world is more interesting than her."

I'd heard this theory of Brice's before, and it didn't impress me. The space people demanded in your life almost always exceeded their appeal.

For years, Brice's mother had been a threat when one doctor or another made Brice angry: "Do that again and I stick her with YOU." But now, at this decisive moment—Lynda was right, at the age of seventy any woman, no matter how hypochondriacal, deserved a decent doctor—Brice couldn't decide which doctor would be better. Dr. Markowitz, who'd actually examine her? Dr. Strub, who'd cheer her up? "It's like I'm holding a cabbage in each hand," he said. "Markowitz . . . Strub; Markowitz . . . Strub." We did some cabbage comparisons for a while. Dr. Strub looked greener, fresher, but Dr. Markowitz might have a richer flavor. Dr. Markowitz was a little weightier, but Dr. Strub was less dense and compacted. His mother on seeing the Markowitz cabbage would say, "Well, that looks okay." For Dr. Strub she'd say, "Oh, what a beautiful cabbage!"

"Put her in with Strub," Brice finally said.

"Are you sure?"

"She's not sick, and he'll make her happy. He's a happy cabbage."

Although we'd never met, I knew everything about Brice's mother. Her name was Kathleen O'Connell Kelvin, but she went by Kitty. Lynda and Brice were her only children, despite her being a painfully good Catholic. Lynda was born when Kitty was twenty-six, Brice when she was thirty-eight. There may have been miscarriages—she had made to Brice an occasional reference to "problems"—but I guessed she was boycotting sex. Brice's father was an accountant for a paper company. His mother never worked outside the home—she watched soap operas and smoked—and his father did the bills and the grocery shopping and arranged the family vacations until 1984, when he fell over dead while pulling up his garage door. Brice was twelve. Dr. Markowitz had also been twelve when his father died, and although this was nothing they'd ever discussed, Brice always felt that his fatherless status had helped get him his job.

When Brice's father died, his sister, Lynda, was already married and out of the house (no dummy she). Brice learned to set his own alarm clock and make himself breakfast. His mother went to bingo two nights a week and had regular lunches with a group of former OLA (Our Lady of Angels) classmates, who put her at the end of the table, facing no one. In 1986 she got so worked up about her parish's new African priest that she moved herself and Brice to another parish. Kitty had days she spent in bed, when Brice fixed her a pack lunch in the morning and delivered it to her room before he left. She wouldn't buy an answering machine, and some days she didn't answer the phone at all, even when she'd made Brice promise to call.

Once Mrs. Barndollar, a patient of Dr. Strub's, had dumped everything out of her purse onto our lobby floor looking for her Medicare card, which she finally found tucked in her shoe. "I don't see how some people survive," I said to Brice later, and his face had glimmered with a guilty awareness. How did his mother survive? I wondered. But I knew. By day she bodysurfed on the hands of strangers and the nice ladies from church, and at night she fed on Brice.

Brice she trusted. Any other family member was judging her, looking for a chance to put her away. She broke a glass removing it from the dishwasher, she couldn't find her car keys, the cat had pooped again behind the sofa: "Mary, Mother of God, next they'll try to put me away! Brice, honey, you'll look after me? You won't let them put me away?" Over time Brice's sister and his cousins and Kitty's sisters and Uncle Nick had become useless to her—and they, in turn, had written Kitty and Brice off.

When Kitty finally walked into our waiting room for her first appointment, the only thing that surprised me was her height. Brice had been right when he said that his mother looked like Katharine Hepburn, a name he never pronounced without adding "the old bat."

"Mrs. Kelvin?" I said, pushing open the window. Her eyes slid imperiously to mine. "You *are* Mrs. Kelvin, right?" She nodded. "I'm Caroline. Brice has told me so much about you. I'm afraid we've got some paperwork for you." I slid the patient information sheet and a clipboard through the window. "You can take a seat and fill it out," I said, nodding toward the chairs behind her.

She stared at me, blinking, and any illusion that she was patrician suddenly vanished. "I'm supposed to fill this out?"

A banker had once asked Kitty, "Did you maybe add the amount of your outgoing checks to your account balance instead of taking it away?" Kitty nodded, and the lady banker waved her hand as if she were wiping clean a board. In truth, Brice's mother had wanted a new dishwasher installed by Christmas, and paid with a check she knew full well would bounce.

"The *entire* form?" Kitty said. Behind her in the waiting room, Mrs. Patel looked up from her magazine.

"Have you ever wondered if she's like, uh, mildly retarded?" Alicia asked Brice, back when the three of us ate our lunches together. Brice looked insulted, he said something like "So your, uh, people aren't?"

His mother had told Brice that his college degree was useless, that he hadn't learned enough to tie his shoes.

"Can I maybe help you?" Mrs. Patel appeared at Kitty's shoulder. "It's not difficult, you sit down next to me and we'll . . ."

No, Kitty was not retarded. Brice's mother was as wily as an outlaw. She knew exactly what she wanted, and she got it.

"She's back in the exam room with the cabbage," I said at Brice's office door. "You can emerge now."

He looked up, and I almost had to turn from the tenderness in his eyes. His look said: *Caroline, you know me better than anyone. Caroline, you're a wonder.*

HAP MARKOWITZ

"Look at this." Will tossed a new patient history form on my desk. "Just generally. Don't get into the specifics."

The patient history sheet was bedecked with ink. There were arrows linking symptoms to explanatory paragraphs scrawled in the margins. Someone had clearly helped the patient fill this out—there was scribbly handwriting in blue and neat, loopy writing in black. I felt for the patient's helper: Did this person believe any of these symptoms, or was the patient saying "Write this down"? The list of surgeries overflowed the available space and continued onto a sheet of notebook paper. "Who is it?" I said. There were certain new patients you knew you'd be seeing all the time, and neither of you would make the other happy.

"Brice's mother," Will said. "Her name's Kitty. Like Miss Kitty from *Gunsmoke*?"

The TV show. There was a moment of silence while I tried to recall *Gunsmoke*.

"Matt Dillon's girlfriend," Will said.

"Wait a minute, wasn't she a madam?" I was trying to be funny, sort of, but Will was tense and awkward. If he were a bird, he'd be flapping his wings. It was more agitation than was reasonable about one miserable patient. Every doctor had miserable patients. You ended up more tied to them than to patients you were fond of.

"I thought she was sexy," Will said.

"Miss Kitty?" I grinned. "How old were you, eight?"

"Not that Miss Kitty. Brice's mother Miss Kitty. I thought it was just her name, and her hair being up in that"—he made a motion around his head like he was wrapping a turban—"but she was sitting there telling me about her feet hurting and I wanted, I wanted . . . I thought of her doing things to me."

Right away I knew what he'd been thinking. I nodded.

"Isn't that sick? Isn't that disturbing? What's happening to me, Hap? I mean, she's kind of creepy and she's *old.*"

"You don't . . . you don't know what'll hit you, sometimes." My voice caught: I was thinking back to Janis in a summer dress when we first met, and the tiny mole I spotted deep in her anterior axilla, at the border of her left breast.

"It's my own fault," Will said. "I've gotten into . . . stuff on the computer. It's like I can't help it, I don't have my own mind anymore, and there's always new stuff there, and stuff that isn't new but I'm just finding it, and I keep looking and looking and I . . ." He brought his hands up to either side of his head and waved them. "It's gotten away from me, Hap. I can't stop myself."

"Can't you get rid of your computer?" I said, wondering how this could happen to a man who had so recently gotten married.

"That's what Al says! Just don't bring it into the bedroom, she says, and, you know, it's not that easy, that stuff's sticky, it's like burrs on your socks, you think you've got them all off and then you . . . Like today." Will looked me haggardly in the eye. "Like with Brice's mother. Brice's mother, Hap! Look at that history! She's a nutcase!"

I had no idea what to say. Honestly, I'd never been on a porn website. Honestly, the sex I fantasized about was sex with Janis. I'd never had a problem in the bedroom, but I had wondered in the past if my testosterone level was low, if that could have been the reason Janis and I never made little Markowitzim.

"When I was married to Harriet, I was fine. I wasn't imbalanced. We had a decent sex life, I didn't think about it every—"

My beeper went off. I glanced down at the message in the window. MURIEL KINSOLVER, STRANGE BUZZING

"Middle-aged crazy," I said.

Will shook his head, looked away. "I don't want to end up like Kudrea." Kudrea was a Romanian plastic surgeon who'd been caught exposing himself outside his ex-girlfriend's apartment. All over the papers, you can imagine.

"Uncontrollable itching," I said, echoing Kudrea's courtroom defense.

"That could be anyone's excuse," Will said. "For anything."

Will wasn't dumb. His medical knowledge might be sketchy, he might have rushed into a marriage that was no good for him, but no one would ever convince me that Will was stupid.

"I think you just have to stop," I said, feeling helpless. "I don't know, maybe a marriage counselor?"

Will looked at me with immense sadness. "That's not it," he said. "That's not enough." I knew I was letting him down, but what else could I say? He was upset that he'd had lusty thoughts about Brice's mother. Didn't lots of men have lusty thoughts? And Will's thoughts wouldn't lead to anything. A middle-aged doctor going after his seventy-plus patient? Realistically, it wouldn't happen. Will's fantasies about Brice's mother would scoot across the sky like fluffy clouds. By tomorrow morning his brain would be perfectly clear.

Will stood, gestured limply at my phone. "Go ahead, answer your page."

~

Janis and I were almost asleep when I thought of the mole that used to drive me crazy. Tonight's sleeveless nightgown offered a glimpse of it, and I lifted my head and gently prodded her arm.

"What are you doing?" Janis said. I told her.

"Here." She extricated her arm from under the sheet and raised it.

"I can't make it out. It's too dark."

She used her free arm to reach for the light. We both looked. The mole was still there, a little drier and less brown than I remembered.

"That drove you mad with desire."

"Yes," I said, "mad." I bent my head to kiss it. "It was close to your breast, and I could only see it in a couple dresses."

"You should have told me. I would have whipped out my whole rack for you."

"Janis!"

"I would have. I would have been super-easy. You don't know. I wanted you from the beginning. You were such a"—there was a tiny pause here I wouldn't think about until later—"nice, clean boy."

"I was shy."

"Of course you were shy. I had to kiss you first, remember?"

She was the only woman I'd ever slept with. I hadn't admitted this to anyone, even to her, but she knew.

"Well," I said, settling my head back into the pillow, "it all worked out."

"It worked out fine. Get the light, okay?" she said, and I reached for it before I wrapped my left arm around her.

She took my hand and put it on her breast, which was our signal, but then she yanked it further and placed it between her legs, past her pulled-up nightgown. The springy hairs, the warmth, the unquestionable moistness—the whole thing was a shock.

"Easy, hunh?" I said, slipping a finger into her.

"Super-easy," she said, her body rotating into mine.

CAROLINE

My bedroom windows were open and Evan was curled with his head on my belly, and I could feel his eyelashes twitch against my stomach. He said, "I've been thinking. Maybe we should stop seeing each other."

"What?"

"Oh, you know," Evan pushed himself to sit upright and looked down at me. It dawned on me he must have a real girlfriend, one closer to his own age, one he could present to his parents and friends.

I said, "I'm sorry you think that."

"Yeah, I'm sorry too. But I think it would be better. Fairer for everybody."

"Who is it?"

Evan blinked quickly. "Girl in the office at work."

"Younger," I said, not a question.

"Twenty-two."

I had an impulse to throw a big metaphorical net over Evan, to keep him with me, but the net would have choked and terrified him; it would have made him hate me; it would have forced him to pretend not to see me at the mall. So I said, "I'll miss you," reaching out my hand to stroke his hairless chest, ripply and firm and probably waxed, although that was a vanity I'd intentionally never mentioned.

Evan said, "Me too." He looked at me in a worried way. "Don't you like me?"

"Are you kidding?"

"Well, don't you want to . . . ?" He stopped, and I knew what he wanted to say: "claim me" or "fight for me" or "argue with me," things I'd never do. I loved that song about showing that you loved someone by setting them free. I might have been the only woman alive who lived that song.

"You're seeing someone else," Evan said sharply, and the charge was so ridiculous that I laughed.

"You think I can't tell?" He scuttled out of bed backward away from me like a crab, shielding his crotch as he stood, then turned his back on me and looked wildly for his clothes.

"Evan, don't be—"

"Well, that's fine. You've got someone else. Fine, I won't have to worry about you." He put on his socks, he pulled his shirt on over his gorgeous shoulders—but this was an illogical way to dress, and it hit me he couldn't locate his briefs. I glanced around and spotted them draped over the arm of my lamp. "There"—I pointed, but he was already zipping his jeans before he belatedly spotted his underwear and stuffed it in his pocket. "You could leave it as a souvenir," I suggested, but this seemed to make him angrier, and he put on his shoes without tying the laces and stomped out.

He knew I couldn't follow him right off. My leg was in its usual spot between the bedside table and the bed. Unless I wanted the

humiliation of hopping naked after him, there'd be lifting and strap-
ping and adjusting—not to mention dressing—before I had a chance
to leave the bedroom.

The front door slammed. I rolled on my side, cast a glance at my
prosthesis, thought, Screw it. Evan's smell was on me. I heard his
footsteps outside, scuff scuff scuff quickly down the steps, and then a
hesitation. And even though he was through the wall and a story down,
I could picture his lip twitching and the furrow of his brow. I could
imagine his small, shell-like ears almost twitching to hear the sound of
my movement. I pushed my head under the sheet. A soft breeze wafted
through the open windows. I had an attic fan that moved air through
the whole house, and I hated the windows being closed. I liked the
noises of cars and insects and fighting cats.

Evan was wondering—I could hear him—if I was putting on my leg.
He was wondering if he should come back up my stoop and across my
porch into the house. He stood still on the sidewalk long enough for a
squirrel to skitter up the drainpipe next to my front bedroom window.

Of course I'd miss him: it was late August, when the night noises
outside reached a peak, when the whole insect world seemed to be in
heat. Maybe the world was keeping me from a man as a counterweight
to all the reproductive energy around me. Maybe the world didn't
want a fertile man to waste his summer seed on me. I believed this, I
felt this, but explaining it to anyone would be impossible. I'd sound
like a person deeply enmeshed in rationalization or denial.

Go on, I thought to Evan. Scoot, skedaddle, get out. But it took
another few minutes before Evan's footsteps moved off and I heard the
door to his car click open and thud shut.

That's the way it is with a breakup. Someone always suffers, and
who suffers more is often a surprise.

~

"I didn't know you had a man here," Mrs. Fussnecker said as she handed in her billing sheet, looking past me at Brice disappearing into his office.

"He's the one you never see." I pointed a thumb at the wall behind me. "His office is behind there." I lowered my voice. "He calls people who don't pay their bills." This was true, but rare: Brice took no joy in calling in reprobates; at times he begged me to do it.

Mrs. Fussnecker bridled, frowning. "Well, I hope he never calls me. He looks like a stickler."

I laughed. "He's really very nice. Good to his mother."

Was Brice a virgin? I wondered. The possibility was intriguing. I'd never figured out what he and Iris were up to physically.

Boredom and proximity and the absence of Evan. Hard to believe the weeds that sprang from that particular compost.

Such graceful hands. I wondered what he did with them all day. From inside his office, I could hear his chair squeak when he moved. Some afternoons it squeaked erratically for no reason. Like a caged animal, I thought. A locked-up dog desperate to be scratched behind the ear. A dog that would lick your hand and whimper.

HAP MARKOWITZ

Will told me that he and Harriet had never had a bad marriage. They bopped along and visited her parents and took their summer vacations to Michigan (Petoskey stones, lakes), they raised their girls, they had sex, of course they had the usual rough spots (discipline, bills), but suddenly Harriet was unfulfilled, she was making friends with weavers and woodcarvers and people whose dinner table conversation revolved around retreat centers and health shakes. She said things like "Consciousness is *hard*." Will was stunned. He thought that sort of shit had gone out with Earth shoes. "What's wrong with me?" he used to ask, and Harriet looked at him with bemused pity. "Oh, Will," she said, "you don't know who you are."

Will and Harriet's older daughter, Chloe, thought her mother had gone crazy. But Chloe's sister, Sarah, was on her mother's side. "You're just . . . *traditional*," Sarah told Will, pronouncing the word as if it were something tainted.

Will and I had been over this a hundred times. It was the central trauma of Will's life, the wellspring, as he saw it, of every one of his problems now. Harriet had holes pierced in her upper ears. She started sprinkling flaxseed in her yogurt. By the time the two of them were meeting together with their lawyers, it was hard to look at her without laughing. She closed her eyes and muttered, she tossed her furry scarf. She couldn't leave Will and still appear sensible, no—she had to go to extremes.

This was the ritual climax of his talk, the moment when his eyes widened and his words sped up and I sensed the danger of flying spittle.

But he missed her. He did miss her. The months between Harriet's moving out and the divorce becoming final, Will would do almost anything not to go home to an empty house. Late at night, he wandered around the hospital visiting his patients. He'd pull up a chair and sit himself at a bedside, terrifying the occasional old lady. He realized that, as much as his patients loved him, he'd never sat down with one to simply chat. People told him about their grandkids, their high school days long ago, listened as Will talked about college and his early, pre-Harriet romances. Late at night in a dark hospital room, the topics could get quite personal. The question was, just who was treating whom?

It was that old and brutal human question: Was there a place in the world for me? When things were going well, you never thought this. When they went wrong, you thought of nothing else.

And then, *there*, between Alicia's legs—Will thought that was his place. There she was in the exam room, bending over, the fabric of her scrub pants tight across her rear. The call to Will was so immediate, he had to think it meant more than pure lust. Years ago, before they had their daughters, Will and Harriet had gone to Costa Rica. All he really remembered about the trip was the tarantulas. The females, their male guide told them, hid themselves in tiny caves, letting the males skitter across the jungle floor trying to find them. The females lived up to twenty-five years, while the males only lasted two or three before some bird or snake managed to eat them. "But the males die *happy*," their guide said. Standing behind Alicia that first day in the exam room, Will thought about those happy spiders. He felt part of the grand scheme of nature. Risk didn't matter, morals didn't matter. He felt like half the universe was a driven thrusting thing like he was.

I looked down at my hands, wondering where his rant was leading this evening. I willed for my beeper to go off. Two nights ago I heard how the true purpose of Will's marriage to Alicia was Will's becoming a father to Jesse; last week I heard how Alicia's mother forced her own henpecked husband to take refuge in the basement.

The night before, Will found Alicia after dinner on a stepladder cleaning the tops of the window frames. "Are you ever going to finish?" he asked her after an hour, but she kept him waiting until he went to bed alone. Her very body seemed to have changed, her introitus dry and constricted, as if he had no business there at all.

Like the damn female spider, Will said, waiting for the male to leave her in her cave in peace. "But the male spider's not tied down!" Will said. "Why should human females get to tie us down?"

"And she wonders why I need the Internet," Will said. "Who wouldn't need the Internet?"

I'd figured something out. If I turned my beeper off and then back on, it made the same sound that it made when I got paged. I did this now to make Will stop. All I wanted was to get back home. Janis had moved our cold weather pajamas to the fronts of our respective drawers: the flannel twins, she called us in the winter.

~

There was a point where loyalty became a sickness, where faithfulness to someone else became a way to destroy yourself. I'd seen that in the spouses of alcoholics. I remembered Howard Dilliard, whose wife, Wilma, had hit him with a car. "You know how she gets," Howard said, shrugging as much as he could in his neck brace. Wilma giggled, said she hadn't really hit him, she'd just tapped him. Later, Howard had a heart attack in his wood shop, and Wilma kept mowing the lawn as the EMTs came and took Howard away. "Have you ever thought that she's killing you?" I thought of asking Howard, but the question seemed too obvious to voice. I should have voiced it. Two months later, stuck at home with a swollen leg and Wilma off God knows where, Howard threw a fatal blood clot to his lungs. Shot by his own gun, in a way.

You saw these things in other people, they seemed obvious. But you thought you were dreaming when you saw them in yourself. I should leave Will? I should start my own practice? Why would I do such a thing?

At about six-thirty on a dim Tuesday in October, the attack started in my office. The staff had gone home. Will was sitting in one of the chairs facing my desk and I was in my swivel chair behind it. We were talking about coding and HumanMed's dropping its reimbursement to Medicare's level and the staff's cost-of-living raises and the college fund that Will had set up for Jesse, and I was expecting any minute for Will to start in on a new complaint about Alicia. It hit me as we talked that Leslie Solganik, my patient with the high sed rate and the positive ANA, had loose bowel movements, so she could have sprue—but she had seen a GI doc, and wouldn't he have considered that diagnosis? Will was saying something about billing for Pap smears and I was trying to remember which GI doc Leslie Solganik saw. Was it Glaxman? Suddenly there was silence and I realized Will was waiting for an answer. "I'm sorry," I said, sitting up in my chair and giving my head a quick negative quiver. "You were saying . . . ?"

A look of fury in Will's face.

"Why should I bother to ask you anything?" he said. "The *Titanic*'s sinking and you're twiddling your thumbs. No! You're not even twiddling your thumbs! You're thinking about twiddling your thumbs. You're wondering if thumbs should be twiddled clockwise or the other way."

There was some truth to what he was saying. I couldn't deny everything. I shifted to the other buttock. "Actually, I was thinking about—"

"Who runs the world?" Will cut in. "The business owners, the managers, the ambitious. The bosses run the world! And why do you think they're bosses? Because they have the guts to understand that ninety percent of the people in the world aren't people. What are they? I'll tell you: they're *sheep*." With that, a spray of his spit hit the blotter on my desk. I reached for a tissue to wipe it off. "Think about it," he said, not seeming to notice me. "Is that nice knowledge? Is that knowledge you want to fall asleep thinking? Hell, no, but you're not thinking it. That's why the world needs people like me.

"I'm the person who gives this office any vision, any plan. Listen, anybody doesn't have vision, they don't have a future. They sit there like rocks, okay? Like you, okay? Either that or they go stark raving nuts. Either that or it's like Rwanda, people are chopping each other up . . ."

I wasn't following this. Bosses to sheep to Rwanda, the leaps seemed a little bizarre. Will might be trying to make a case for holding the middle ground, but at this point he hardly sounded moderate himself. Still, there was something riveting about passion, something no one ever saw in me. ". . . chopping each other up like Tutus and Hutsis . . ."

"Hutus and Tutsis," I said without thinking.

Will looked at me as if I were piddling and despicable. "What'd I say?"

"You said Tutus and Hutsis. It's really Hutus and—"

"Typical," he said. "Just typical. Goddamn self-righteous bullshit about something that doesn't even matter. It's like those fucking ears. You're not even good at ears!"

"No one's complained," I said, half joking, trying to dodge his metaphorical fists.

"They're afraid to complain! They think they'll hurt your precious feelings. Helen Bittwater had Alicia check to see if you'd broken her eardrum."

Thud. A blow had landed. "I didn't, did I?" I saw again the wad of dried brown wax in Helen Bittwater's ancient ear canal, heard her little squeals as I flushed it.

Will scoffed and shook his head, as if my even voicing the possibility of a mistake demonstrated my weakness.

"One thing I thought about a couple months ago," I said, pleased at the calmness in my voice, the deftness of my redirection, "is that we should have an office manual. If we had an office manual, a lot of these questions could be handled as policy."

"Fine, you write it. Make yourself useful."

My face burned, but I kept quiet.

Will stood up. "And make sure you put down ear irrigation as a nonphysician procedure. I don't want to see one fucking ear."

"Of course," I said, and Will walked out.

I didn't hurt Helen Bittwater's eardrum. If anything, I didn't get all her wax out.

I shouldn't have to put up with this, I thought. But I knew I would.

This wasn't about me and Will, I told myself. This is about Will being miserable with Alicia.

CAROLINE

Alicia missed their breakfasts together, Jesse's and hers. In their old life, she'd get him up at six-thirty, fix his egg and toast and pour out his orange juice while he took his shower, and then he'd sit across from her at their fake-wood kitchen table as Al had her coffee and yogurt. It wasn't that they had a lot of time together—they were out the door each morning by seven—but every morning had been the same. Will wasn't there asking if his toast was done, reminding Alicia to write down patient complaints so he didn't have to listen to a laundry list, telling her to go light on his Cheerios.

When Will went out of town for an internists' update, Alicia got up and showered early to make breakfast for her son. The smell of the toast as she buttered it was almost intoxicating.

"What's this?" Jesse said, his chair scraping as he pulled it out.

"I made you your old breakfast."

"Dad wouldn't like me eating eggs." *Dad*: to Alicia, it felt like a slap when Jesse called Will this. Had Jesse really been that lonely? Wasn't Alicia ever enough? She had tried so hard to be everything for him.

"Give me a break," Al said. "You two don't have a problem with Doritos."

Jesse sat. He didn't reach for his fork.

"What about those cheese curls? You two eat those cheese curls like they're brussels sprouts."

"Cheese curls and Doritos aren't high in cholesterol, Mom," Jesse said. "Cholesterol is an animal product."

"They're high in saturated fat and sodium, right?"

Was it the money? Was it the fact that Will was a doctor, and Jesse, A-plus student that he was, automatically respected that position? "Eat," she said, sitting across from Jesse. "One egg won't hurt you."

He gave her a look. He ate the toast, drank the orange juice, and was halfway through the egg before Alicia realized that he was eating around the yolk, leaving an unpierced orange button in the center of the plate.

"I grabbed it off his plate and popped it in my mouth and ate it," Alicia told me.

"What did Jesse do?"

"He just left for school. He walked out the front door and barely said good-bye."

I felt bad for her. You can't get things back, I thought, imagining her watching Jesse's shrinking form through the front window. I thought about waking up the first few mornings I was with Evan, how I hopped into my bathroom and smiled at myself in the mirror, holding up my hands to inspect my shaking fingers. Now those days seemed as distant as my childhood.

∾

Brice said that that morning when he left for work his mother was standing in the kitchen clutching her belly, saying that today he had to get her in with Dr. Strub. "Not that I care," Brice snapped. Still, it was strange: usually she stayed in bed until after nine.

"You worry about her," I said.

"I don't want to," he said quickly, with a small smile.

Brice's smile had been getting to me for some time. He didn't smile often, and when he did, it was quick and apologetic. Rarely would he offer a smile with any hint of happiness and hope. There were unhinged-looking people who showed all their teeth in a smile that was almost rectangular; people who smiled like movie stars, baring their top teeth in an aggressive way; people who smiled ruefully with their mouths closed; and then there was Brice, whose smile was a toppled parenthesis, his upper front teeth barely showing and a glimpse of the pointy canines on each side. It was just how Brice's mouth was shaped, I told myself, a look shaped by genes, not need, but there was a caution in that smile that broke my heart.

I tried to find a slot for Brice's mother. Dr. Strub's schedule that day was full, and I wasn't allowed to add a patient without checking with Alicia.

"Where is the pain?" Alicia asked Brice. "Is she eating? Is she going to the bathroom? Does she have a fever?" She waved at the people in the waiting room. "Your mother, no offense, your mother has a high level of somatic awareness. There's no point in screwing up Dr. Strub's schedule for somebody who's not sick."

Brice stood there with his sad smile, as if he deserved this abuse. "What about after lunch?" I said. "She's hurting a lot and she's—"

"A fruitcake," Alicia said, interrupting.

I gave Alicia a pleading look.

"It's nothing to be ashamed of. Everyone has a fruitcake relative." She made a bitter spitting sound. "People even marry fruitcakes!" She reached for the next chart on my ledge. "Huntingdon!" she called out through my window.

~

It was late in the workday on a Friday in early November. The last patients were back with their doctors. Kitty had sent Brice in with a Tupperware container holding an oddly shaped bowel movement she wanted Dr. Strub to look at, and Brice and I had been hiding the container in its plastic Wal-Mart bag in each other's spaces all day.

"Is my mother free?" Jesse was on the phone.

"Are you still in Georgia?" I asked. Jesse said yes. He was at a debate tournament, his first national level bout of the year.

I found Alicia restocking gowns in an empty exam room. She almost ran to the work area.

"Did you break?" Alicia said eagerly into the phone, taking a seat in my chair. I had learned what "break" meant in the debate lingo: reaching the elimination round. "You did? You went to the semi? You went to the *final*? Are you kidding me, you went to the final? So? So?" I bent over to peek at her face, but she didn't look back at me. "What do you mean, 'decent'? Did you win?"

She screamed. She flat-out screamed, she leapt to her feet and jumped around, she threw her head back and whispered, *"Yes yes yes,"* and shot her phoneless fist into the air.

Brice emerged from his office with a puzzled frown. "I think Jesse won his debate tournament," I whispered. I had last left the bag with his mother's specimen in the bottom left drawer of his desk, under the records of disputed billings.

"And you were good at the cross, that's what did it?" Alicia was saying into the phone. "How about the second negative, did your partner . . . ?"

Brice rolled his eyes and disappeared back into his office.

"Oh my *God*!" Alicia screamed. "Jesse, I'm so happy I can't see!"

Her eyes were closed. Her eyes were closed and her face squinched and her head back, the phone pressed tight against her ear. She was swaying. She could be one of those people at a Pentecostal church possessed by The Spirit.

Alicia was crying, fat streaks running down in her cheeks. In my whole life I'd probably never felt that happy. It was impossible for me to imagine the lack of self-consciousness that would let a mother scream about her child over the phone.

It sounded as though Jesse was telling his mother to calm down.

"I can't help it, honey. You don't have kids, you . . ."

"Here," I said, reclaiming my chair, "give me the phone. You're making your mother mad with happiness, you know that?" I told Jesse. "She scared Brice out of his cave, you believe that? Oops, here comes your stepdad to see what's going on. Listen, Jesse, congratulations from all of us." *He won*, Alicia was mouthing to Dr. Strub, doing a little dance. "I hope someday you're fighting for confirmation on the Supreme Court," I said into the phone. "We'll testify for you."

"Don't do drugs!" Dr. Strub said, leaning over my shoulder. "Don't cavort!"

"Did he say 'cavort'?" Jesse said.

"You cavort all you want," I said. "Our lips are sealed."

Dr. Strub snatched the receiver. "Dude," he said into the mouthpiece, "you done good." A big grin spread over his face. "Right. Take my bad grammar as a compliment."

"Oh, Caroline," Alicia said, throwing her arms around my shoulders from behind. It felt surprisingly good to be hugged; I lifted my hand and laid it on hers.

"That debate camp was worth it," I said to Alicia.

"Everything was worth it," Alicia whispered, and I remembered years before when she'd taken a second job to save money for an educational trip to Yellowstone for Jesse. I glanced toward Dr. Strub and winced, thinking of her cracks about his you-know-what.

But Dr. Strub looked as exultant as Alicia. He said into the phone, "Hell, colleges are going to be fighting to give you a scholarship!"

Maybe it wasn't great being sterile. I glanced past Dr. Strub and spotted Brice standing in front of his office, holding his mother's Wal-Mart bag aloft and pointing at it with a grin. "Good one," he mouthed.

Poor Brice's mother, poor Brice, poor me. I felt like crying for us all.

CAROLINE

Brice's mother had nothing wrong with her GI tract. Ultrasounds and MRIs and scopes, three-day stool samples, radioactive meals, bloodwork for diseases neither Brice nor I had ever heard of: everything was normal.

Shortly later she got chest pain. Dr. Strub put her in the hospital for observation.

Brice was very good at keeping himself occupied while his mother had tests. Sitting in the CCU waiting room below the harvest cornucopia wreath, he recoded a stack of charts, finished two crosswords, and organized a new list of his favorite twenty movies. This one was a little different, although *Godfather I* and *II* and *Doctor Zhivago* stayed on top. He didn't realize until he got in bed—alone at home, what bliss—that Joan Crawford movies had gone off his list completely. He hadn't considered even one! Jesus, should he feel guilty? Leaving off films starring his mother's favorite actress had been unconscious.

"Really, this is it," Brice said. "I'm declaring myself D-I-V-O-R-C-E-D from my mother. What's she going to do next, fake a stroke?"

HAP MARKOWITZ

At dinner one night at Giuseppe's, Janis told me about her dream. In her dream she gave birth to two seal pups, but the doctors walked away too early, and she was stuck with two more inside her.

"I hate it when the bulbs are in," she said. The week before, she'd replanted 640 tulips. "I start watching too much Animal Planet."

"What happened to the seals left inside you?"

"I don't know. The last thing I remember I was screaming at the doctors to come back."

What could I say to a dream like that? A childless woman, an inhuman birth, the doctors too busy or uninterested to stay.

"The pups were adorable," Janis said. "White and furry with those big black eyes." She rolled her eyes, and I looked away. Was I the father? Surely I was not the father.

"You're right, too much Animal Planet." I picked up my menu to deflect the conversation. "You're not going for the veal again, are you?"—which I meant as a joke, because at Giuseppe's Janis always ordered veal piccata.

Janis said, "I think I'm done with veal. Animal Planet again." I looked up as she disappeared behind the menu, the top of her hair flaring in a nimbus of light from the candelabrum on the wall.

I said, "Was I the father?"

"There really wasn't a father, there was just the ..." She set the menu down. "How's the eggplant Parmesan? Have you tried that?"

"The rollatini's better."

"I'll do the rollatini." Janis pushed the menu to the edge of the table. "That was a sad dream, wasn't it? I had it last week. I was waiting for a chance to tell you."

We'd had nights together at home. I realized she'd been waiting to tell me in a restaurant, with strangers in booths around us, with Giuseppe's wife, Kelly, approaching us with her order pad. Janis said, "I think it was a dream about waste."

"You having to scream at the doctors," I said. "That's what gets me."

"I mean, I loved the two pups that came out. It was just that there were the other two stuck inside me, and—"

"You two ready?" Kelly said. I went vegetarian like my wife did, and we didn't talk about anything else of import, we talked about the weather and Janis's nieces' children and what Janis wanted to plant next spring, we talked about the same things we always talked about, yet there was a giant bubble between us, glimmering and iridescent, and both of us were careful with our voices lest we break it.

CAROLINE

I wasn't imagining things, Brice's mother said. That was real chest pain. *Was*, Brice thought: good. Past tense was good. Definitive tests that showed nothing wrong: good.

"Oh, Caroline," he said, passing his beautiful hand through the curls atop his head, "I'm tired."

Iris was gone for good, she'd moved on from Iowa City to California. Brice had no one to talk to, no one to see movies with, no one to snuggle during his evenings in his mother's basement. "Snuggle"—he used that word.

I could heal him, I thought. Maybe. At least make him ache less. What harm could there be in that?

~

"Hi, Caroline, how are you?" It was Mrs. Markowitz on the phone. I never knew quite what to say to her; she was such a quiet woman.

"Want to talk to your hubby?" I asked.

"Oh, don't bother him. I just need some information. What do you know about hepatitis C?"

I gestured for Lucy Chen to hand me her billing sheet, tore off her copy, and waved her good-bye.

A friend of Mrs. Markowitz's from the garden club had gone to give blood, because another woman in the club had chronic leukemia, and that started everyone thinking about the responsibility of donating blood. At any rate, two days after the friend donated, the blood bank called her and said they were throwing her blood away, because it tested positive for hepatitis C.

"Your garden club meets now?" I said, surprised, because it was almost November and plants were turning brown. Mrs. Markowitz said oh yes, people had more time for meetings off-season.

"The blood bank's sending her information," Mrs. Markowitz said, "but it'll take a few days and I knew I could ask you. Hap's so busy. Please, don't bother him with this. Or I can just wait."

It was a viral infection, I told Mrs. Markowitz, trying to remember the things I'd heard the doctors tell patients. Sometimes it didn't do anything bad, other times it could cause long-term liver problems and maybe even ... "liver cancer," I almost said, but I stopped myself. "Well, some liver problems," I said, twisting my computer monitor so Asa Walker could see the openings the week of March 10.

"How do you get it?"

"Thursday at two," Asa whispered, pointing, and I typed in his name.

"One quarter from blood transfusions back before they could test for it, one quarter from sexual transmission, one quarter from IV drug abuse, and one quarter no one knows."

I looked up to see Brice at the side of my desk. I put up a finger to tell him to wait a moment.

"Your friend's husband should get tested," I said into the phone, remembering Dr. Markowitz lowering his voice and leaning across my desk to give a last message to an unhappy-looking patient. "We'll set you up with Dr. Noverkian, he's a liver specialist," Dr. Markowitz had said. "The medicine's nasty, but sometimes it's worth it."

"Oh, I'll tell her," Mrs. Markowitz said quickly. "Thank you."

Brice made a face and drummed his fingers on my desk.

I mouthed to Brice: I'm talk-ing. He glared. Like a spoiled six-year-old, I thought. The last person I wanted to sleep with, I thought.

"Can you get Dr. Strub to sign for more Hismanal?" the drug rep at the window said, passing me a form. She turned to the woman in line behind her. "You're a new patient for Dr. Strub? You'll love him. He's really nice and he *smells* so good."

"My mother's on the phone," Brice hissed. His eyes, already squinty, narrowed more.

More pain? I mouthed.

"Who's a good liver specialist?" Mrs. Markowitz said over the phone. "I'll tell my friend."

I looked at Brice. His eyes were closed now, his hands still, his palms turned toward his legs.

How can she do this to him? I thought about Brice's mother. How dare she? *She should get cancer*, I thought automatically, but in Brice's mother's case this didn't seem like a good idea. I looked at Brice's hands again, pale and pointing like arrows at the floor. I'm not his safety net, I thought. I'm not his savior. I felt a little sick, because if I wasn't, who else would be?

~

That year Alicia did Thanksgiving for her whole family, like she always did. By Thanksgiving noon, the turkey was in the oven, the creamed mushrooms and cranberry relish were made, and she'd already been outside and swept leaves off the driveway. She was peeling potatoes and dropping them into a pot of salted water when Jesse walked in from the den. "Grandma called. They're going to be late."

"Late? How late? Did she say why?"

"She says Grandpa's sleeping in."

"That's why I didn't set dinner earlier!" They were supposed to eat at three. "Goddamnit, he can set his alarm!" Alicia peeled the potatoes like she was attacking them. "Did she ask to talk to me?" Al kept up her whacking and looked Jesse in the eye. She knew her son too well: he couldn't lie. Jesse gave an awkward shrug.

"Typical of my mother to try and avoid me," Alicia said to me.

All four of her siblings were coming. Her parents were picking up Kenny and Lena, because Kenny's car had a shot carburetor, and of course they'd also bring Chelsea (she lived with them), which left only Dick, who would probably forget Thanksgiving anyway, and Briana's gang, but they were always late.

"Can you imagine?" Alicia asked me. "I had fifteen pounds of pota-toes, I was up till two a.m. brining that turkey, and now they're telling me they'll be late? And I'm thinking everything's going to be dried out and disgusting. God, I don't know why I bother. Why do I bother? Because I'm the botherer. *Let's ask Alicia, she'll do a nice Thanksgiving.* And does my family even appreciate me? No, they think I'm a bitch. It's an insane family."

Will appeared in the kitchen, his hospital rounds over. "What's all this banging going on?"

"I'm trying to do something nice for people!" Alicia screamed. She saw Jesse and Will exchange glances, and it made her crazy to see them smiling. She grabbed the pot of peeled potatoes and swung it onto the stove top and somehow the whole thing fell, water and potatoes pelting her legs and potatoes bouncing on the floor.

She had to change her clothes upstairs and Will invented a story (pot too heavy, potholders slipping), because Briana's gang showed up early.

"I can't stand it," Alicia said to me. "I feel like I'm dying."

HAP MARKOWITZ

Janis was Will's patient, the way that Harriet had once been mine. Alicia so far as I knew didn't have a doctor. Will didn't see Janis often, just for an occasional cough or sprain, things I thought might need a medication or an X-ray that I didn't feel right ordering myself. When Janis's mother died, Will gave her a few sleepers. Because she listed him as her primary care doc, Will got reports when Janis saw specialists. This meant he knew from Dr. Noverkian about her hepatitis C before I did. Caroline and Alicia must have known too: they opened the mail, and I couldn't imagine they'd let a letter about Janis pass through their hands without reading it. Human curiosity was normal; I didn't begrudge it. What I did begrudge was Janis leaving me in my bubble of obliviousness for over a week as I chatted with Alicia and Caroline about her garden plans for next year and told Will about the musical she and I were going to see that weekend. For those nine days, everyone but me knew my wife was ill. Human pride was normal too: no one wanted to be shown up as ignorant. And I was. My one consolation was that I suspected Brice had not found out. He seemed more isolated from Caroline than he once was, and she and Alicia might not have shared their knowledge with him, instinctively protecting Janis as one of their female own.

The day after Janis told me about her hepatitis C (at another restaurant, behind another menu, as if this were news of nothing more consequential than a bug bite), there was a bitter part of me that spoke a little longer with my patient, Sue Nelson, than I needed to, that followed Sue Nelson to the lobby, that gave her a sidelong glance when she lifted her hair over her fur collar and pulled on her gloves and said that I should stop by her gift shop. Sue was attractive, divorced, healthy—a little bossy, but a man like me could use that. I could imagine her calling me to help unpack some new shipment in the back room at her store. Sue Nelson and I could have backroom assignations for years— she could even put a sofa in the back for us—and when I retired and decided to move to Santa Fe, Sue Nelson and I would go hand in hand to Janis and tell her we were taking off. "It's for the best," I'd say to Janis. "Sue knows me better than anyone. And I knew you wouldn't want to leave your garden."

~

One night in early December we were coming home from Meijer, where we'd bought Legos for Janis's nephew's birthday and coffee yogurt for me and ibuprofen for Janis. It was dark out but spookily warm—some kind of front was coming in—and our car windows were cracked open. Since Janis had told me about her hepatitis, it had been hard to look her in the eye. Two times thus far I had given her weekly injections of the hepatitis C treatment, ribavirin and interferon, with (I hated to admit this) a certain glee. There! I thought as I plunged the needle into her buttock. You should have told me!

The ibuprofen eased a little the side effects of interferon, fever and aching. Dr. Noverkian had also put Janis on an antidepressant.

"I know what my hepatitis C was from," Janis said as I turned right out of the Meijer parking lot. "Drugs."

Like a cannonball into my abdomen. What would she tell me next? She spent her days as a prostitute? She'd fallen in love with another woman? It took her nine days and a threat from Dr. Noverkian to tell me about her hepatitis C at all; another week to persuade her to try the interferon. Dr. Noverkian's letter to Will, which I eventually saw, stressed the importance of my being tested, and said that my wife had been "urged" to tell me her diagnosis. (I was tested; I was healthy.) The letter also listed the cause of Janis's hep C as "idiopathic," meaning its cause was unknown. There was an old medical joke about "idiopathic": that it meant the doctor was an idiot and the patient was pathetic.

But I was the idiot. I was pathetic.

"Drugs?" I said. A thought hit me. "Marijuana doesn't count, you know." We grew up in the sixties and seventies, and normal good kids did try things, although I'd never imagined that Janis did. She'd never mentioned it.

"It wasn't marijuana."

"Cocaine doesn't count, either," I said, glancing toward her. "Not unless you inject it."

"I did inject it. And not just cocaine, it was . . . various mixtures." She extended her left arm and pointed. "Here."

Her arm was as white and unscathed as a roll of exam table paper. My mouth went dry. "You're kidding."

"No. I injected drugs maybe twenty times over about six weeks when I was a senior in high school. It was that boyfriend I had. Zuni. I've mentioned him."

"The one who changed his name from Todd and said his dog was half wolf?" A classmate of her big brother's. All through college she'd barely dated, because of the trauma of Zuni.

Janis nodded. "I couldn't say no to him for a while. It was like I lost my self."

I should have known, or at least have sensed it. There was a thick silence whenever Zuni's name or its echo came up—when her brother visited, or a cable station ran a show on a cult leader like Charles Manson or David Koresh, a piece she'd always watch in a thoughtful, grieving way, as if (I saw this at that moment) she herself could have been one of those young bewitched women.

How did I miss it? What was wrong with me not to see it?

"I got my AIDS test back," Janis said. "It was negative. Dr. Noverkian said I should be checked to be on the safe side."

"You told Larry about Zuni and the drugs." Anyone who admitted ever injecting drugs got checked for HIV. My voice had gone even flatter. Larry Noverkian was an excellent hepatologist and a compassionate guy—but he was religious, Catholic, active in the local antiabortion physicians' group, and it killed me to think of him looking down on Janis.

"I didn't want to hide it anymore. He couldn't have been nicer. He drew the blood himself."

"Did he wear gloves?"

"Everyone wears gloves." Larry and I and other doctors in our generation didn't grow up using gloves to draw blood, and it hurt me that Larry felt he needed them with Janis. Although of course he needed them with Janis: my wife had hepatitis C.

"I always . . ." Janis hesitated. "I kind of thought it was justice that I didn't get pregnant. I knew what I'd been like with Zuni, and you can think of not getting pregnant as a punishment, and I always thought maybe that's what I deserved."

I couldn't drive. My vision went funny as if I were looking through glass brick, and I had to pull over and put on the emergency blinkers. "You think you deserved to not get pregnant?"

"Maybe in a karmic sense. You know. 'The wheels of justice grind slowly, but they grind exceedingly fine.'"

I closed my eyes and covered my face with my hands. For a moment I couldn't talk, but the cool air through the car window eventually calmed me. "You think because you shot up drugs with some Pied Piper when you were seventeen, you don't deserve to have children?"

"Hap"—Janis's voice curled—"don't be mean."

"You're wrong," I said, and this came out sounding harsh. I pressed the buttons and the car windows—both mine and Janis's—glided up. Janis's eyes were wide and bloodshot and she looked ready to bolt out of the car. "You're punishing yourself for something you did before you were even formed. You were a kid! He was older! I'm sure not getting pregnant was me. I don't have sperm, or if I do, they sit there like dead tadpoles."

A flash of shock hit Janis's face, and she reddened. I realized she'd never thought it might be my fault that we didn't get pregnant. "Oh, no, Hap. With another woman, you could have had a child."

"I didn't want a child with another woman! I didn't want another woman. All I've ever wanted was you."

She said nothing. She sat staring at the dashboard, her right hand up to her mouth, biting the soft area between her thumb and her first finger. "I guess you have me. For better or worse."

My beeper went off. I shut it off, didn't even read the message in its window.

"You're all I ever wanted," I said again, my voice soft now, and she nodded without looking my way. The air outside turned abruptly cold and I turned the key in the ignition, started the heater. Someone honked as if we were in their way, although we were fully off the road. Soon Janis was calming me, telling me it hadn't been that bad, after a while you get used to anything, it wasn't on your mind every minute each day, it was background. "Has our life been unhappy?" she said. "I've been happy. Haven't you been happy?"

"Of course I've been happy, but you, you . . ." I was struggling with a memory now, a mental picture of her sitting on a bench facing the river that runs through Midburg, looking haunted. "This kookiness in your past: you were a child, you were trusting, it was nothing your fault, but it's colored your, your . . ."

Her face seized up in a terrible way, and I saw it would be ruthless to say more. It would be like telling Caroline the pathology on her amputated leg was benign. *It's all a mistake, don't worry!* It was too late; the damage was irrevocable, and now all Janis and I could do was pick through the debris.

"I should have told you," Janis said. "I wasn't sure how you would take it."

How I'd take it? No more faith in me than that? The car had gone stuffy, the back window fogging up. Someone else honked—three quick jabs. They probably took us for parkers. "Let's not worry about that now," I told Janis. "Let's go home."

We drove numbly through the night, around corners, under green lights, past front-yard nativity scenes and Santas, past Speedways and drugstores and fast-food establishments, until we turned left onto a nicer street, onto our street, a lovely street where driveways severe in their straight whiteness sprang from the sides of the road.

The flannel twins. The innocence in that phrase seemed to come from another life.

CAROLINE

Sometime before Christmas, Brice asked if his mother could be added on for abdominal pain. "The same pain?" I said, but Brice looked so sad and worried I asked Alicia to approve the visit. In my opinion, Alicia owed me: I listened to her complaints for what seemed like hours every day. I had even listened to her through the office Christmas dinner, when her whining about Will and his schedule embarrassed everyone there.

She responded with a note left on my desk.

NO

NO

A THOUSAND TIMES

NO

Minutes later, Brice emerged from his office. "Any luck?"

"Have your mother come in at five," I said. "I'll put her on as Strub's last patient."

I thought there would be fireworks, but there weren't. I thought Alicia would shoot me dirty looks all afternoon, but instead she sat at her desk and nattered on about the shopping she had left.

Then, at four forty-five, once the last patient before Kitty had arrived, Alicia ran to the lobby and locked the front door.

"You are out of control." I hissed through my window at Alicia.

"I told you no! I told you a thousand times no!"

"I checked with Dr. Strub."

"You did not check with Dr. Strub!"

"I did!"

I had—although admittedly after Brice's mother was already on the schedule. Alicia went tearing down the hall to him. When she returned she was even angrier. She opened the front door for Brice's mother, took her vitals and deposited her in an exam room, then slammed into her seat behind me.

Dr. Strub told Brice's mother to eat more fiber.

"I hope you're happy," Alicia said to me and Brice once Kitty had left. "I hope both of you are hoppy-fucking-happy."

Dr. Strub left, Dr. Markowitz left, Alicia left.

I knocked my fake foot against the his door frame. "Hi, Brice. Hoppy-fucking-happy yet?"

He didn't look up from his computer. "That was a new line to me," I said, and there was a hint of a reaction, a twitch in Brice's shoulders. "What're you doing?" I asked.

Brice turned the computer screen to show me Herbert Cassidy's billing record. His insurance had denied payment for an office visit. Probably some coding problem, Brice said: Brice would have to go through Cassidy's chart and revise the bill before he resubmitted it. "See how thrilling my life is?" he said.

I shouldn't worry about him, Brice said. Tact had never been Alicia's strong point. Remember when she called Mrs. Southerin Mrs. Suffering?

"She's changed," I said, wincing. "She isn't funny anymore." I felt my face twist, the corners of my mouth going down and my eyes squinching and blinking. Was I about to cry? I hoped not. "Listen," I said. "You're not responsible for your mother. You're your own person."

He looked up at me then, and the flash of gratitude in his face was almost painful to witness. "Thank you, Caroline," he said, and he smiled his sad smile.

No. Don't do that, Brice. You deserve more than that, Brice. Before I knew it, I was on Brice's side of the desk leaning over, my chest under my white sweater (which I'd really gotten too big for; I wouldn't have worn it if I had planned this) in front of Brice's nose. "You sell yourself short," I said. "You're always selling yourself short."

It was probably too much breast for him. His chair rolled back and hit the credenza. I grabbed for Brice's hands, pressed them between mine. "You're a special person, Brice," I said.

That didn't sound right. Very, very special. Like Calvin Barnes, who drooled and smiled in my third-grade class. I could hear the fan in Brice's computer behind me, the ticking of the clock outside his office on my wall. I said, "I think I like you more than anyone on earth."

Looking back, I almost can't believe I said that, but at the moment it seemed true. I'd like to say that my offering myself to him was nothing more than a good deed, a desperate attempt to snap him into joy. But it wasn't that simple. The tragic uselessness of his beautiful hands had a magnetic effect on me. He was like a ruined mansion I could picture cleaning and painting and refurbishing into glory, and already on his lap I was flushed with anticipatory pride, imagining the completion of my vision. That pride pushed me, I suppose—that and the fact that I hadn't had sex with anyone since Evan.

Brice looked half astonished, half terrified. *Me?* his eyes said. *Me???* Yet, he was forcing himself to look back at me (I respected his guts in this) and I knew that he would find my face sincere. *Caroline? Caroline wants me?* I glanced again, embarrassed, at my sweater—acrylic with tiny darkish pills studding the front of it, a thing I needed to throw away—but Brice didn't seem to be aware of my clothes at all. His hands between mine were warming up; his aster-blue eyes were gazing into mine, and before I knew it I was saying how beautiful his hands were, how I liked to think of them moving over me.

"Not that you're picky," Brice said, and I must have looked so hurt he immediately apologized and bit his lips together, coloring them even more. His cheeks flushed.

"They're just, you know, regular hands," he said. "I mean, my hands."

"They're not," I said, pressing them to either side of my face. "Nothing about you's regular." At that moment this was true, and this was good.

HAP MARKOWITZ

"You know what I feel like?" Janis said one day after we'd finished our Christmas shopping. "Bland Canadian food." There was a new Tim Hortons restaurant in town, and we drove there.

Tomato soup, egg salad on a white roll, Boston cream doughnut. We ate in silence in our car in the parking lot, the heater on and the radio turned to NPR. We went back there maybe once a week. I will think of those foods and those days for the rest of my life.

HAP MARKOWITZ

The week before Christmas, Janis came down our stairs in her open-toed slippers and slipped. Her foot caught in the banister and the rest of her pitched forward.

I was at the hospital doing rounds. I didn't hear the crash. But when I got home and found her with her foot up, I was relieved at what I found: a broken big toe, a thing that even I could fix.

The toe looked terrible—bruised and misshapen even after I buddy-taped it to the toe next door. But it would heal. In the meantime, it wasn't the pain that bothered Janis. "I won't be able to sleep," she said. "I can't tuck my ankle in."

It turned out that every night as she spooned in my arms she brought her left foot in front of her right and tucked her left Achilles tendon between her first two right toes.

"How come I've never noticed this?" I said. "How long have you slept like that?"

"I don't know. Forever."

She cradled herself, I realized. And here I'd thought I was the cradler.

I spent maybe an hour total every year with most of my patients, and I knew them better than I knew Janis. I could recite Elsa Winters's eating habits, for example, in zestful detail. I felt like crying. "Do you have any other quirks?" I asked. "Do you always start in one part of your mouth when you floss your teeth?"

Janis seemed to find my distress amusing. "I'm pretty normal other than that foot thing."

"You don't clean out your belly button with a toothpick, do you?" (Kathryn Wilson). "You don't eat eight raisins soaked in gin every morning?" (Herb Wonderleigh).

It was a Wednesday, and she was almost recovered from the effects of the shot I'd given her Sunday night. That dose I'd tried to do something new: I'd envisioned myself injecting her with not just medicine, but hope. "You're cute when you're worried." Janis smiled, cuffing my face with the back of her hand. "No wonder your patients love you."

～

The Friday morning between Christmas and New Year's, I walked into the office after hospital rounds and found Caroline conferring with Brice in his doorway. She turned around abruptly when I opened the back door. "Dr. Strub called," she said. "He needs you to go back to the hospital to get him."

Will's car must not be starting, I thought. "Me?" I asked, thinking of the patients waiting in the lobby (quite a number, by the look of our parking lot). "Why not Alicia?"

"Alicia's not here. I called their house but there's no answer." Caroline glanced quickly over her shoulder at Brice, then returned her gaze to me. "You think I should go over there and check?"

We stared at each other a moment, remembering Alicia's comments at the Christmas dinner: "... didn't know I was marrying my father ... Ooh, don't upset the Boss. ... Will, why don't you have another drink and be fun for a change?" I said, "You're sure Will's at the hospital?"

"He called. He said he took a taxi to get there."

"Did he say anything about Alicia?"

Caroline shook her head.

"Did he sound ..."

"Okay," Caroline said too quickly.

In an emergency, I was usually pretty calm. I didn't assume the worst. But this time my voice had a quiver. "I don't think they've been one hundred percent happy." I was running through my lawyer patients in my head, thinking—if Will had done anything crazy—which one I might discreetly ask for the name of a criminal attorney.

"I'm going over to their house," Caroline said, reaching for her coat hanging on the rack by the door.

Will was waiting for me outside the hospital, head down against the wind, hands tucked under his arms. As he got into the car he kept his face turned away from me.

"Are you okay?"

"Little car accident," he said with an apologetic smile, and as he looked toward me I saw a bruise below his right eye.

"Don't tell me Alicia hit you."

He gave a jittery laugh. "No, I did this myself."

"Is Alicia okay?"

"She's fine. Just a little upset I was out till three, is all."

He would tell me more later. He was glad Caroline had gone to check on Alicia. Maybe after work—if Alicia made it to work, she might not want to see him—Caroline could drive her home? Maybe after work I could drive Will to an appointment?

CAROLINE

I didn't talk much about my missing leg—it wasn't interesting, really—but I expected it to bring me some respect. By and large, my lovers came to my house. My day-to-day leg was basically a metal post down to the foot, certainly not made for intimacy or sleeping, and—whether or not someone was with me—I always took it off when I went to bed. My bathroom was ten feet away, and I had a zippy hopping path along the furniture. My shower was one of those old-fashioned tile cubes, and it was easy to balance myself—keeping my hands free for washing and showering—by propping my stump against the wall. I could have gotten various pull bars installed around the house—my medical insurance would have paid for them—but things like that just seemed like giving in. There was a cabinet around the bathroom sink to lean on, a chair rail in the upstairs hall and railings on both sides of the stairs. Some evenings I took off my prosthesis as soon as I got home, and some weekend days I didn't put it on at all. This wasn't laziness. The inner lining of a Bali push-up bra was the best thing I'd found for padding the inside of the prosthesis, but sometimes the stump got sore despite the Bali. Also, my balance was different without the weight of my fake leg, and I wanted to always be mobile—or potentially mobile—on one leg alone. In case of fire, in case of disaster, in case of war. It was logical if you thought about it, but people didn't.

"You're a real fireball," a lover might say. Or: "Nothing slows you down, hunh?" Or: "Geez, my uncle had just his foot cut off and he went around in a wheelchair." Everybody said *something*, and I didn't realize how much I needed that praise until Brice was in my bed.

We were relaxing after making love when Brice noticed my spare leg propped in the corner. "What's that?"

I followed his gaze. "Oh! That's my spare."

Brice said, "It's a little creepy."

"Creepy?"

"Not creepy, exactly; unnerving. Could you cover it or something?"

Ridiculous. Half of me wanted to get out of bed and stow the thing in a drawer, just to show lazy Brice how easily I could get around, and half of me thought to hell with him, that leg was part of me.

"I'm not covering it or something," I said in irritation. "That's my party leg."

A high-pitched laugh. "Your party leg? That's weird."

"See the shoe on it? It's designed for a two-inch heel. I wear it if I'm dressing up. You've seen it, at the office Christmas dinners."

He fell silent. He was facing me and the party leg was in his view beyond my shoulder, and he pushed himself up in the bed so that my breasts would block the sight of it. Of course I noticed.

"I'm very proud of that leg," I said. "You think you can wear the same leg for flats and high heels? My regular leg was covered by insurance, but the party leg I had to pay for."

"Oh."

"You don't think it helps a woman's self-respect to wear heels?"

"I never thought about it."

"Well," I said, disappointed, "I guess you wouldn't."

HAP MARKOWITZ

The Friday that I fetched Will and his bruised face from the hospital, I drove him to his appointment after work. "Where are we going?" I asked.

"You'll see," Will said.

On the drive he filled me in. The night before, he'd gone to bed a little late—he'd been on the computer, he admitted it—and Al was already asleep. When he tried to wake her, she said, "Get out of here! Just get out of here!" So he did.

Looking back, he could see how tired Alicia was and how Christmas must have seemed like a wall ten feet high she was supposed to climb over without a ladder, but at the moment it was only Will, Will, Will.

The purring car, the dark slushy streets, the glowing candy canes hanging on the streetlights. Will drove downtown and over to Fifth Street, where girls flitted like snowflakes into his vision. He wouldn't get infected by a blow job. He'd check their lips for any sign of herpes. He veered into the middle lane, suddenly shy, and then he circled the block maybe five times, convincing himself to pull over.

Two black girls were on the curb, one tall and dark in a miniskirt and boots and a shorter one with big smooth hair and furry jacket. Two girls. Will's breath got short and he touched his wallet, not sure what these things cost. He pulled to the right and rolled down the passenger side window and the girls bent over.

"You busy?" he said.

"Not too busy."

"Why don't you get in?"

The short one was already reaching for the passenger door. "What you looking for?"

"Should we go somewhere?" Will said. "I thought we could get in the back—"

"Dr. Strub?" said a voice, and for an instant Will thought it was his conscience.

It was the taller girl. Her face appeared in the door behind the short one's. He knew that face. He knew the girl's mother—Esther Tinklepaugh—although he couldn't remember the girl's name. What was she doing here? Where had he seen her before?

"What're you doing here?" Esther Tinklepaugh's daughter said. "Aren't you married? You should go home."

"We can have a good time," the shorter girl said, ignoring her. "What do you want us to do?"

"It's Lucinda," the tall girl said, thrusting her face over the short one's shoulder. "I saw you last Christmas, remember? Bronchitis."

Wait a minute. Wasn't Esther's daughter trying to pass the police exam? Had she flunked it? Had she had to resort to . . . ?

"Then a light went on!" Will said to me. "You get it? It was a sting!"

Lucinda said to just go home. "You gave me that antibiotic that starts with B, kind of a horse pill, leaves a bad taste in your mouth?"

"Biaxin."

"That's right, Biaxin! I love Biaxin. Second day I was better." She tapped the shorter girl's shoulder insistently. "Antibiotic. He's my doctor."

"Your doctor?" The woman jumped back. "Doc, you shouldn't be out here. The women out here aren't clean."

"We're clean." Lucinda jabbed her partner. "It's okay, I know what you were doing, Doc. You were checking us to be sure we're healthy."

"That's right," Will said, but he was frozen and couldn't move the stick shift, because suddenly he could imagine his photo in the paper and the snickers and the jokes, like the Romanian surgeon with his itching.

Somehow he got the clutch down and the stick moved and he screeched off, the girls actually jumping back, and he turned right at the first street and went straight until he hit a stop and had to turn left onto a one-way street. No idea where he was. Alicia's scolding face was in front of him and the hospital chief of staff was saying, "Jesus, Strub, you're worse than Bill Clinton," and the cute nurses on Five West were gathered together casting glances his way and giggling. There was a light to his right and maybe a street to turn onto—wasn't he going east now, farther from home?—and he turned hard and there was slippage and a noise and nothing.

Now Will got to the meat of the story. Now his talking slowed down and he looked in my eyes. I knew he was coming to something he wanted me to be amazed at, although I almost couldn't hear him, my brain still buzzing with the news that he was ready to invite two prostitutes into his car. What was he thinking? Was he really another Kudrea?

"That's not possible," a man said, and Will felt something firm against his forehead, and he realized his hands weren't on the steering wheel at all. He could wiggle his fingers and feel fabric and something warm beneath it, but that was impossible because he was driving. Wasn't he driving? Also, he seemed to be talking but the noise wasn't coming out right.

"That's not possible," the man said again.

Not possible? Will picked up his head. God. I. Am. Such. A. Loser. Was that right? He couldn't tell.

"It's possible!" he said, and that sentence made sense, that was a real sentence. Then he realized his car was stopped, the front end of it shorter than it should be, a shaft of light illuminating a horizontal strip of brick. His door was open and the inside car light on and there was this guy leaning over him, feeling for the pulse in his neck, and the guy must be a paramedic.

"Where's my air bag?" Will said, and he tried to pat the steering wheel but the air bag was open and the steering wheel trapped beyond it.

Will had to tilt his head to see the guy beside him. Round face, balding head, nice, peaceful expression. "What's your name, son?" he said. Son? Will thought. This guy looked maybe thirty-five.

"William."

"William, Jesus didn't give his life for losers."

"What?"

The calm man said it again.

Will said, because it would be embarrassing to miss this: "You're not an angel, are you?"

"Hardly." He pointed through Will's windshield. "I'm Pastor Roger. You hit my sign."

"Zion Bible Church," Pastor Roger said. "You broke our sign of perpetual light. Don't worry, we've got excellent insurance."

"We're here," Will said to me, pointing at the brick and broken glass.

$\sim$

"Who's in this Zion Bible?" I asked Will a week or so later. Earlier that day Alicia had appeared in my office, closed the door behind her, and said that I was Will's best friend. "You're reasonable," she said. "Can't you talk to him?"

Will had been going for counseling with Pastor Roger almost every night. That Sunday he had attended the early service and the service, and on Wednesday he dragged Alicia and Jesse to evening prayers. Zion Bible was big—they'd just built a new sanctuary—and people were nice enough, but there was no one there they knew. Mostly people from New Paisley, on the eastern side of town. Our office and Will's and my houses were south.

"You really convinced about this Zion place?" I asked Will.

Silence. "What's your point?"

"No point, I was just talking."

"Alicia tell you I got saved?"

I nodded. "And now he says he's saved and he wants to share the good word with us," Alicia had said in a tone of despair.

"I'm different, Hap. Things have changed for me. I believe in Jesus Christ."

"I believe in the tooth fairy."

I wondered—during the long pause that followed this comment—why in the world I had said this, how it would taint our future, what I could say now. "Sorry," I said. "I didn't mean any disrespect, Will. Just a stupid joke." He said nothing. "You know me," I added, making a hopeless face.

"Zion Bible's a good place, Hap," Will said slowly. He fixed my eyes. "You should try it."

It was impossible to know if he was kidding—I hoped he was kidding! My God, he'd been to seders at my house!—and I looked away and ignored the comment.

"Is Zion Bible hooked up to some denomination, at least?" I said. "Bob Fullerton from the Lutheran church out on 722—you know he's my patient, right?—Bob Fullerton said Pastor Roger won't join the clergy council."

Will gave a dismissive snort. "Doesn't play well with others. Why should Pastor Roger get forced into some council? He's got meetings every night as is. He's quite a guy, Pastor Roger. He made that church out of nothing. He's got vision."

You bet he had vision, I thought. Walked out in the middle of the night and there was a doctor in a Lexus who just crashed his sign.

~

I used to believe in God. It was a no-brainer, something I couldn't not do. Growing up, I went to shul almost every Saturday. I could read Hebrew as easily as English. When I chanted the prayers, the ladies in front of me fluttered and said I should be a cantor. I went to services every Saturday through college and on the High Holidays through med school. But after I got married to Janis, whose family rarely went to church, I stopped going to services myself. I still fasted on Yom Kippur and occasionally snuck into the local synagogue to mark the anniversaries of my parents' deaths, and I would have defined myself as a nonobservant, God-believing Jew. But when Will hit that sign and in his desperate voice told me how his life had changed, I got doubts. It hit me that belief in God could be nothing but self-delusion, another of the lies we humans told ourselves to keep on going. I thought of laws carved on stone tablets that appeared out of the sky, a man alive in a fish's belly, a tower tall enough to pierce the clouds, lame men walking, dead fish multiplying, Jesus strolling across the water, and everything implausible in the Bible seemed impossible. The Bible was supposed to be God's truth? Give me a break, it was a bunch of far-out stories.

Religion was just too easy. It had the answers, it had the tales, it had a nice place for you to go after you die. People were too damn fond of comfort. They talked about getting a massage: "Oh, it was heaven." A massage was heaven? I hoped not. A sensual pleasure should not be confused with a spiritual reward. I could see heaven's appeal for certain populations (coal miners, slaves, Palestinians), but for well-fed, prosperous Americans, yearning for any afterlife seemed ungrateful. Why wasn't this heaven here?

Mrs. Jenkins was looking quite cheery. People talked a lot about "color," and it was one of those ineffable things for which medical science had no good explanation. Mrs. Jenkins had good color. Two months before, she was in the hospital with diverticulitis. "You look great," I said, pleased.

"I am." She cast me a quick, shy look, and confessed that she'd gone to a new church and she'd been saved.

An epidemic! "You don't go to Zion Bible, do you?"

Janis had not been able to explain saving to me. I asked her about it the night before and she got uncharacteristically huffy, as if I were mocking *The Ed Sullivan Show* or hula hoops, remnants of her childhood to which she was irrationally attached. She acted, I suppose, the way I did when she went on and on about the insanity of a kosher kitchen at home and shrimp at a hotel bar mitzvah party, an incongruity neither I nor any other of the Jewish attendees found particularly disturbing. A couple of her aunts were saved, Janis said. Nice aunts. There was nothing *wrong* with being saved. It could help people.

My relief—Mrs. Jenkins goes to Central Nazarene, not Zion Bible—made me positively chatty. "Can I ask you something?" I said, and Mrs. Jenkins smiled in encouragement. "How does saving happen? Is there a procedure for it? Do you, I don't know, stand in front of a panel of ministers or go sit in one of those confession boxes and take a test?"

A funny moment. We were grinning at each other, we were trying, but the gaze that passed between us was as blank as if one of us were talking Swahili.

Mrs. Jenkins took a breath. "You don't go to church, do you?"

"I'm Jewish."

"Oh, you're *Jewish*." Her eyes lit up, and I wondered if she'd heard that Jewish doctors were the smart ones. "My church loves the Jewish people."

What kind of statement was that? It was like saying a school loved cole slaw. But Mrs. Jenkins, apparently unaware she'd said something baffling, moved quickly on: "Being saved is accepting Jesus in your heart. It's a personal thing, one day you feel it and you know God loves you and Jesus died for you and you're going to live your best in God's world and when you die you'll go to heaven."

"Being saved leads to eternal life."

Mrs. Jenkins nodded happily.

I was disappointed in her. Thinking you'd live forever was just *tired*. As long as humankind had been human, I thought, no one wanted to believe that his own death would be their actual end. I felt a sudden surge of affection for my own faith, because as far as I could ascertain, the Jewish line on the afterlife was: *Well, we don't know.*

"What about here?" I said. "What about this world? You don't think the earth itself is wonderful?" I'd been reading natural history— whales the size of sailing ships that live on microscopic plankton; tectonic plates grinding and shifting; mitochondria toiling in our cells like inexhaustible hamsters on wheels. I pictured a God who looked like Charlton Heston shaking his head: I do and do and do for you kids, and what thanks do I get?

"Oh, the earth *is* wonderful, God made it to be our way station, but heaven is where he takes his children home."

I nodded. Who was I to deny her the solace of her belief? Mrs. Jenkins was good-hearted and direct and sympathetic, the sort of woman who, hearing of my Jewishness, was even now thinking up a substitute for the sausage-and-cheese breakfast casserole she dropped off each year before Christmas. I said, "If you hadn't been saved at your new church, would you be going to hell?"

"Oh, I'm sure of it. I'm not that nice, Dr. Markowitz. I've had all kinds of ungodly thoughts. When Orson left me and the kids . . . well, it was bad. I was bad."

"What about me, then? Am I going to hell?" I was feeling reckless. And safe, somehow: Mrs. Jenkins and I had a history. We'd laughed together about our urinary habits: she was good on long car rides, I was not.

Mrs. Jenkins shifted on the exam table. "See, that's where maybe I have some disagreement with my pastor. I think if a person's a good person and he wasn't born Christian, well, then he can get to heaven without accepting Jesus. That's my personal view. And you're a good person."

She made me an exception. I put my stethoscope in my ears and prepared to listen to her chest. But after only one breath, she started talking.

"Now, a Christian . . ." she said, "a Christian has to accept Jesus. There is no way except by me, that's what Jesus said."

"But we Jews get a free pass."

"Dr. Markowitz, Jesus was a Jew!"

My wife's a Christian, I almost said, but I stopped myself. Janis's aunts believed in heaven. Janis herself? I didn't know. "Quiet a moment, let me hear your heart." Ka-dump, ka-dump, ka-dump—surely a miracle. "What about Hindus?" I said, removing the stethoscope from my ears.

"You're going to get me in trouble!" Mrs. Jenkins made a comically nonplussed face. "I'm not a theologian, Dr. Markowitz. I'm just a believer."

Just a believer. I forgave her for dooming Janis. "Good for you," I said. "Lie down." Her breasts and abdomen and rectal were normal, as were her reflexes and the pulses in her feet. I wasn't sure what was more remarkable: that all her sixty-two-year-old parts were normal, or that my other patients with missing kidneys and diseased hearts and scarred lungs kept ticking on. Life was tenacious. Life wanted life. "Good for you," I said again, pleased with that phrase.

Maybe in my heart I was a pagan. It was life itself I wanted to worship. A thousand-year-old slime mold could be my god. I told Janis this later, at our kitchen table.

"I'd pick an oak tree, maybe," Janis said, her cup of tea in front of her, her chin on her left hand. Her gray-streaked hair was pulled back by a navy headband, she wore jean overalls over a T-shirt, and I could see why our neighbor Charlie referred to her as Mother Earth. Outside flakes of dry snow swirled in the air, as if the ground were an impossible goal. "That big tree in front of Steel Elementary."

"What about the resurrection? What about virgin birth?"

Janis shrugged. We both looked out the window, watched a sparrow pick at the dried seeds in the center of what used to be a flower. "I think of them as winter appetizer plates for birds," she'd told me once about her daisies. Plants, she knew how to pick 'em. "Virgin schmirgin," she said. "Metaphor."

Women. I knew how to pick 'em.

CAROLINE

I had a line at my window, and Alicia had disappeared again into the basement, where I suspected she went to cry. Will was never home anymore, she said. Will had something every evening at Zion Bible. "Brice!" I called. "Can you take a couple patients to exam rooms?"

He appeared beside my desk, giving me an intense look. I was tired of those looks, so I ignored him.

"My mother's bleeding," Brice hissed. I looked up. His eyes, already squinty, narrowed more.

From what area? I mouthed.

"From her vagina, okay?" Brice said, too loudly. "Her va-gi-na?"

The new patient on the lobby side of the window paled and stepped back.

The phone rang. "Can you go downstairs and get Alicia?" I said to Brice. He didn't move. Women his mother's age shouldn't bleed from their vaginas. This could actually be something bad.

"She's had pain for *months,"* Brice said. "Why didn't anybody listen?"

"Look, I've got to go," a new voice said. "Here's my billing sheet and ten bucks for my co-pay."

I looked up at Brice. "We'll skip Dr. Strub," I told Brice. "I'll get your mother in with a gynecologist right away."

HAP MARKOWITZ

I was in bed with the paper when Janis emerged from the bathroom. Maroon flannel tonight. I was blue. She shut off the overhead light, leaving only my reading light on, then stood with her hand on the bedroom doorknob and announced, "I'm going downstairs to check the doors."

"Don't go," I said from behind my paper.

"I knew you'd say that," she complained. "Why do you have to say that?"

"Your toe." I lowered the paper and looked at her in surprise. "Why go downstairs and walk on your broken toe?"

"My toe's okay. I like to check the doors. I feel better if I check the doors. Why do you have to tell me not to do it? Why can't you just say to yourself, Oh, that's Janis's thing? Why do you have to insert yourself into everything?"

Out of the blue. I was stunned. Surprise could make me meaner than anger. I set the paper down. "You want me to uninsert myself? You'd be happier if I went away? If I were *dead?"*

Hard to remember what we said next. Soothing noises, disavowals, excuses. She was still sleeping on her left side, which meant I was on my left side too, and maybe that was what we blamed it on, jokes about the wrong side of the bed. We talked about her sore back after lifting bags of soil, the stress of my interceding between Will and his furious wife. Janis never went downstairs to check the doors.

~

A few days later, Will came by my office after work. It was time to tell me the whole story. He wanted me to share his truth. Before he met Pastor Roger, he had an addiction problem.

"Addiction?" I was startled. Susan Galsworthy the oncologist had had a Vicodin issue; Joe Matsumoto the ER doc used to shoot up speed. Drug abuse wasn't unheard-of in physicians, but . . . Will? I felt sick, realizing that again I'd missed a pathology. Who knew what else I wandered through unsuspectingly? Maybe Caroline was really a compulsive gambler. Maybe Brice spent his evenings dressed in women's clothing.

"This is a little weird for me," Will said he told Pastor Roger. "Usually people come to me for advice."

Will said to Pastor Roger, "I'm addicted to Internet pornography." This wasn't what he meant to say. *I surf a lot. I like to look at girls.* "Addicted," "pornography"—those were strong words.

"But words are the beginning of healing, Hap," Will said.

"Pornography?" I said, flooded with relief that I hadn't missed drugs. "That counts as an addiction?" Immediately Will's anguish—which I'd missed, looking back, when he told me about Miss Kitty—became achingly clear. He'd been hurting then and I had missed it. He had tried, in his backhanded way, to tell me, but I hadn't heard a thing.

"Look," Pastor Roger told him, waving at a photo on his desk of a blond bombshell in a pink sweater, "I'm married. And Cyrinda and

I, we don't have kids yet, we have time, and we do"—his eyes glazed— "we do a lot. That's what you've got to understand: you're part of a Christian marriage, and God wants you and Alicia to have great sex. You're disappointing God if you don't. Those websites, they're Satan trying to lead you out of your marriage. God wants you back in."

Wasn't it God's hand, Will said to me, that pushed him into Pastor Roger's sign? God's hand that made Pastor Roger get out of bed at midnight to go check that he'd locked the sanctuary door? God's hand that made Will stop for a fake prostitute who knew his name?

Pastor Roger, Will said, was thirty-four. Beneath his round monk's face he was skinny and not too tall—he'd look like a kid in a bathing suit, and Will didn't want to imagine him with Cyrinda—but there was something compelling about him, an invisible cloak of authority that made him seem older and bigger. It was probably his eyes: he looked at Will steadily and held his gaze forever, so it was always Will who looked away.

I tried to see Will the way Pastor Roger might. The thick graying hair, the chiseled face, the slight droop at the corners of his mouth: you would cast him as a doctor in an ad. How did a man as apparently adult and sober as Will get hooked on porn? Not to mention his marital blessings, with a wife young and attractive enough to be featured on a website herself.

The sin, Pastor Roger would think. The Devil pulling Will down.

"What was it like getting saved?" I asked Will. "How did it feel?"

It happened on Will's third appointment with Pastor Roger. The branches of a tree tapping the pastor's office window sounded like Jesus calling. As he and Pastor Roger prayed, Will felt a sensation like warm honey spreading over his chest, and just that quickly he *understood*—it wasn't thinking, it was feeling—that Jesus was his savior, that Jesus loved him, that Jesus had plucked off his heavy backpack of sin and tossed it away like a pebble. "I mean, this'll sound silly, but remember when you were a kid and your mom rubbed that eucalyptus stuff on your chest when you had a cold? It felt like, I don't know, super-eucalyptus, like my whole body became this curtain waving in the wind. And it was God's wind."

"Do you feel it? Do you feel it?" Pastor Roger said, putting his hands on Will's forehead.

When things had settled down, when the event was over, Will sat in his chair and Pastor Roger told him about Brothers in Christ. "See, the beauty of it," Pastor Roger said, "anytime one of you feels the pull of Satan, you call up a buddy and get help. Satan hates it when God's people get together. A lot of times just praying on the phone's enough, but sometimes guys go out for coffee, play a round of tennis, watch some football."

Pastor Roger rummaged in his desk, extended a pen across his desk. "This is your Buddies in Christ pen, get it? A Bic. Keep it in your pocket. You lose it, you go to any drugstore and pick up a new one. Or, better yet"—he held up a box—"come back here."

An instant network and a logo, I thought, horrified and impressed. This pastor was one smart guy.

Will took the pen out of his pocket. He handed it to me across the desk, watched me inspect it, reached out to take it back. "Cool, hunh?" he said.

It was a regular Bic pen, came in a pack, six for two dollars.

"Shall we pray?" Pastor Roger said at the end of each of Will's visits, and they bowed their heads and Pastor Roger prayed for Will's continued strength and thanked Jesus for the gift of his salvation.

"Any more super-eucalyptus?" I said. Will smiled. No, no more of that, but with each prayer Will felt like one of his mother's crystal glasses cradled and dipped into warm sudsy water: he left the church feeling transparent and agleam. "You could make a noise with your finger on the rim of me," Will said. "I'm that clean."

"Really," I said, feeling an envious ache. I wouldn't mind feeling that clean, and I had never felt that dirty.

"And his sermons," Will said. "You figure any Sunday there have to be ten thousand possible topics, but all the sermons I've heard he's aiming straight at me."

∼

Fernando Villegas had sick-sinus syndrome, a condition where the heart's intrinsic pacemaker, the sinus node, functioned erratically. At times Fernando's sinus node sped up for no reason, other times it slowed down, and the irritating thing about this was I couldn't use meds to prevent Fernando's fast beats without risking his slow beats getting slower; and when his heartbeat became slow, Fernando got light-headed and tired. His cardiologist wanted to put in a pacemaker, but Fernando, whose mother was a Christian Scientist, had yet to be convinced.

"It's not like I believe it, but I think of it, you know?" Fernando said about Christian Science. "It makes me, I don't know, reluctant. I think the cardiologist is getting a little mad at me."

He probably was. Fernando's cardiologist was a windbag: I almost hated to help him out. But I liked Fernando. "Think of the pacemaker as a floor," I said, moving my hand in a quick horizontal line. "They put it in, they set it to seventy-two, and that's the slowest your heart is going to get. We can fiddle with the pills for the fast heartbeats, because you're guaranteed not to drop below seventy-two."

Fernando's whole body relaxed. "A floor," he repeated. "That makes sense."

"It's no big deal. They slip the wires into a blood vessel under your collarbone and down into your heart and then the transducer goes right here." I patted my right upper chest. "They make a pocket for it under your skin."

We chatted a couple more minutes, and I listened to his lungs and his heart (racing, at this moment). A satisfying visit. Fernando was happy, I was happy, and as I walked out of the exam room I had a realization: Will had found his floor. "Getting saved," whatever that was, was Will's equivalent to a pacemaker for his soul. It wasn't a big deal, the idea slipped right into him and settled.

Patients with new pacemakers tended to get nervous. *How do I know it's working? Does my rate need to be set higher? What if people notice the lump on my chest?* Some people with new pacers were afraid to fall asleep or to move their arm.

They settled down. A few months later, they rarely checked their pulses. They went back to grabbing kitchen cans to practice flexing their biceps, the lump in their upper chest no more exciting than a kneecap. Will, I thought, would someday be just another pacer patient. He wouldn't be running off to meetings every Wednesday and closing his office door to pray. He would be normal. He would be Will again. In the meantime I saw the attitude to take: sympathetic, vague, reassuring. It would work out.

"Think pacemaker," I said to Alicia, pleased to offer her my theory. Hard to say if she was convinced. Caroline said Alicia had basically stopped talking.

When Janis appeared to be asleep that night—back on her usual side—I lifted the covers and tried to make out her feet. I wanted to know if once again she'd hooked her Achilles tendon between her toes. "What are you doing?" she said drowsily, not opening her eyes. And then, before I could answer, she said, "Yes, okay? Yes."

CAROLINE

By February, Brice's mother was healing from her uterine cancer surgery and waiting to start radiation treatment (thus far, her disease hadn't improved her); I had ended my affair with Brice and found myself on an awkward footing with him at the office; and Dr. Strub had joined the advisory council at Zion Bible, which was just one step below the church board. In the meantime, I had had two revelations:

1. Men are made to sow their seed, and women are made to want the men who sow it.
2. There's a lot of harrumphing in the world.

I wasn't sure how much number 2 was related to number 1—maybe quite a bit, because harrumphing was an attempt to draw attention and disseminate your opinion, which was actually what sowing the seed required. But harrumphing wasn't totally male, as proven by the cute drug reps in their pumps and red suits who told the doctors that the

LDL reductions with Lipitor were just *amazing* and the safety profile was *unmatched* and the availability was . . .

Now, Brice:

I thought that I could repair the ruined house of him, but the place had rotting timbers and squirrels living in the attic and, really, its interior held little charm. Brice was, I'd come to see, in some essential way not a real man, and this hurt me to realize—it wasn't what I expected that day when I walked into his office and plunked myself on his lap. I thought that I could wake him up, but even wakened he was hazy and indistinct. Hugging him was like hugging a cloud.

Another way to put it: The imperative wasn't there. For most men, their penis and where they put it was the center of the world (see number 1). Not Brice. In bed with me, he acted like some old married guy torn between his wife's demands and something on TV. Trying to look past me, wrinkling his forehead for no discernible reason, turning his head as if he were attempting to catch a sound. It was disconcerting. I wanted to explore him, shine a light down in his basement and sit around chatting in his living room and hide out in his upstairs closet. He, on the other hand, didn't seem interested in the inner me at all. Paradoxically, he didn't know when to leave my real house. We'd go to bed and hours later he'd still be sitting in my kitchen reading through my *Entertainment Weekly*s.

After five or six assignations and Brice's endless fretting about his mother's surgery and recovery, I had had it. Not only that, but I was struck with the overwhelming foolishness of sleeping with someone I worked with. Did we want to end up like Dr. Strub and Alicia? Plus, we could get fired. Neither of us had the protection of being a doctor.

I'd act like nothing ever happened, because, in a way, nothing had.

I decided to change myself. No more seed seeking, no harrumphing. That was why I finally said yes (he'd been hanging around my window for years) to the one patient I pretty much knew had to be impotent (radical prostatectomy for cancer), Fred Langford. Fred had told me the best joke I knew:

Q: If you're dying in the dining room, what should you do?
A: Go to the living room.

Which, if you think about it, is a less bossy version of Henry James's "Live all you can . . ."

Fred was seventy-two. Although he walked as quickly as a thirty-year-old, I thought he was his real age in wisdom. He'd been a career Army guy, served in both Korea and Vietnam, lost a son to lupus and a daughter to alcohol, lost his wife in a freak accident (she fell through their attic trapdoor and impaled herself on the vacuum cleaner), and still, as his joke implied, managed not to be bitter. He had an average face, an average body (which meant a potbelly), a medium amount of gray hair, and twinkling green eyes. I thought he was the most relaxing person ever. Our first date (Saturday) we wandered around a flea market before having pie at a restaurant owned by someone Fred went to church with; on our second date (Sunday afternoon) we went bowling. That night he stayed at my place and shared my bed. No sex, but some very pleasant cuddling. I liked him enough that I smiled and chuckled and said, "No, he's my boyfriend," when Mrs. Haggerty on Tuesday asked if she'd seen me looking at Fiestaware with my father. Fred was thrilled when I told him this. He reddened and did that flustery thing with his mouth.

About my leg he'd said on Sunday night, when I removed it, "Why, that leg's heavy! It feels like a normal leg!"

My mistake with Brice, I realized, was that I'd pushed myself on him. Harrumph, harrumph. That was a kind of arrogance, a way of saying I knew what Brice needed more than Brice himself did. I decided to no longer exhort people to be or do anything. I started saying, "Should I schedule this mammogram?" not "It's time for a mammogram!" Instead of "What day's good for your test?" I'd say, "Do you want another appointment?" Always giving people a choice, not a command. It was interesting, because people's response to me changed. I'd become a rare human, a fully absorbent being, and people seemed to sense their freedom. They started telling me the truth. The pills they said they took but didn't, the medicines they borrowed from their sister, the blood on the toilet tissue they wanted to ignore, the odd metal pipe like a kazoo they'd found in their son's room. Often, just saying a thing out loud made a difference for them. One visit Miriam Reynolds talked about her teenage daughter's throwing up every morning. The next she whispered to me that everything had been taken care of.

You couldn't force things on people, I realized. The things people have to do, they do themselves. It was Brice's choice to keep living with and for his mother. He took half days off all through her surgery and hospitalization. Once he was back in the office, she'd call from her hospital bed to report on her pain and bowel movements. "Tell her I'm not here," he'd tell me, but a second later he was picking up the phone in his office. "Yes, Mother," he'd say, rolling his eyes as I frowned at him from the doorway, but his fingers on the receiver curved tenderly, and he spoke loudly enough that both Alicia and I could hear everything he said.

I still had a reaction to Brice's hands. They looked frail now, not elegant, and the memory of sitting on his lap that day was excruciating. Thank God no one ever saw us together. We would have looked like Jack Sprat and his wife. Even a clown (and I wasn't one) didn't want to be unintentionally funny.

My friend Sandi asked about him once. "What about that guy from your office? Bruce?"

"Brice. Wimpy. Wasn't worth it."

"Most of them aren't." We laughed, enjoyed the nasty thrill of writing off an entire gender.

I felt sad for him. Brice had once had a great advocate—me—but now he had only a coworker. My hopes had been dashed, and, with them, some of Brice's hopes too. "You're still my friend, Brice," I said on his last visit to my house. "I really like you." That's what I said, but both of us knew it wasn't true.

~

From the get-go Alicia didn't mind Pastor Roger—she loved it when his Dallas Cowgirl–style wife, Cyrinda, elbowed him over something he said—but the rest of the church people were merciless. They were Jesus zombies coming after her.

Don't get her wrong, she loved Jesus. She believed in God. Still, there had to be a limit. Will was throwing himself into Zion Bible the way she'd never seen him throw himself into anything. Well. The way that once he'd thrown himself into her.

A church on the move, the literature called it—and it was spiffy-looking literature, because someone in the congregation owned a printing company. There was money in that church, if not much education. Pastor Roger had this spiel about sitting in the basement of the family restaurant where he'd just held his first service and asking God to bless his ministry but only so far as God saw fit, and by golly, Pastor Roger knew he was a regular guy, a sinner like the rest of us—ask Cyrinda if anyone ever questioned *that*— but God had blessed him beyond anything Pastor Roger had ever dreamed of, because now he had a ten-thousand-square-foot church with a sign of perpetual light and two associate pastors and a youth ministry program serving two hundred twenty kids each week and three weekly services that together drew twelve hundred. "Twelve hundred *souls*," Pastor Roger said, dropping his voice and leaning into the mike. "Twelve hundred souls who love the Lord Jesus like I do."

I didn't mind Dr. Strub the way Alicia did. He seemed to me like a man bundled up in cotton, relieved that he couldn't be hurt but at the same time slightly deaf. He was certainly more challenging to schedule. He'd started asking his patients about their religious beliefs, which seemed to extend every visit five minutes and agitated both the Weinsteins (obvious) and the Martins (Jehovah's Witnesses, and shouldn't Dr. Strub have figured that out from the "No Blood Products" notations on their charts?). He told me to add on any new patient who said that they were from Zion Bible, even on days he was overbooked. Pastor Roger referred to him married couples who were having "restoration therapy"—Zion Bible's version of marriage counseling—to be checked for VD, and because our usual patients had little need to be checked for that, we had to order special supplies. "Ah," Dr. Markowitz said when he spotted the shipment of brown culture plates used to check for gonorrhea, "the Christians."

Donating ten percent of a person's yearly income to Zion Bible was a tithe. Donating fifteen percent made a person a Super-Sizer Tither. Will was Super-Sizing. There was a reception at Pastor Roger's house for Super-Sizers, and Will had donated a year's worth of Super-Sizing in six weeks. Really nice reception, Will said. Cyrinda made her vanilla twist cookies. Alicia should have come.

Pastor Roger did a sermon about the whole shepherd/pastor thing, and Al sat there thinking that she was a naughty sheep, wandering off and looking over the cliff, making her way past rocks to get to a clump of clover. She didn't want to be penned in, staring up the asses of the good sheep. She wanted her freedom and her green deliciousness and her view.

It was a relief to have the premarriage Alicia back. All her anger focused on Dr. Strub had made her a little scary, but in scattershot her anger had a certain daring charm. I laughed out loud when she told me about her meeting with Rosalind, the bigshot in WINNERS (Woman In Nurture, Nourishment, blah blah blah), the group that put on potlucks and bazaars. The two of them went for a Saturday breakfast at a Burger King, and Alicia started with a bang by saying "Shit!" when she dribbled coffee on her shirt.

Rosalind was blond and radiant. She wanted Alicia to accept the gift of Jesus and obtain eternal life.

"Is that what Will did?"

"I'm sure it is. With Pastor Roger."

"And you did it too?"

"I was only four years old when I accepted Jesus in my heart. I was lucky. I was raised up in a Christian family."

"So what about me?"

"Just pray. Say the words and open your heart." Alicia did an imitation of Rosalind praying, her eyes rolling heavenward under her closed lids.

"The thing is," Alicia said to Rosalind, "I'm not that bad. Will had a problem, he was lost, but I'm by and large found, okay? I go to work and I don't cheat on Will and I love my son and I'm a general good person. And then I read about, oh, Son of Sam and he's in prison and now he says he's saved and I think: This is ridiculous, you get to kill and rape and torture, and then you say, 'Oh, boo-hoo, now I love Jesus,' and all of a sudden you're going to heaven? That's crazy. And why do I need saving, anyway? Can't I just get grandfathered in for good behavior?"

Rosalind raised several scriptural objections.

And Alicia replied, "That's what your Bible says Jesus says, but how do you know they quoted him right? People get misquoted all the time. And Jesus didn't talk in English, so how do you know it's the right translation? And maybe he was talking in a general sense, saying, 'Be good like I am,' not saying, 'I'm the one, kids!' I mean, for a guy that's supposed to be God, don't you think that only-by-me stuff is a little egotistical?"

Apparently, Rosalind's wide eyes went even wider. "Alicia, don't you understand? Christ wants us to be his covenant bride, just like God took the people Israel to be his bride. How could you not want to accept that—having a husband to provide for you, to adore you, having a warrior husband to protect you, and . . ." Rosalind's face was beaming and blissful.

Alicia said, "Geez, you haven't been married long, have you?"

"I'll pray for you," Rosalind said, setting down her breakfast sandwich.

"You do that," Alicia said cheerfully, happy to notice that Rosalind didn't eat another bite.

"I don't know that I'd believe all the stuff that they do," my new friend Fred said about Zion Bible, "but the way I figure, at least they're making an effort."

HAP MARKOWITZ

Will found out about Janis's druggie past too: Noverkian had sent him the patient history. "She made some mistakes, Hap," Will said. "We're human, we have a fallen nature, we all make mistakes. Adam and Eve and the apple, right?" This reference made me blink in grateful surprise, because in relating "fallen nature" to Adam and Eve and not to Jesus, Will was showing me respect.

We both were trying. For a while, anytime Will said anything that might be remotely construed as Christian, I'd get a distant look and find a reason to hurry off. After a couple weeks I realized this wasn't fair, that Will's Christianity—and it was a sin-believing, the-endtimes-are-near-and-only-Jesus-can-save-you version, one I suspected a great many of my Christian patients didn't share—had, at least temporarily, become part of who he was, like his height or the color of his eyes. It would insult him if I asked him to change it. It would be like setting up Kenneth Tucker, my choir director patient who asked me for a monthly AIDS test, on a date with Sue Nelson. It wasn't the brand of Christianity I'd have picked for myself, but clearly Will was in a state where he needed it. He'd always had immoderate instincts—passing out drunk in med school, taping rows of unpaid parking tickets to his kitchen wall, falling for Alicia. What appeal would a moderate religion have had for him? And if life for most people was a pendulum with varying arc lengths, a near-disaster with a fake prostitute must merit quite a swing to the other side.

In February, I did pass on to him a bottle of wine I'd received from one of my patients at Christmas, thinking this might give his pendulum a shove back.

CAROLINE

Brice emerged from his office looking ragged, his cuffs rolled up instead of linked at his wrists. "My mother's on the phone. She was in the ER this morning for leg pain. They told her to see Dr. Strub this afternoon."

I wrinkled my nose. "Could she see the gynecologist?" Dr. Strub's schedule was packed, and Alicia would have to be persuaded.

Brice said, "They told her to come here. Can you pick her up on one?"

I punched the button. "Did Brice tell you?" Kitty said. "I was sound asleep—sound asleep!—and then I got this terrible . . ."

Wilma Barndollar waved at me through my window, pointing at her husband, who was taking a seat in the waiting room. "Make sure Dr. Strub asks about his piss," she whispered.

"... the doctor was so nice. He said I was his favorite patient he'd seen all ..."

I wrote *Ask re prostate* on a Viagra Post-it note and stuck it to Mr. Barndollar's chart. Line two lit up.

"... he couldn't believe how old I was, and I said, 'What, did you think I was ninety?' "

"Drs. Strub and Markowitz, can you hold, please?" I said to line two.

"... so nice! And he's the head of the whole emergency department, he ..."

The UPS man was at my window, the handle of his trolley visible. "Supply run!" he said. I forced a smile, scribbled my signature on his sheet, and gestured for him to put the boxes in the corner of the waiting room until I had time for unpacking.

"... when I told him I had cancer, he really got concerned, he ..."

Out of the corner of my eye, I saw Brice poke his head from his cave. Alicia was at the far side of the waiting room, ready to call a patient, and I waved at her and held up a piece of paper. *Kitty Kelvin, ER this AM, leg pain, see doc today.* Alicia crossed the waiting room, snatched the note from me through my window, growled, set the note on the ledge, and attacked it with her pen. Before I could read her response, she'd turned her back to me and was calling Mrs. Haggerty.

ADD HER AND DIE

I felt sick. Even if it was a joke, it took a certain obliviousness to write a note like that the day after you'd been worshipping.

It made Kitty's day to think the ER doctor liked her. No one in our office liked her at all, not even her son. "Dr. Strub is full this week," I said into the phone. Alicia turned to me and smirked. I heard a thump, which must have been her giving the box of supplies a celebratory kick. My voice dropped. "Why don't you call the ER," I said to Brice's mother, "ask the nice department head if he could recommend a new doctor for you?"

An hour later Brice was beside my desk. "How dare you send her to a different office? How dare you? Half my parents are dead, okay? Your parents are only dead to you."

~

Very quickly, the Zion Bible people got used to Alicia. They didn't have much choice. Will pledged to pay for the Youth Activity Barn the church wanted to construct on their back acre. Alicia had thought Will's and her discretionary income would go to a country club membership, not a barn. Everyone at Zion called Will Doc. Alicia was Mrs. Doc. Jesse they called Baby Doc.

People seemed to simply assume that Al was saved. Who knew, she said one day—maybe she was. There was a moment during a Christian rock service (the chiropractor sponsored bringing in a band from St. Louis) when she felt a kind of soaring sensation. Maybe that was what being saved felt like. She went with it, at any rate. Just easier to tell people she was.

Pastor Roger's wife, Cyrinda, got pregnant, and when she came to services she sat in the back pew and periodically disappeared. "She doesn't look nauseated," Al said. "It's an excuse."

She said that to people at church too, she told me proudly. She said all sorts of things. About Kent Lanier, who came to the Zion board wanting to put recycling containers in the parking lot: "Oh, that shirt's such a good color for him! Pinko." About Brenda Crabbe, whose tunelessness was a secret only to herself: "Was Brenda singing 'Amazing Grace' with us? I couldn't tell what she was singing."

"Ooh, Alicia!" people at church would say, giggling.

She and Will were generally doing better. He could be the saint, she could be the saint's manager. The tobacco stocks they continued to own, tips for the paperboy, getting rid of the incompetent office cleaning crew: "Believe me," Alicia said, "there are things a saint doesn't want to know." "Will can't rein *you* in," Pastor Roger told her once, smiling, but later he gave two sermons about biblical submission, the wife giving in to her husband's will the way the husband gives in to God. Alicia sat there and took it, but both Sundays Cyrinda spent the sermons in the bathroom.

Jesse and another senior were the lead debaters on their team. They flew to Dallas, Chicago, Memphis—all trips that Will paid for. Alicia thought it was a sense of obligation that made Jesse go without complaining to church on Sunday mornings. That, and the fact that he was gone on debate trips so many weekends. Jesse spent his evenings looking up evidence on a laptop Will had bought him. He might be on the UN website, on some congressman's link, or LexisNexis reading the work of some crazy philosopher. Good debaters like Jesse, Al told me, attacked not just an idea itself but the assumptions under it. "Let's say his opponent argues that getting rid of unions leads to slavery. Well, Jesse argues back that slavery is okay."

"Yeah, right," I said. "Just like women as beasts of burden is okay."

Alicia snorted. "Jesse says Pastor Roger's very fond of his own assumptions. Will doesn't buy that submission stuff, either," she added firmly. "I mean, he's not completely gaga."

Alicia said she'd love to know what went on in Pastor Roger's marriage. Sometimes she caught Cyrinda staring at her husband in the pulpit with a bright and speculative look, as if she were imagining her life if he suddenly died. Alicia had to look down at her hymnal to keep from giggling. Cyrinda was no angel, no angel at all.

~

It took Brice several weeks of asking, but he finally got Dr. Strub and Dr. Markowitz together in his office on a lunch break, on a day when there was ice on the roads and the attendant cancellations. Brice had used the ice ax on both the front and back stoops that morning. During the meeting, Brice left his door open and I heard them. Al was at her lunch in the break room. Brice said, "You'll probably want to shoot the messenger, but . . ." I heard papers being rustled.

"Again?" they said.

I knew the issue. Office receipts were down.

Even more, Brice said. Even with the ear cleanings, the extra labs from the VD checks, the shots, the church people. This year Medicare reimbursement had been cut, and even though the doctors were seeing more volume—"Your patient visits are up too, Dr. Markowitz," Brice said encouragingly—the money wasn't there.

I imagined the doctors looking at each other. "Maybe I should join a synagogue," Dr. Markowitz said.

"Maybe you should," said Dr. Strub.

Dr. Strub said, "At least, Jesse's got a chance for that debate scholarship at Tecumseh University." There was a silence. I pictured the doctors looking at each other again. Who knew, really, what went on between them? I imagined there were times they talked about me, but I didn't want to know what they discussed.

Brice said, "I almost hate to mention this, but it's cost-of-living time in two months."

"We cut that as a last resort," Dr. Strub said. "Absolute last resort."

CAROLINE

"Dr. Marcus won't talk with me," Brice said. Dr. Marcus was his mother's new doctor.

I didn't look up from typing hospital visit data into the computer. Brice was at my right shoulder, close enough I could feel the heat off his leg. Everyone else had left.

"Dr. Marcus isn't answering my phone calls," Brice said.

Your parents are only dead to you. Like it was my fault. Like I'd killed them. I yearned for an old-fashioned typewriter, so I'd have a carriage to throw.

"Why should she?" I said. "She's your mother's doctor, not yours."

It was a relief when I sensed him pivoting toward his cave. Then his voice rang out. "The worst thing I ever did was sleep with you."

"Yeah?" I finally turned to look. "Me too."

I wasn't done for the day, but I shut down the computer, locked my desk, headed out the back door. I had a hard time unlocking my car: I couldn't get the key to fit in the slot. I headed toward Fred's, then remembered he was filling in for someone at league bowling that evening. I went to Applebee's and sat at a table by myself, took myself to a movie. I didn't want to go home and hide the way I knew Brice had. I forced myself back to the world.

HAP MARKOWITZ

There was no light on, no noise in the house. It was almost seven on a bitterly cold day. The kind of weather you'd need a backhoe to dig a grave in. Terrifying. "Janis?" I called. "Janis?" Not out the back door, not out the front, not in the kitchen or on the sofa. I bounded up our stairs.

She was curled on her side in our bed under the covers, eyes closed. Yes, yes, she was breathing.

"Janis?" I said. She moaned a little and her eyes opened. "Are you okay?"

She looked at me with a dazed expression. "I fell asleep."

"Why are you tired?"

"I don't know, I just am. I went to the library after lunch."

"It's Friday!" I said. I gave her the shot on Sundays; by Friday the side effects should be over.

"I'm a human being, Hap. You have to let me be tired."

The house was too quiet. Janis closed her eyes again, and I wanted her to kick at the sheets, yawn, clap her hands, breathe loudly—anything.

I reached past her for the clock radio. "Seven-o'clock news," I said, switching it on. "I want to hear if there's anything new about Iraq." This was a lie. I couldn't have cared less about Iraq; all I wanted was to wake up my wife.

CAROLINE

I first heard about succinium when Alicia got back from a Womanly Woman's Conference in Pittsburgh. She went there for a weekend with three other women from WINNERS—all of whom shunned her, she reported with delight, after she had a glass of wine at dinner. One of the speakers had talked about lovemaking in a Christian marriage, and in the middle of her PowerPoint about scent and negligees and food she made a reference to "some vitamins" that helped female response.

After the talk, Al beat her way through the mob of tittering women and asked the speaker: "What vitamins?"

The woman stared at Al for a beat or two, then brightened. Hadn't Al heard of succinium? It was natural, the woman said—natch-rul: she had an accent—a natch-rul substance used in every cell of the body. It sped up your metabolism and calmed you down and regulated your cycles and made you feel just—

"I've never heard of it," Al said. "I'm a nurse."

Al was a nurse? Oh, wasn't that a blessed occupation. Think of all the people she could help! "Because succinium," the speaker said, "succinium . . . well, people just don't know."

By then the speaker was rummaging in her big floral bag, searching for a card, because all she'd brought with her this weekend was her Womanly Woman's material and not her His Way line. As Al often said, in something close to admiration, "These Christians have a million angles."

"Do you have e-mile?" the speaker said.

"I do have e-mile," Al said back.

"You devil," I said to Alicia, and we laughed.

Later, I told Dr. Markowitz what Alicia had said to the succinium lady. Disappointingly, he only smiled.

HAP MARKOWITZ

Will appeared in my office after work on a Monday. Pastor Roger, I thought at first, must have moved on to Monday meetings with more freshly saved parishioners. Then I realized that Will wanted to talk about Pastor Roger himself.

At the previous week's BIC meeting Pastor Roger had asked for prayers for himself and his marriage. Will looked at me with his eyes wide, as if the shocking import of this news was obvious.

Cyrinda had had a miscarriage, the BIC guys knew that. She didn't smile much anymore, they knew that. Pastor Roger was working so hard—cooking so many pies, the ladies said—that everyone wondered out loud how he did it. But what didn't they know? Was Cyrinda running around? With whom? Was Pastor Roger tempted? (How could he have *time*?) Was he on the Internet like Will had been? In the BIC room, there had been a sudden electric charge in the air. Every man there, Will knew, would now be afraid to say hello to Cyrinda.

"I kind of feel bad for her," Will said. "She might as well put a sign around her neck that says 'In Quarantine.'"

Poor lost lamb, Will thought about Cyrinda. The day before he'd taken a seat in the pew behind her. The light through the stained-glass window highlighted the fuzz on her face. He'd yearned to reach out a finger and stroke it.

"No," I said. "No, Will, you absolutely do not want to touch that woman. Do you hear me? Absolutely not."

CAROLINE

Fred was a weekly churchgoer. I went with him a couple times, but the services did nothing for me. A sermon about how everyone needed faith, a sermon about treating people kindly—nothing different or new. The minister was a balding man with an earnest manner, the liturgical reader a middle-aged woman who frowned and adjusted her glasses before she spoke.

"Gone there for years," Fred said, when I asked him how he'd picked this congregation.

"Do you like the sermons?"

"I just go there," Fred said. "Makes me think about things, I guess." For him, Fred said, going to church was like sitting in a waiting room in front of a door in front of God. He sat there for a spell each week seeing if the door swung open. It hardly ever did, but at least he'd be there if it happened.

"Do you believe in heaven?" I asked Fred.

"There's got to be something. A soul holds a lot of energy; it's not going to go poof and disappear."

When I pressed him more about his beliefs, I didn't get much. "I don't know," he said. "'I was hungry and you gave me food, I was thirsty and you gave me water.' That's about it."

"What about Jesus? What about the virgin birth?"

"That's about it," he said.

~

Alicia said, "So I said to Will, 'If your income's down, why don't we sell succinium? As a service. Because we want to help people.' "

Her husband was not eager to sell vitamins in the lobby. "Why not?" Alicia said. "Because your buddy Hap won't like it?"

Al was down eight pounds (she reported her weight to me daily). She'd had lowlights put in her hair and a new cut that cost eighty dollars. She was wearing Opium, a scent recommended by Womanly Woman. "I'm an industrious woman, O master of the family," she'd said to her husband. "You should use me. Don't you think my son who won a full-ride debate scholarship to Tecumseh U. gets some of his drive from me?"

She marched to the door of Brice's office, told him about succinium and asked him what he thought.

"I'm not getting mixed up between you and the doctors," Brice told Alicia. If anything, he said, he'd have to side with the physicians. After all, they were the ones who signed Brice's paycheck.

Brice was scared, I realized. He knew the finances of our office better than anyone, and he was worried about our business and his job. He needed the place more than I did. What did he have? A crazed mother, a sister who ignored him, two girlfriends who'd dumped him (I put myself in that category), a stack of old movies. I had my house and Fred, and even if my nights with Fred didn't contain the sexual relief I craved, I was getting plenty of affection.

I knocked with my hand on the frame of Brice's office door. Unlike before, I didn't bang with my leg—I had ruined that private joke by using it the day that I seduced him.

"What's up?" he said.

I sat. "I'm sorry about what I said to you. About sleeping with you being a mistake."

He looked at me with wary hopefulness.

"I . . . liked you. I still like you. I thought sleeping together might be good for both of us, and . . ." I faltered.

"And you're not picky," Brice finished.

"That's a little insulting, Brice."

"To who?"

Good point. We looked at each other and smiled.

~

I felt better about Brice, but I was tired. Outside of everything, I was the absorber, and around me there was fear and anger. At some point the stains and the grit and the odor were too much, and I wanted to be washed and rinsed and squeezed.

Fred showed up in the office waving an advertisement about Costa Rica he'd found in the Sunday *New York Times*. Volcano, cloud forest, sea: ten days in April.

"I got on their website. It's cheap because it'll be rainy season. A torrent every afternoon, that's it."

Costa Rica. "Is it hot?"

"Tropical. It's a great country. No military." What a funny comment, considering that Fred had been career Army. He leaned forward through my window. "We'll see monkeys. Don't you want to look up and see monkeys?"

HAP MARKOWITZ

"Cyrinda came here," Will says breathlessly, taking his usual seat across from my desk. "As a new patient. To see me."

"Did you know she was coming?"

He shook his head no. Although it was probably because of the week before, when, at the Wednesday Nightbites supper, Cyrinda was at a round table by herself, and Will thought it would be the Christian thing to join her. Other people might sit with them, once Will had broken the ice. Al was home with what she called a chest cold, although it seemed like a simple runny nose to Will. She always had an excuse for Wednesday dinners.

Will sat across from Cyrinda, empty chairs between them on both sides.

"You know how I feel?" Cyrinda said. "Like I'm a balloon on a string, and I'm way way up there, you can hardly see me, and any second there's going to be a solar flare that zaps right out and pops me."

Will said to me, "And then I said something weird, I don't know why I said it, I was unwrapping my silverware and I just . . . said it."

"What?" A sharp little word—"What?"—and my heart sank, I was thinking that he told her that he loved her.

"I asked if she was faithful."

Even worse. I heard a grunt escape me.

"But she is, Hap, she says she is. And then we started talking and she said how usually when a couple has problems, the parents of the husband or wife side with their own kid, right? But her family doesn't. They think Pastor Roger is a saint."

"That's extreme."

"It *is* extreme," Will agreed. "This Christian life is harder than it looks."

We looked at each other ruefully. "All life is hard," I said.

"Anyway, I sympathized with her, you know, and then today she shows up in my exam room and says that Pastor Roger thinks she's depressed. She asks if I can give her one of those happy-happy-happy pills."

He got through her office visit in seven minutes. He didn't even listen to her lungs.

This will be the rest of my life, he thought as he left the exam room. Always, these small fires to be snuffed out. He hadn't had a disaster yet, but he understood how quickly a fire could consume him. The bookmarked websites he'd had to delete, the fine hairs on Cyrinda's cheek, her high arch in her strappy shoe, her eyelashes tangled in a clump of mascara . . . Like wads of burning Kleenex tossed his way, things he had to jump up and down on to stamp out.

"Aren't you proud of me?" he said.

CAROLINE

As usual, Rabbi Kerchner was looking at me with a little smile, and I could sense him bouncing on his toes as I marked the charges on his billing sheet and handed the paper to him through my window and waited for his words of wisdom. "Have you joined the center yet?" he said.

He swam every day, and once I'd made the mistake of telling him that in the summer, I swam in a local lake. Now he wanted me to join his rec center through the winter. I didn't like a pool—the chemicals were smelly and I felt confined, like a caper bobbing in a jar.

"No pool for me," I said.

"But you have to keep up your shoulders in the cold months!" Rabbi Kerchner cried. "After all, the legs are only the paddles of the body. The heart is in the arms."

". . . and if you could make a list of ten movies I could pick up for him on the way home," Alicia was saying to Brice behind me. "I just phoned him and he says he'd watch movies. Ten DVDs you think a highly intelligent young man would like." Alicia was having a crisis: that morning Jesse had announced he wasn't going to school that day and wasn't getting on the plane for the debate tournament that evening. He said he was sick, but Alicia thought he was faking it. Serious debaters didn't miss big tournaments—what if Tecumseh heard and wanted to take away his scholarship?

"I'll have to tell that to Dr. Strub," I said, wondering if Rabbi Kerchner was even aware of my missing leg. "Tell him his anatomy book needs an update." Dr. Strub was not a fan of Rabbi Kerchner and his insistent, cryptic advice; he referred to him as the office weirdo.

"I don't care what the movies are rated," Alicia was saying to Brice. "He's mature, he can handle sex and violence."

Rabbi Kerchner smiled. "Words are only words, but a metaphor is a cagey stalking beast."

"I don't even know what Jesse likes," Brice said. "Is he into comedies? Drama? Action? I'm tilted toward drama myself, but . . ."

"Cagey." A funny word, because it indicated a kind of intelligence you wouldn't associate with something trapped and imprisoned. Or maybe you would. Maybe making the best of your imprisonment was the whole point. I could have talked about this with Rabbi Kerchner—he would have been delighted—but Mrs. Musgrove was already standing behind him clutching her billing sheet, eyeing him with dislike and suspicion. I handed Rabbi Kerchner his appointment card. "Brice, you old meanie," I said over my shoulder. "Don't you want to do something nice for little Jesse?"

"Hello, sweet lady," I said to Mrs. Musgrove, because it always works to greet people as opposite to what they are.

~

I tried to make Brice's mother into a joke. She was in our office less often ("Hello, sunshine!"), having gynecologists and radiation specialists to pester, but she continued to be an avid presence on the phone. "What's the suffering this week?" I might ask Brice.

Or: "How about this title, *The Unbearable Sufferingness of Kitty Kelvin?*"

"That was a strange movie," Brice said, turning away. "The *Unbearable Lightness* one."

Was I exhorting him? (Not that it worked.) Maybe. Brice felt like a special case to me. Getting him to laugh at his mother would be one step toward getting him away from her. There's an incredible magnetic power to a sick family. I know that power, and it takes an atom bomb to break it. For me, it took my almost dying, and I can see like a movie myself in front of my parents' house with everyone on the porch watching as I walked backward away and my leg flew off and turned in slow motion in the air and then ker-plow—it exploded in a fireball between them and me, and I was pushed away so fast you could see the empty stick figure space my body made blowing through a thousand houses and the camera swooped through the holes after me until it found me sitting on my own sofa with my face sooty and my clothes torn and hanging—but I'd done it, I was alive on my own sofa, I was totally away.

That's what Brice would have had to do, and he couldn't. Knowing Brice, cancer would not have been enough.

"Oh, gosh," my boyfriend Fred said, shrugging and chuckling when I told him how Brice set his alarm for two a.m. to be sure his mother was back in bed after her nightly visit to the bathroom. That was an appropriate response, in two words managing to acknowledge, accept, and rue Brice's limitations. Of Brice, I always expected too much. I never told Fred that Brice and I had slept together: too much humiliation in that confession, too much pain. "I overreached," I would be saying. "I thought I could save him."

"Oh, gosh," Fred might say.

HAP MARKOWITZ

Will said that the sermons in Pastor Roger's Israel series were beautiful, beautiful. Will thought of me all the way through them, how lucky I was to be a Jew.

"Lucky?" I said. "Hunh."

Pastor Roger's latest was "Zion Restored." It took Will a while to get into it, because Pastor Roger rehashed the whole Old Testament—the serpent and the fall and Moses and the exodus and King David—before he finally got to the point about Zion Restored, which it took Will a moment to recognize as heaven. Zion Restored, Will said, is what would exist once Jesus returned and the world got through its seven years of tribulation and there was the battle between Jesus and the Antichrist and the world of sin was wiped out.

Pastor Roger, Will said, hadn't gotten all excited about Y2K. He knew that the "new millennium" was only a man-made date. The conditions weren't yet ripe for the Final Days. Once the Israelites had rebuilt their Temple in Jerusalem and Israel itself had spread across all the land God had designated for it, then we'd have the Rapture. Pastor Roger didn't think the Rapture meant people would be whisked up to heaven while they were driving, their eyeglasses and keys left in the car—oh, no. Pastor Roger thought—

"Wait a minute," I interrupted, "people really think that? They think they'll be—" I waved my hand in an upward tornado motion.

Oh yeah, Will said. Hadn't I heard of the Left Behind books? I shook my head in incredulity, thinking there was no limit to the things people will believe.

Pastor Roger believed, Will said approvingly, that the Rapture would be a spiritual, not a physical, experience, that Jesus would reveal himself to all his believers at one time, that he would make himself known to them, that he would enfold them in his arms in safety, and then the believers would stay on earth, protected under the umbrella of heaven, converting unbelievers, helping their loved ones. A missionary time like no other, Pastor Roger said. It would be easy to save people then, he said. People would see the chaos around them and they'd *realize*. They'd yearn for the peace and beauty that was Zion.

Will had a new way of saying it, Tzee-OWN. The Hebrew pronunciation, he said shyly, looking at me for approval. I nodded: he indeed had it right.

In Tzee-OWN restored, Will said, Pastor Roger said there would be no suffering. No jealousy, no weeds to pull, no aching knees, no worry you'll get fat. No sin! No fights with your spouse, no hearing yourself say things you know you shouldn't. You'd see old friends you hadn't seen in years; meet new people you'll feel like you've known forever. No neighbor's wife will tempt you; all your neighbors' wives will feel like sisters. You'll have all the time in the world to talk. When you're tired, you'll lie down with your spouse—maybe your spouse who got to Zion before you—in a wonderful bed. You like your mattress soft? It'll be soft. You like your mattress hard? It'll be firm. You like it hard and your husband likes it soft? Listen, the same bed will feel firm to you and soft to him. It'll be better than the Atlantis in Bermuda, than the Montreal Four Seasons. (In his old days, Pastor Roger said, he was in hospitality, and let me tell you, these were fine hotels!) You wouldn't have to toil. You won't have "stress." You'll forget what that word means! S-t-ress. Isn't that an odd word if you think about it? Str-ess. Someday you'll hear that word and think: What could a strange sound like that mean?

The bed. The mattress soft on one side, firm on the other. That detail somehow moved me, made me blink tears from my eyes. I could see, at that moment, the joy Will felt in believing. I yearned to believe myself.

At the same time I wondered why Will was telling me this, what he hoped for in response. If he converted me, would that earn him an extra star on heaven's blackboard? "Time will tell," I said, meaning nothing—saying words whose only purpose was their vagueness.

"Time *will* tell," Will said, nodding, and his eager voice touched me. He seemed to have no concern that time might let him down.

Cyrinda was better, Pastor Roger had said to Will after services, pulling him aside outside the front door and speaking in a low voice. Less snappy. It wasn't magic, though, a medicine like that. Vale of tears, the Bible said. But what could we expect from a fallen world?

∽

I sat in my office with my arms crossed, angry at myself for agreeing to this meeting. "Of course you have doubts," Kirby the distributor said, snapping open his briefcase on top of my desk. "Everyone has doubts, at first. Doubts are normal. But once you try the product, once you feel the changes, then you'll find your doubt can be a sales tactic. Think of how you'll sound: 'I'm a doctor, I'm a scientist, I said show me the studies, and the studies looked real good, almost too good, but my buddy Will said—and I love Will, Will's the bomb—"Hap, you've got to try this for yourself." And I did, for just one month. One month, what could it hurt? And you know what? I felt better. I felt so much better I gave His Way with Succinium to my wife, to my kids, to my employees. I even gave it to my mother-in-law! And every one came back to me, every one, and said, "Dr. Markowitz, this stuff is amazing. This stuff makes me feel like I've got wings." And I thought, I've got to offer this to my patients. How can I not offer my patients this natural, God-created compound? Moses brought the Ten Commandments down the mountain, didn't he? He didn't keep them for himself. Jesus shared the loaves and fishes! He didn't sit there in the boat gobbling down halibut.' "

"I'm Jewish," I said, glowering, aware that this whole scene had a comic aspect, but not willing to admit the humor in it at all.

"I don't care if you bow down to the God of Fruits and Nuts!" Kirby said. "You've got to at least have heard of the loaves and fishes."

I managed to look totally blank.

After a moment of befuddlement, Kirby brightened. "Ask Will. Ask your buddy. He knows all about the loaves."

CAROLINE

One Friday morning Alicia came running around the corner of the office. "Hildy Kahn is down," she said in an urgent whisper.

I couldn't imagine it. "In the bathroom," Alicia said. "She's fallen and she can't get up. Brice!"

Our scale couldn't weigh Hildy, and it went to four hundred pounds. Hildy used a walker and carried a bandanna to wipe her face. She never left the office without a crack about Dr. Strub looking down on her. There wasn't much immediate appeal to Hildy, but every once in a while she showed up with a newspaper clipping that made me feel guilty about not liking her more. For Brice she brought in a reminiscence of Audrey Hepburn. For me she found an article about paying off your mortgage early.

I clicked on the answering machine and hurried down the hall between Alicia and Brice. The doctors were already with Hildy.

"What if we got you through the door?" Dr. Strub was saying. "You think you have a chance of standing in the hall?"

"If I can lean against the wall, I can." Hildy was remarkably calm.

"Brice and I will each get a shoulder," Alicia said. "This happen much at home?"

"Oh, a couple times Gordo's had to call 911."

"I'll get her right leg, you get her—"

"Knees, go for the knees!" Hildy snapped. "You grab my ankles, there's too much stretching. Sorry." It hit me that Hildy's maneuvering her body through the world required ceaseless energy and planning. I felt a sudden sympathy for her complaints about our front ramp and our chairs.

"Nice of you to do something exciting for me, Hildy," Brice said. "Ninety-nine percent of my time, I'm stuck in my office the size of a hamster cage."

"One, two, three . . ."

"I was reading about dynamite," Dr. Markowitz said. "Very interesting. What they want for open-pit mining is *heaving* power. They don't want to be blasting rocks into the next—"

"What if we get your legs this way and you roll . . ."

"We'll pull. You two can push on her, her . . ."

"Ass," Hildy said.

"Buttocks."

"Buttocks? Jesus, that sounds even—"

"One, two, three, *heave.*"

"Are you okay? Are you dizzy?"

"Brice, you get the wheelchair."

Mrs. Jorgenson was standing at the opening to the lobby. "What a good team you are," she said as we wheeled Hildy past.

"We're dynamite," Brice said.

"Open-pit," said Alicia.

Mrs. Jorgenson's forehead wrinkled in confusion: the five of us looked at one another and smiled. As late as February there were moments in our office like this one, moments of cooperation, of happiness and peace.

The next day Brice told Alicia and me the doctors couldn't afford our cost of living.

CAROLINE

Within a month, His Way with Succinium had taken over our waiting room. I had to move the patient education racks to the basement. There was the basic His Way display with bottles and brochures, and then the ancillary displays of His Way for women (Eve's Elixir) and His Way for men (Adam's Advantage) and His Way Nourishing Balm and Penetrating Lotion and Brisk Body Scrub. One day Dr. Strub had come in and said, "We're selling it," and the next week all the bottles and tubes were out there. I didn't know what Dr. Markowitz thought. Once I asked him a question about "the His Way line" (as Kirby the distributor called it) and Dr. Markowitz simply shrugged.

"I'm almost getting orgasms again," Alicia said. "At least with a vibrator."

Kirby had given Brice a bottle of Eve's Elixir to take home to his mother. "She likes it!" Brice said. "Says it helps her bowels."

"Just so she doesn't come back to this office," Alicia said to me. "Just so Brice buys it here and takes it home."

"Tell you what," Dr. Strub said from over my shoulder as I filled out a His Way receipt for Anna Zukowski. "If they're here for an office visit, we'll take off three dollars on any His Way purchase."

"Is that allowed?" I asked. It struck me the insurance companies and Medicare might not want people setting up office visits just to get a His Way discount.

"How can it not be allowed?" Dr. Strub said. "They're here to see us anyway. This'll encourage people to buy now and not put it off." He looked up from me and out the little window. Geoffrey Waite was standing there reading the label for Adam's Advantage. "Wait'll you try that stuff," Dr. Strub said. "Your diabetes? Those sugars are going to come down like you're on a waterslide."

Geoffrey frowned skeptically at Dr. Strub's retreating back. "This stuff ain't cheap. It as good as he says?"

"He's convinced." I leaned forward conspiratorially, dropped my voice so Alicia didn't hear me. "I take a generic One-A-Day myself."

~

One morning I came in early to get some filing done, and found Dr. Strub was early too. It almost scared me to see his car in the parking lot—he wasn't usually at the office until nine—but when I got inside he seemed fine. When he'd reached the hospital that morning he'd learned that both his patients had been discharged by their surgeons, so he found himself with extra time. He nodded at the empty chair beside my desk. "Mind if I sit?" He leaned forward, pushed aside a stack of charts and the latest *People en Español* (I was brushing up for my trip, although I didn't recognize half the celebrities), and rested his crossed forearms on my desk. He was settling in. My filing would have to wait.

A beautiful, clear morning, the light through the lobby picture window slanting through my small window, making the dust in the air sparkle. You could believe that spring was coming. I hadn't yet turned on the lights.

One night when they were med students, Dr. Strub said, Hap was stitching up drunks in the minor-trauma room of the ER when somehow—Dr. Strub still didn't understand this—Hap nearly sliced off his fingertip with a scalpel. It was hanging by a hinge of skin, and he came running to Dr. Strub in the X-ray reading room, where Dr. Strub was tailing the radiologist. He wanted Dr. Strub to cut off his glove, because if he pulled it off himself the fingertip might come with it.

"Jesus Christ," the radiologist Dr. Strub was trailing said, rolling his chair away from Hap. "If I wanted to see things like that, I'd be a surgeon."

Dr. Strub went back with Hap to the minor trauma room and used a pair of scissors to get the glove off. "Hap, you gotta ask one of the ER guys to stitch this," he said.

But Hap wouldn't bother an ER guy. It was a weekend night with gunshot wounds and heart attacks in the acute areas, and he was the only worker in minor trauma. He had two head wounds and an arm laceration to stitch (those patients were drunk and snoring) as well as a nasty bedsore he'd been getting ready to debride.

There were all kinds of suturing supplies around them, Dr. Strub told me. Hap had looked at Dr. Strub hopefully, but Dr. Strub felt queasy and he couldn't, couldn't do it.

Hap did it. Stitched his own fingertip back on. "I watched him, that's what I did," Dr. Strub said. "He didn't use any anesthetic. He put in these wobbly stitches, washed his hands, put his gloves on and went back to work on his drunks."

I didn't know what to say. I could picture it perfectly: Dr. Markowitz stitching up his own hand was the sort of thing he'd do. He probably barely flinched as the needle went in. Later, he probably never mentioned to anyone what he'd done.

"He was always a better student than me," Dr. Strub said. "Better student, better doctor, better husband. I took this pretest on lupus last week, got two out of eight questions right. Hap knew them all. He's dedicated. And it just hit me about a month ago when I was out walking—you know I've been walking lately, mostly Sugarbush Park, trying to keep the weight off with Al and me eating out so much—anyway, it hit me, I was walking up this hill: How could I be going to heaven and Hap's not? It's not fair. A wretch like me."

Did I know how he got saved? I thought I did, although I realized as Dr. Strub repeated the story that Alicia's version was less damning, focusing as it did on dirty websites and leaving out his approaching an actual (fake) prostitute, a woman I could picture immediately when Dr. Strub told me her name. "You didn't," I said, wincing, the almost comical depths of his plight making me like him more. "I did!" he said. He'd told all kinds of church people this story, he said, and I could see that in its unexpurgated form it was an excellent redemption narrative, starting with bad intentions and ending with the grace of God. Also, it featured coincidence, public humiliation, and no actual sex—all narrative advantages. Well, that story was another one of God's gifts to him, Dr. Strub said, because it glossed over the truth. The scariest things from his unsaved days were the things in his own mind. "It wasn't that I looked under the rock"—Dr. Strub looked into his lap, the morning light glinting off his watch and wrist hairs—"I saw the muck under that rock and I wanted to eat it."

I said, "Oh, gosh."

We were silent for a moment. The thing was, Dr. Strub said, was that part of Hap's stitching himself up was vanity. Vanity was part of his drive. For example, he really didn't need to go into the hospital in the middle of the night every time a patient of his was admitted. None of the other attendings went in. The residents could handle the new patients until morning, and if they had questions they called the attending doc at home. But Hap felt compelled to cast his big, weary shadow across each patient's bed. He had to arrive sighing at the office the next morning. Wasn't Dr. Markowitz always complaining that he was tired? He didn't have to be. His tiredness was a choice.

There was even vanity in the way Hap said he didn't know something. "Acute intermittent porphyria? I don't remember if it affects the liver. Good question. Let me look it up." As if Dr. Strub should applaud Hap's admission of ignorance, the way he'd scurry off to find an answer.

Still, Hap never held anything back. He never said "Go look it up yourself!" when Dr. Strub asked him a question. Weekends Dr. Strub asked him to do call, he always said yes. When Dr. Strub was married to Harriet, Hap always helped her with her coat. She adored him; Dr. Strub used to tease her that she'd married the wrong partner. Dr. Strub sometimes wondered what Hap thought when she left him. Maybe he could have told Dr. Strub what he was doing wrong. "I should have asked him," Dr. Strub said.

It was half an hour before Alicia and Brice would arrive and I would be turning on the phones. I had no idea where Dr. Strub's soliloquy was going. My mind wandered to Fred's birthday, whether he'd be offended if I bought him some new shirts, and suddenlyDr. Strub was talking about standing in the middle of a path at Sugarbush Park weeping, the sun warming his cold hands, the leaf bits on the path working their way between the treads of his shoes.

"I'm sorry," I said. "You were . . . ? It was . . . ?"

"Doubly damned," Dr. Strub said. "When I was walking and I thought that Hap must be doubly damned."

Dr. Strub ran down the hill and out of the woods and into his car and drove straight to Pastor Roger's office. "Of course he's not damned," Pastor Roger said, and this startled Dr. Strub so much he started laughing. "Listen," said Pastor Roger, "during the tribulation, every Jew will get his chance to accept our Lord. Remember, the Jews are God's chosen people. God made them a promise, and God doesn't change his mind."

Had I read the Song of Solomon? Dr. Strub asked. He seemed excited now, his hands leaving my desk to form a globe or heart—some rounded shape—in the air. That was one sensual part of the Bible, that was a book some people wanted to ignore, but what those prudes forgot was that the Song wasn't just the love of a man for his bride, it was the love of God for Israel, his people. That love was deep. That love was a pool you could dive right in and never touch the bottom of.

"See, we're dependent on the Jews, not them on us!" Dr. Strub said. "They have to rebuild the temple in Jerusalem for the Messiah to return. Pastor Roger's been there, he knows. He was trying to get Zion Bible to send some money to this group in Israel that's working on the rebuilding, but people are selfish, they think the here and now is important. It's not. The real world for us is the Zion to come."

Which brought him to his point, Dr. Strub said. Because there were no coincidences. Because God had a way of pointing with his index finger. Because as Pastor Roger talked to him that Sunday afternoon in the office, he was leaning back in his chair and worrying something plastic in his right hand. The thing in his hand made a rattling noise, and Dr. Strub finally asked him what it was.

Pastor Roger looked surprised. He opened his palm to reveal a small white bottle. "Vitamins," he said. And then, almost in apology: "I've been a little tired."

"Think about it." Dr. Strub stood, leaned toward my window, gestured toward the lobby rack of His Way with Succinium supplies.

One of those magic moments, Dr. Strub said, when ideas combined like nuclear fusion in his mind.

CAROLINE

I looked up and there was Jesse in my window. "Look at you," I said. "Our newest coworker."

He was done with the high school debate team. He'd debate in college, he said, but high school was worthless. Alicia was terrified the debate coach at Tecumseh would decide that granting his one scholarship to Jesse had been a mistake. The coach had basically said as much, telling Jesse he would have to revoke the money if someone better came along.

Jesse needed something to do with his time beyond watching movies, he needed supervision, he might need money for college, and so the doctors and Alicia cooked up a scheme to get him working in our office, despite Brice's squawking about expenses and work duplication. Jesse's hourly paycheck, Dr. Strub said, would come straight from the His Way proceeds. The doctors and Al had written a job description and pulled together furniture, bustling around in a hopeful but apprehensive collusion, as if they were planning a surprise party for the neighborhood grouch. Jesse would use a table in the office basement. He'd work three afternoons as week, pulling charts and filing. On the day he was to start, Al carried a vase of fresh flowers downstairs to put on Jesse's desk.

Jesse himself looked remarkably meek for someone who'd caused this much turmoil. "Come on around," I said, nodding at the door from the lobby, and Jesse emerged in his mother's and my office. His hair had gotten long and messy, and he was wearing a wrinkly dress shirt with the cuffs open and a twisted hemp band around his left wrist. I asked him if he missed debate at all and he shrugged. "I got tired of arguing."

It was all a game, he said. Nobody cared about what they were debating. The topic this year was UN peacekeeping, and after hearing about riots and disorder in Kosovo, people jumped around in excitement because it helped their argument.

"I mean that's crap," he said. "Crap."

He was still looking forward to college debate, if the people on the team there were as intelligent as the coach swore they were. He gave me a look. "I'm tired of arguing. I'm not tired of my brain."

Interesting. He was growing into just the person I'd hoped he'd be. "Did you watch Brice's movies?"

"I liked Brice's movies. Brice's movies got me through a lot."

A compliment for Brice! I felt a surge of relief that someone besides me would be Brice's ally in the office. "Tell him that," I said, not realizing until later that this was an exhortation. "He'll be pleased."

HAP MARKOWITZ

As a favor to Will, I added on his Pastor Roger as a new patient. He hadn't seen a doctor in years and just needed to be checked out.

"Dr. Markowitz," Pastor Roger said when I walked into the exam room, blinking as if he'd just walked into brightness. "Will's told me about you." He looked like a cartoon monk: short, round body and a fringe of hair. The top of his head was so naked I touched my own for reassurance. He extended his hand. "Lots of His Way products out there. I appreciate that." I wondered if Kirby-the-pusher was a member of his congregation.

Pastor Roger wasn't sleeping and his feet were throbbing. His wife had for the last two weeks been staying with her parents, although he and Cyrinda were going to a Christian counselor in Indianapolis and trying to work things out.

"Christian counselor": the two words flowed together from his mouth as if he'd said something totally unremarkable.

It turned out Pastor Roger was from a family that owned two popular restaurants in Columbus, The Hearthside and Jo-Jo's, places Janis and I knew. We covered all his physical complaints, and our conversation wandered.

"You know chefs? Chefs are funny people. We had this guy named Rudy, studied in Paris after he graduated from Cornell, and the only time he was happy was in September, because that's when the Bosc pears came in." Pastor Roger hesitated, looked down at his hands. "Cyrinda's my Bosc pear. I am helpless in front of that woman."

The church was great, the church had grown beyond his wildest expectations, but what he really hoped for was something long-term. "That's what we had at The Hearthside. We'd do the wedding dinner and twenty years later the anniversary party and fifteen years after that the retirement gala with the kiddie menu for the grandkids. That's how I envision Zion Bible. You know, being there for people over time. If there is time."

"Will says you're an excellent manager." *If there is time?*

"We try to keep the menu up-to-date." Pastor Roger gave a small smile. He looked and sounded so modest and appealing I thought I must have misinterpreted his earlier comment: this guy wouldn't worry about the end of the world. He shifted on the exam table, crackling the paper beneath him. "That was how I always thought of marriage too. Being there, time."

I knew Will revered him, was maybe even afraid of him, but sitting in this small room in front of me, Pastor Roger was an ordinary human being. Admirable, grieving, lost—a man a lot like me.

I said, "My wife's a Bosc pear too."

Pastor Roger gave a twist of his mouth that could be sympathy or his own pain. "Will says she's been sick."

"She's on medicine," I answered quickly, wondering exactly what Will had said to Pastor Roger.

His exam was unremarkable except for signs of stress: his pulse and blood pressure a little up, patches of eczema on his arms, tooth-shaped indentations in the sides of his tongue. I drew blood, talked in vague terms about antidepressants (maybe at some point, he said), told him to get daily exercise, and gave him a pamphlet on sleep hygiene, but I liked to think that if anything in that visit helped him, it was the moment when he knew I understood the pain inside his marriage.

"I saw your pastor," I told Will later. "Nice guy."

A disturbed look crossed Will's face. To him, I realized, calling Pastor Roger nice was like calling a chef's masterpiece "tasty." Maybe Will was prone to hero worship. Maybe—my mouth twitched—he had used to hero-worship me.

Will smelled different. It hit me as we passed in the hall that there was a new and lemony scent to him. "Where's the Old Spice?" I said, stopping.

He looked sheepish. "Kirby gave me some stuff to try. Adam Body Spray." He shrugged. "We've got it in the lobby. Alicia likes it."

A young man's spray. It smelled like a gleaming metal coffee shop, not a wood-paneled, cozy bar. Of course Alicia liked it. It hit me I should at least peruse the displays in the waiting room, something that I'd studiously avoided. Body spray! God knew what else we were selling. I understood our practice got a cut of everything, but that made selling it even more distasteful. I imagined Alicia in the lobby, pointing at the display: "Wouldn't you like some Adam Body Spray, help fund my cost of living?" Snake oil, sheesh. Thank God it was Will's *meshugas* and not mine. I didn't plan to suggest the products to anyone. A few of my patients might try things without asking me, but if they told me that the products had helped, I would be noncommittal. "Maybe it's the vitamins, who knows?" I'd say. "Maybe it's the passage of time."

CAROLINE

Fred and I were sitting on the sofa at his house watching *Wheel of Fortune* when he turned to me and said, "You're a young woman. You shouldn't have to give things up for my sake."

I said, "I like *Wheel of Fortune*."

"I'm talking about sex."

The nights we shared a bed, I nestled on his chest and he put his arm around me. Sometimes after he fell asleep I rolled away from him and masturbated. But it was like there was metal plate separating our upper from our lower bodies. He never touched me below the waist, I never touched him below his. I didn't want to embarrass him, remind him of the things he couldn't do.

"I want to make you happy." Fred held up his hands and wiggled his fingers. "I have fingers. I've got a tongue."

HAP MARKOWITZ

I came upon Janis on the sofa in front of the TV, the remote in her hands. "Sharks?" I said, because there were bunch of swarming fish on the screen and their eyes looked beady. She was watching Animal Planet, her new favorite channel, no longer for just after the bulbs were in. She used to watch Bravo or the news.

"Salmon," Janis said.

A male announcer's voice was speaking: "The males swim in a frenzy, jostling and sparring for a chance to fertilize the freshly laid . . ."

Janis raised her right hand and clicked off the TV. "At least you have my nieces and their kids," she said. She looked at me, sucked in her lips until they disappeared.

More regret? More angst? Frankly, I was sick of it. I'd seen patients with entire dead families who acted less miserable than she did. I took a seat at the far end of the sofa. "Janis, you've got to get over this. It's useless for you to sit around and brood. It's crazy to ask, *Why us?* I mean, why *not* us?"

She turned away and in profile her lips billowed out like tiny parachutes. "That's tactless."

I looked down at my hands. My skin looked surprisingly old, ripply and finely crosshatched. I wouldn't make a very good lamp shade. Janis had always had lovely hands, unmarred by even her gardening (she wore leather gloves)—pale and plump, with tapered fingers, like hands in a Renaissance painting. Her hands would be lovely in a casket, I thought, and this thought was so horrifying and unbidden (Jews didn't display their dead, and I had only seen open caskets at visiting hours for my patients) that I sprang up and plopped myself down beside her, I wrapped her in my arms, I assured her—over and over, to the point of making her mistrust me—that she was, she would be, okay.

CAROLINE

Alicia wanted Jesse to take yoga with her. It would help him relax, improve his flexibility, keep up his muscle tone. He hardly got any exercise. He didn't want to do yoga, she persisted, he said no, she insisted, he got angry, Dr. Strub got involved as a mediator, and then Jesse said the thing that devastated his mother: "Why are you always trying to improve me?"

A good question. Alicia said it made her think about her own mother. Her mother's line was "too bad you . . ." "That's a lovely sweater you knitted, honey, too bad you picked that hairy yarn." "You look beautiful in green, too bad you still have that cold sore." Nothing about Alicia was ever right. She'd tried so hard to not act like that with Jesse. She pointed out the exceptional in everything he did. But maybe she was only concerned with his excellence, not his whole being. Maybe she wasn't letting him grow into the beautiful tree he could be. She was always trimming him, lopping him, not letting him take his own shape. Her mother in her, hurting him.

I felt for Alicia more at that moment than I ever had. It must be terrifying, I thought, to have a child. Thank God I didn't have a son or daughter to mess up. Who knows what family craziness I'd pass along? Alicia's mother had at least nestled each barb next to a compliment, although maybe that had made the barbs hurt more.

"He'll be okay, Al," I said, because all of her worry, I knew, revolved around his quitting the debate team. "He needs to rest a little.

He'll beready for debate again in college. And look how happy he is working here." He was happy running up and down the steps ("Exercise," I'd say to Al, pointing), standing at Brice's office door talking about which movie he should rent next, looking over Al's shoulder and pointing at lab values and saying, "Ooh, that's a bad one, isn't it?"

"It took me five years to get through college and another five for med school," Dr. Strub said to me and Alicia. "Let him struggle a bit. It's a phase."

I was impressed and slightly surprised, as I always was when Dr. Strub made sense.

"Do you know how many parents in the course of history have worried about their kids?" Dr. Strub continued. "You tell me. How many kids really turn out to be ax murderers?"

"Ax murderers, hunh?" Dr. Markowitz said from behind him. "That's setting the success bar pretty low."

Like a comedy team sometimes, as Alicia said.

HAP MARKOWITZ

My Bosc pear. My biggest fear through the years had been losing her—when Harriet left Will, I thought I'd literally die if Janis ever left me. Hepatitis C from IV drug abuse. Now I saw that if I'd lost her without knowing about this, I wouldn't have known who she was. Her self-sufficiency that was really brokenness. She was a porcelain cup that had fallen to the floor and shattered, was reassembled and glued together. Good enough. Held water and coffee. If you didn't look closely, you'd never see the seams.

I should have seen the seams. I should have looked more closely.

If she believed something, maybe she'd be less broken. Maybe belief was not quite glue but a matrix into which shards of plates and cups and old mirrors could be placed, forming a new beauty out of broken-ness. Maybe, for her, that was all I could hope for. Or for me.

The display had been in our lobby two weeks before I finally picked up a bottle of His Way Basic Starter vitamins and headed back to Will's office. Will was sitting in his chair staring at the wall—was he praying?—and I hesitated a moment until he looked up. "'His Way'?" I said, holding up the bottle. "Who's 'His'?"

Will set his mouth peevishly, not answering.

The label encircled the white plastic bottle horizontally. The front of the label, done in black and white with purple-blue shading, showed the midsection of a robed figure, its hands extended out both sides, palms open, its fingers emitting golden rays that coalesced as a yellow wash at the back of the bottle, where the ingredient list and instructions were printed. I held out the bottle to face Will. "Doesn't this look like Jesus?"

He blinked. "Maybe it's a Greek god. Apollo."

"I don't think Apollo has rays coming out from his fingers. I think that's a Jesus-saint thing."

We got twenty-five percent. A quarter of all His Way income came directly to our office, an amount Kirby swore we could get a tax break on because we were setting up our lobby as a personal business. I should have worried about that, but I didn't have the time. It was an issue for our tax guy, not for me.

"Give me that." Will took the bottle and inspected it. "You can't be sure it's a guy," he said. "It's just someone's middle."

"But it's *His* Way," I pointed out, "which implies that the figure is a male. If it were *Her* Way, the person in the robe could be Mother Nature."

Will gave me a look. "You think too much. It's a label."

"I thought you said this business of yours was nonsectarian."

"Christian vitamins? Christian *vitamins*? What are you, crazy?"

"There's a Christian marketing tool implied here."

"Hap, Hap, Hap." Will shook his head. "I never thought you were a fanatic."

"It's my office too!"

"Of course it is. That's the whole point. It's not *my* business. There's plenty of profit for both of us."

"Right," I said, spitting off the *t* at the word's end. My voice astonished me with its fury. "And we Jews only care about profit, right?" I hurled the bottle at him, and it bounced off his tie and disappeared, with no noise to announce where it had landed, and this was so odd it sent both of us looking in Will's chair and on the floor, and whatever drama was in the moment fizzled away. By the time I left Will's office, I felt like an idiot. Throwing things! It was melodramatic. It was like a girl. I started to laugh, although in truth I wanted to cry.

"You don't understand," Will kept saying, in a bizarre comment I didn't think much about until later. "Pastor Roger loves the Jews, he loves them."

CAROLINE

What Fred liked, it turned out, was doing things that made me whimper. "You make that noise, I know I'm doing fine." His inventiveness was perverse and delightful. He had quite a stash of goodies: videos, DVDs, weighted metal balls, dirty old Japanese magazines releasing puffs of dust that made me sneeze. Once he brought a cucumber to bed (ridiculous but fun), and from then on we would wander in the produce section as he watched me get turned on. He wasn't without feelings, he said. He didn't have the relief of an erection and climax, but he still got the warmth and the humming. It was unbelievably sexy to watch him above me, his face furrowed in concentration, as if he were trying to start up a machine, or thread a needle, or fit two mitered joints together. *Come on, baby. Come on, baby . . .*

There you go, baby. There you go. Kissing me all over my face. *There you go.*

HAP MARKOWITZ

I started seeing more patients, upping my coding, making sure I scheduled ear cleanings for separate visits. I didn't actively promote His Way, but when patients said it helped them, I said, "Good!" Will and I chatted about general things—not his or my problems. I stopped hurrying to get home to Janis and her nature programs. The office had become my sanctum. Maybe it always had been.

Will asked me if it was okay for him and Alicia to plan a summer trip to London with Jesse. "Of course," I said, feeling a little disappointed: not that Will and Alicia would be going off, but that Jesse would be gone too.

Jesse was a shot of life for us. The first week working he was tense and serious—the Little Me I remember—but within days he was waving over Caroline's head at his mother, flying around the office with a "What, me worry?" smile. (It was a bit like Will's smile, actually; I could see why people thought Will was his real father.) When I was in my office and could hear his laugh from the far side of the lobby, it was hard to imagine him either as a debater or as someone miserable doing anything. He seemed totally at home. He branched out from pulling charts and filing to checking blood pressures (Caroline taught him how to do this). Once he hovered near the exam room door before I went in with the patient, bulging his eyes and pointing at the number he had written on the chart. "What are you going to do? Will you recheck it? Will you prescribe anything?" My practice wasn't influenced much by this prompting, but Caroline said that Will was scheduling blood pressure rechecks so frequently that Alicia was actually complaining about the number of add-ons. Brice—who Will and I had had to overrule to bring Jesse on—was even more transformed. He seemed—I almost couldn't believe this—happy. I realized I had never seen Brice happy. Almost every time I walked past his office, I picked up an unintelligible but cheerful snippet of a conversation he and Jesse were having:

"Harvey Keitel as a parish priest!"

"The dude abides."

"When he throws back the sheet at the asylum and there's that guy with the rhinoceros head, wow."

"Just a general kind of funny-looking guy."

"Movie talk," Caroline said, smiling.

"Do you know which movies?"

"Well, the funny-looking guy is *Fargo,* and I think the rhinoceros is something from the seventies. I only pick up about ten percent."

"They're going to run out of movies, you know," Will said, plunking a billing sheet on the corner of Caroline's desk and bustling away. "They're going to scrape the bottom of the movie barrel."

"We already have!" Jesse called.

Just then Will's patient Rabbi Kerchner bounded through the front door, shaking his head and blubbering his lips in a mock commentary on the cold. What was it about him, I wondered (not for the first time) that made me embarrassed we shared a religion? He made a beeline for Caroline's window, waved his arm in an expansive way at the racks of His Way. "What's this about, eh? Now you're a drugstore?"

Caroline lifted her face to him and smiled. "Nuclear fusion," she said, and even as the rabbi and I shot each other inquiring glances, she smiled placidly and didn't tell us more.

HAP MARKOWITZ

One Monday morning when I reached the office there was music in the lobby I didn't recognize as LYTE-FM. It was low-pitched and choir-y and had lots of ebbs and swells. No patients were waiting yet; I stood in the lobby for a moment to listen. I made out the sung word "cheeses," which seemed odd, but then I recognized what they were really saying. I strode to Caroline's window. "We're playing Jesus music now?"

Caroline didn't look at me. "Apparently."

"What is this, a new radio station?"

"CD."

I navigated around the His Way displays and boxes and the wall to emerge by Caroline's desk. "Where's the CD player?" She pointed. *Songs of Praise and Hope from the St. Louis Gospel Tabernacle.* "Who brought this?"

Caroline shrugged, although I was sure she knew. Part of her brain already seemed to be off on her trip to Costa Rica. The day before, when I located the bottle of injectable B-12 for her, she said, "Gracias."

I pressed the eject button.

Alicia emerged from the back hall. "Hey, what happened to the music?"

"We see Hindus, Jews, Buddhists here," I said firmly, appealing to Alicia's business sense. "Muslims too." (Perhaps four of them, although I wasn't sure about Mr. Aziz.) "Any music here should be nonsectarian."

Alicia shot me a venomous glance and snatched the CD from my hand. "You're worrying about our music now? You should spend your energy worrying about our business. Where's my cost of living? Where's Caroline's cost of living? You talk to Will about the music, if it matters that much to you. You talk to Will."

"You might want to button your white coat," Caroline said, nodding at my shirt, and I saw that I had dribbled my coffee.

I seethed all day and through my evening phone calls. I kept ducking my head in the lobby to hear what we were transmitting (LYTE-FM—thank you, Caroline), and at six that evening I was just about to head down the hall to settle things once and for all with Will when he appeared at my office door. "How was the weekend on call?" he said, as if this whole day hadn't happened, as if I hadn't caught him and Alicia at noon whispering beside her desk.

"Not bad," I said. "Actually, I had a miraculous weekend. I went out walking at the Deerline Reserve and I was sitting on a bench, catching my breath, and an angel came out of my pager."

Will gave me an uncertain smile.

"I couldn't tell what sex it was. I guess they're eunuchs. Wearing those robes . . . Looked like Apollo! Anyway, it told me there was this computer chip buried in the woods that contained the word of God, and I should dig it up and put it on my hard drive."

"Don't make fun of me." Will's face went stony. He took a step forward into my office. "You hate His Way."

I raised my eyebrows concedingly. "His Way I find dicey, yes."

The muscles around Will's right eye twitched. "Look, Hap." The final *p* was like an explosion. "I know you don't understand my religion, I know you hate succinium, I know you're sad and you've lost your way and Janis's condition is preying on your mind, but that doesn't mean you get to play games with me. Listen, since I hit that sign my life is better, my life is happy, and if you resent that, I'm sorry, but it's true."

My God, maybe I did resent it. I realized the sleeve under my left arm was sticking to my skin from sweat. Maybe I'd always resented his happiness. Maybe my misery was nothing more than the chronic misperception of a bitter man.

"It's not my job to judge you," Will was saying, "but you're my friend and I even talked about you with Pastor Roger, and he, he . . ."

"You talked about me with Pastor Roger? Why would you do that?" I liked Pastor Roger; I wanted him to like me. Humiliating to imagine Will presenting me as some kind of problem case to Pastor Roger.

"Hap." I hated that voice of fake concern.

"You've known him for four months," I said. "You've known me for twenty-eight years. Why in the world are you talking to Pastor Roger about me?"

"About your religion, okay? I was thinking about being saved and I was worried you—"

"You were worried about my *religion*? What do *you* know about my religion?" I was yelling. "You're always telling me what you think; what about what I think? You know what I think, really? I think you know as much about God as you do about lupus."

His pupils dilated. He actually shook his fist. "You go to hell!"

"Superfluous!" I threw my hands up. "Overkill! I'm sure you think I'm headed there already!" I wasn't sure how much Will heard of this, because by then he was shouting back. You're lazy, he said to me, you're obstinate, you act like billing a patient is a crime. What would our bottom line be without His Way? Who kept this practice going except for Will? Where would I be if I had to make it on my own? "You can't even get yourself paid for cleaning ears!"

"Oh, yeah? At least I'm cleaning out the right . . ." The word didn't come, I was scrambling down the slope of incoherence, looking around madly for a branch to grab. "Orifice!" I shouted in something like triumph. "I'd go for the right orifice!"

It was a funny word. It was a funny word and we were each saying funny things and making ludicrous gestures (fists waving, hands flapping), and at the exact same moment we burst out laughing. I put my face in my hands and Will doubled over and for a good two minutes we couldn't speak.

We were too entwined, Will and me. We'd known each other too long. We fought like an old married couple, dirty but with a celebratory zest. Janis and I should have fought so well. We should have fought at all.

~

Pastor Roger was sitting on my exam table, shoulders hunched and his shirt sloppily untucked. "Well, I got my birthday present. Cyrinda filed."

I was surprised. The coldness of her timing made me think she must be either truly miserable or crazy.

His hands clenched the end of the table, ripping the paper. "It seems trivial now, with everything going on around the world, with the terrorists and the . . . I mean, I keep thinking I've got to be like Jeremiah, go out from my people and speak."

Trivial. What a lying word. Losing Cyrinda was not trivial to him, it was the destruction of his dreams. I said, "I'm sorry. About your marriage, I mean."

"Yeah, well." Pastor Roger tapped the ring on his left hand with his right index finger. "We'll still be married, as far as I'm concerned. She just, she just . . ."

I waited. "You should hear him preach!" Will had said. "What a speaker!"

I said, "How did you meet?"

"She was a waitress." He smiled faintly, met my eyes, and looked quickly away. "Cocktail waitress, actually. I was the evening manager at The Hearthside. She had some personal problems, this guy who . . . I used to try to help her. I helped her and we got together and we . . . It was too much of an easy life. Lot of alcohol, you know, bad hours, different temptations. My brothers can handle it. Actually, it's my sister that's the real manager, kind of surprised my dad but that's how it is." His gaze returned to his hands, he twisted the ring on his finger. "Anyhow, that's how we started. Maybe she's jealous of the church, I don't know, she doesn't want everyone judging her because she's the preacher's wife. That can be a problem in a church. The Brothers in Christ guys are okay, but those women, man, those women can be ruthless. Cyrie had some woman from Nurture—Rosemary, bless her heart but she's a biddy—anyway, Rosemary told her she shouldn't wear sleeveless tops. You believe that?" I thought of Janis and her mole, and I did. "Someone else wrote me a letter . . . I mean, here you've got the biggest threat to our world since communism and people are upset about Cyrie's upper arms? I stand in the pulpit every Sunday and I try for perspective. Some Sundays it's hard. Some Sundays I'm talking to convince myself."

"Those are probably your best sermons."

He looked at me, obviously startled. "How did you know?"

I shook my head, not sure.

"Thank you," Pastor Roger said, and I saw that I wasn't imagining that his eyes were tearing up. I knew that in a moment he would ask me about Janis, and my eyes would fill too.

~

One day as I drove home from the office, I thought how Janis had changed. If you looked back on the year until that moment, it hadn't been a tragedy. Her hepatitis C was a not-uncommon disease, it had been identified, it was being treated, we were more honest and tender with each other than we had ever been. But Janis was not happy. People would say that she was "depressed," but that term to me seemed pitifully inadequate. I needed something to particularize what she was doing, to help me make sense of her response. It was like she . . . it was like she . . .

What I needed was a metaphor.

I passed a couple of serious bikers wearing their helmets and black shiny shorts despite the chill, and it came to me: Janis had stopped pedaling. We'd been going for years on our road together, each on our own bike but in tandem, and suddenly she was no longer beside me. I could only grab her handlebars and pull so far. I could get her off her bike and carry her on my back, but I wouldn't have the strength to get us up the slightest hill.

I pulled into our garage breathless—as if I'd biked, not driven, up the rise to our house. *She's stopped pedaling.* Why? I didn't know, but it was her choice. I closed my eyes. *El na refana la. Please, God, heal her.*

It was—I remembered this from religious school as a child—the prayer that Moses offered for his sister Miriam after she'd been stricken by God with leprosy. God gave Miriam leprosy because she and Aaron, Moses' brother, had been saying nasty things about Moses' non-Hebrew wife—and this punishing episode was included in the Bible, if I recalled my college biblical history course correctly, by priestly descendants of Moses who wanted to make their rival descendants of Aaron look bad. "Every verse in the Bible is there for a political reason," my college professor used to say, a view my religious school teachers might not have shared. The thing was, I didn't care what politics had gone into this verse. This prayer could have been written by the Hebrew version of Richard Nixon and I would still have loved it.

I sat in my car in my garage and prayed. *El na refana la. Please, God, heal her.*

I wanted those words, I wanted that language. I wanted, I supposed, that metaphor.

∼

Will and I told Brice and Jesse about our fellow resident, Jake Coburn, who used to push the static button and move his beeper over a drunk from head to foot, saying, "Yup, you check out fine." We told them about the cardiology attending who described to us, in vivid detail, how his hemorrhoids bled on the anniversaries of traumatic events in his life.

One day I caught the boys—that's how I thought of them, "the boys"—at the door to the basement, and asked them if they were excited about the new Harry Potter movie, which I read in *Time* magazine would be coming out next month.

They eyed each other gleefully. "We'll see it, but not the first weekend."

"Oh," I said, seeing my mistake, "you mean Harry Potter's a little young for you?"

"He's fine, we love Harry," Jesse said, "but we think of his movies as a little commercial for us."

"You're highbrows," I said, and the boys nodded happily. "You don't go to conventions dressed as Darth Vader."

"Generally not."

Brice said, "Maybe Princess Leia."

"I prefer Yoda myself," I said solemnly, turning down the hall, delighting in their snickers as I lumbered off.

Children. I understood why people wanted them in their lives.

Although really, thinking about it, Brice was not of childish age.

CAROLINE

It turned out Brice's mother was in a nursing home because the radiation she'd taken had given her intractable diarrhea. Brice didn't mention this to anyone: Al heard about it from a woman in WINNERS who worked as a hospital social worker.

"I went to visit her," Alicia said.

"You're kidding."

"I know, it was crazy. But Pastor Roger had given this sermon about loving the least lovable, and I thought . . ."

At the nursing home, Kitty told Alicia that Brice hadn't visited her for days. She said, "No one cares about me at all." She asked for white-and-red peppermints, smashed up so she could suck on them without choking. Peppermints were soothing, she said. Peppermints would surely help her bowels. Al went to the grocery right away. She un-wrapped a bag of peppermints one by one, put the candies in a Ziploc bag, and took a rolling pin to the lot of them. She packaged up the bits and trotted them to Kitty the next day.

"Too big," Kitty said, sucking on a shard of candy she had picked. "Hold up the wastebasket for me."

"Try a smaller one," Al said.

Kitty did. "Still too big. Wastebasket. I can't eat these. You take them home. What I need is Esther Price chocolates. No nuts."

It was sunny when Al went in but when she got out it was sleeting. Bad enough Kitty had demanded, then rejected her efforts, but . . . chocolates! No one with diarrhea should eat chocolates. Poor Brice, Al thought as she got in her car. She sat there several minutes with her eyes closed, listening to the clicks and scratches of ice hitting her car.

Alicia had turned her chair around to face my back. "Caroline?" she said. I'd been listening as I typed diagnosis codes into the computer, but now I turned around. "You know I never understood how you could cut your parents off completely, but after dealing with Kitty and the peppermints, I swear I understand it. You probably had to."

I nodded, surprised at the catch in my chest. "I had to." She was quite beautiful, Alicia, big brown eyes and shiny dark hair that curled like monkey fingers on her shoulders. I hadn't really looked at her in ages.

"Brice can't," Alicia whispered, gesturing at the wall beside her. "I wish he could."

HAP MARKOWITZ

I said, "Alicia went to visit Brice's *mother*?" Even I had rejoiced when Brice's mother left our practice, and I had only had to deal with her on weekends.

"I don't know, some do-goody thing," Will said. "But she won't go back. I think now Al's probably praying for Kitty to be put out of her misery."

"Understandable."

"Oh, one interesting thing"—Will turned at my office door—"Kitty told Al that Brice doesn't come see her because he's got a girlfriend."

"A girlfriend? Brice?"

"Spends about every evening with her down in his basement, I guess," Will said, with a suggestive click of his tongue.

~

Almost April. "Janis really wants to visit Zion Bible?" Will shot me a look mingling shock and respect. He must have thought that Janis wanted Jesus. I felt guilty, as if I were misrepresenting her motives, although I wouldn't have minded her feeling as if she'd been dipped in warm water and cleansed. Maybe she did secretly want this. Who knew my wife's true motives? Not I.

Just curious, Janis said. A couple of the Garden Club women were talking. Will's church ran movies followed by discussions Saturday night and passed out doughnuts and coffee Sunday mornings. They'd hired a hotshot landscape designer to do a meditative labyrinth. It sounded like an amusement park, Janis said. Something to see.

I thought of Pastor Roger's restaurant background. Entertainment in his blood. The Hearthside had had a Liberace-style pianist on weekends.

That Sunday I was on call and I flew through the hospital, almost forgetting to visit the demented patient with pneumonia on Four South. When I got home, Janis was in the garden seated on her red stool, a bouquet of pulled weeds on the ground beside her. It hit me belatedly that this was a perfect spring day. "It was okay," she said. She wiped the sweat from her forehead, leaving a smear of dirt. "The place is huge. They've got a drum set on the altar and cup holders in the pews." She raised her eyebrows. "Israeli dancing. We had a demonstration."

"Ay-yi-yi," I said, startled. I'd seen Pastor Roger several times in the office now, and he'd said nothing about Israel to me. I wondered if the dancing involved actual Israelis, or even actual Jews.

"You can't escape from Pastor Roger. They have projections of him on these big screens, and his name's printed underneath. Quite the little showman." On one hand, I was relieved Pastor Roger looked disreputable to Janis. On the other, I was disappointed that she hadn't seen him as I had, sitting at the end of an exam table talking mournfully about his wife. There must have been a Pastor Roger and my Roger.

"He's my patient," I said. "I like him."

"Your patient?" Janis said in surprise. There was a visible satisfaction she got upon learning that a public person was my patient. The conductor of the local orchestra really wowed her. She reached for a weed with her right hand, drew up with a wince. "I can't bend that way. It's like there's a cinder block in my guts. Guess it's my liver. What I have to do is"—Janis rotated on her stool, stretched out her left arm—"but I don't have the grip in that hand."

"Let me pull it." I reached in front of her and pulled the thing out, displayed it in the air for her, hairy roots dangling.

"That's not the weed!" Janis shrieked. "You pulled up my blue lungwort!" It was a panicky moment before I realized she was laughing, not crying. "Devil, be gone!" she said, shooing me away.

"Here, I'll put it back."

"Some doc you are. You say you'll help and you pull up my blue lungwort. You'd better tamp it down and water it." She nodded at the plant, who clearly resented its trip out of the ground and was refusing to stand straight.

"It is one of many," I said, relieved to notice similar plants around it. "That's true. Not a tragedy."

The tamping helped. The dirt had a good smell. Above us, baby leaves rustled. In that instant I believed that I understood Janis. I said, "I saw a stepping-stone at Lowe's nursery that said you're nearer to God in a garden than anywhere else on earth."

"Yeah, I've seen that." Janis didn't sound particularly moved. She reached for a plant with spiky leaves, yanked it out. "Die, thistle, die!" To me, the grip in her left hand looked fine. She peered at the weed, made a considering face.

"You know, you're right," she said. "I do feel quite godlike."

She was better, I thought, my chest filling with breath. *El na refana la. Toda. Please, God, heal her, thank you. Thank you, God, that you have brought us to the spring.*

CAROLINE

One morning I found a torn-out piece of notebook paper on my desk, phrases written on it in Brice's blocky print.

Viper Venom Time
Or Just the Night
Flying by Law

I walked to Brice's door and held the paper up. "Does this mean anything?"

"Oh, God, I'm sorry," Brice said. "I don't know, some stupid time-killer. Shh, don't tell the docs."

Jesse came tromping up the stairs, a stack of charts in his hands. "Caroline found our list," Brice said.

Parvati's Pastiche
Honestly, Trees
But Every Bird
Notes from an Undesignated Place

"Oh." Jesse looked over my shoulder at the list. "Do you like it?"

"They're titles to imaginary movies," Brice explained.

File Under Love
My Life in Red

I said, "I like *My Life in Red.*"

"Don't you?" Jesse said. "I love that title so much. It's a dream title. Brice thought it up."

"Do you guys have plots for these movies? *My Life in Red* could be anything—lust, murder, betrayal . . ."

"No plots," Jesse said cheerfully. "Titles alone."

"Or love, or the life force," Brice said, getting up from behind his desk and approaching us. "There's nothing that has to be violent about red. It could be positive, like the girl in the red coat in *Schindler's List.*"

"But doesn't she die?" I said.

"Yes, but the red shows you her vitality."

"He's kind of yogilike these days," Jesse confided, nodding at Brice.

"My favorite is *Honestly, Trees,*" Brice said, taking a place at Jesse's other side. "That's Jesse's."

"That's really the only one that's all mine. I'm not the title maven you are."

"You have other strengths."

"But of course. I can quote Foucault."

"And I can't?" I noticed that Brice's hand had appeared on Jesse's far shoulder. *"The judges of normality are present everywhere."*

"That's a quote." Jesse slid his eyes in my direction. "I taught him that, you know. I teach him everything."

"The whole idea was to be cryptic and beautiful," Brice said, nodding at the paper. "I have to say we pretty much succeeded."

Jesse and Brice. I don't know how the doctors and Alicia kept themselves from seeing it.

HAP MARKOWITZ

Now, really, why should a liver filled with chronic low-level inflammation feel like a cinder block? Maybe like a tennis ball, that slight give. But Janis said cinder block. I don't know why I didn't listen.

In bed, spooned, my arms encircling her arms, her ankle and foot notched together, I could have easily slipped my hand under her elbow and poked at the edge of her liver. I could have. I have no idea why I didn't. That's a lie, of course. In the words of the lady psychiatrist who used to meet with us residents monthly so we didn't forget our souls: "Massive fear, massive denial."

CAROLINE

We saw howler monkeys, capuchin monkeys, poison dart frogs, toucans in flight tipped forward by their heavy bills. We were rained on so hard, the water got in our eyes. One day we went on a day cruise on the Pacific with a raucous bunch of half-naked Germans who gawked at us for half an hour, clearly titillated by our ages and my prosthesis. Finally a blond woman with spooky blue eyes started in with questions. Were we father and daughter? Was this leg an accident, or something with which I was born?

"Are you my daughter?" Fred said.

"I hope I'm not your daughter." I looked at the blond woman and snuggled into Fred. "Believe me, he doesn't treat me like a daughter."

Odd what their witnessing made of us—turned us show-offy, daring, naughty—not our usual proper public selves. When patients spotted us in Ohio at a craft fair, we could indeed have been father and daughter.

Was it the heat? Was it being in a strange place with strangers? Every moment was swarming and rising—like a wave, I thought, like life—with a regularly irregular rhythm that could be mistaken for repetition. The hot breeze, the sun on my closed eyelids, the slap of water on the boat's side, the splatting punctuation of the Germans' cries. The waves swarmed and disappeared and swarmed again, monotonous, irrepeatable. *I'll never have this moment again.*

I wouldn't have thought that there'd be comfort in this thought.

"Let's go in," I said to Fred, unstrapping my leg, and I'm not sure what gave me more pleasure, the colorful fishes below me or the open-mouthed glances of the Germans when, after our swim, Fred pulled me into the boat and I pressed my stump into his crotch.

While we were waiting to board our plane home in the San Jose airport, Fred struck up a conversation with a man who was retired U.S. Air Force. Three years before, the guy had moved to a house he built on the Pacific coast, where he lived like a rajah on his pension. He had a maid who cleaned and cooked him dinner five days a week. He didn't pay her much but she was happy.

"You and your . . ." The man's voice trailed off. "You ought to move down here."

"Girlfriend," Fred said, and out of the corner of my eye I saw the guy give Fred a quick thumbs-up.

"Well, I don't know," Fred said on the plane home. "Think we have a future in the tropics?"

We'd never talked about ourselves as being anything long-term. I wondered if Fred's question was a joke, a proposal, or simply idle chatter. "I just hope we have a future," I said. I was rattled and said the first thing that entered my head.

His eyes narrowed slightly, as if he was as confused by me as I was by him.

"I could live here," he said, although by that point "here" was somewhere over the Gulf of Mexico. "I can see it."

~

When I got back to the office, I expected a general hubbub. I thought everyone would want to see pictures. I thought Al would ask about the weather, Jesse would wonder if I'd seen a sloth, that I could make Brice squeal with my story of the hundreds of bats around the nighttime birdfeeder. Instead, no one said anything. When I walked in that first morning, Brice and Alicia looked up like I was shouting as I came in a library.

"Did you hear?" Brice said, stepping out of his office as I hung up my coat.

"Hear what?"

"About Mrs. Markowitz."

My throat tightened. I wanted right off to get rid of the worst possibility. "Did she die?"

Alicia got up from her desk. "She has primary cancer of the liver. Hepatoma."

"For sure?"

"They did the biopsy last week."

"How's Dr. Markowitz?"

Alicia shook her head.

But when Dr. Markowitz arrived, he seemed jolly. Before I could ask about his wife, he was peppering me with questions about Costa Rica: What was a cloud forest, exactly? Did the country have good relations with its neighbors? What were the roads like?

The lobby started to fill with the morning patients. I had a week's worth of charts and paperwork on my desk. "What about health care?" Dr. Markowitz said. "Did you see any hospitals or . . ."

"How's Mrs. Markowitz?" I cut in. "I was sorry to hear she . . ."

Someone tapped me on the shoulder and I turned: Jesse. He grinned, waved at me, and reached for a stack of charts on my desk. "Basement," he whispered. I heard the creak of Brice's chair.

Dr. Markowitz made a quick, almost furtive wince, then brightened. "It's okay. Now she can get a transplant."

"A liver transplant?" I said, startled.

Kelly Waterhouse was rapping on my window. Leslie Solganik was behind her, tilting her head to better see me over Kelly's shoulder. Blood pressure check, she mouthed. Since Dr. Markowitz had diagnosed her sprue and put her on a gluten-free diet, she was absorbing her meds enough to be tapering off her pills.

I realized Brice was behind me. "Anything for downstairs?" he said.

"I gave Jesse everything," I said, not looking at Brice.

"Primary liver cancer pushes you *way* up on the transplant list," Dr. Markowitz said.

"Excellent," I said, and he answered with a festive bounce and swivel and headed toward the back hall and his office.

"Who is it?" Kelly Waterhouse said eagerly. "Anyone I know?"

"Dr. Markowitz's wife has cancer of the liver," I said, wondering as I said this why I was telling her.

"Liver cancer!" Leslie Solganik winced. "He needs to talk to my friend Sam. They put a special device in Sam that gives him chemotherapy straight to the liver. Give me a paper, I'll write down the specialist's name."

"Oh, here's something to file," Brice said, seizing an envelope from the weekend's pile of incoming mail. "I'll run it down."

A transplant? I thought. Is that realistic? Mrs. Markowitz's age, her hepatitis C, the scarcity of organs, and the rarity of a perfect match: the whole thing sounded impossible. Yet Dr. Markowitz had walked off with such confidence.

Leslie Solganik said, "Liver cancer, you have to know the right doctor."

The office seemed to shake as Brice bounded down the basement stairs.

CAROLINE

Brice pulled together the previous month's income report for the second Tuesday of the month, and the April numbers were the best the office had had in three years. "See," he announced to me, "Jesse's helping us!"—a funny thing to hear him say, since he was the person who hadn't wanted Jesse hired. Brice told me that Dr. Strub's earnings were flat, but Dr. Markowitz was a little up, and a nice boost came from the recently added His Way antiaging skin care line. One of the dermatologists had made some nasty comments in the hospital doctor's lounge about the His Way lotions, Dr. Strub told me, but Dr. Strub didn't care. Over $7K a month to the bottom line and an added quarter of that amount to Pastor Roger's Reclaiming Zion Fund, he said. Our repeat customer rate was running about sixty-five percent—phenomenal. Brice cut the checks for Zion Bible, Dr. Strub told me, and that money—close to $2,000 a month! Pastor Roger was ecstatic!—was a little secret I didn't need to mention to Dr. Markowitz, because, after all, Dr. Strub had introduced the products to the office, and the vast majority of the patients who bought His Way products were his. Also, the office would get a charitable tax deduction on the money it sent to Zion Bible. And anyway, Dr. Markowitz had enough to worry about.

I wasn't sure why Dr. Strub was telling me this, maybe because Dr. Markowitz was hurrying out every day after he was done with patients and Alicia was always too busy to talk when Dr. Strub approached. Dr. Markowitz seemed newly interested in his own billing: he had started keeping track of his daily hospital and office visits in a notebook on his desk, and he popped into Brice's office every evening to check on his collections. Brice and I thought that he was fretting about weeks he'd have to miss if his wife got a transplant. "Look," Brice had heard Dr. Strub tell him, "don't worry. The His Way products will make up for any downtime you have, guaranteed, and if you've got to be off more than a few weeks we'll credit any His Way profit to you."

"That's very generous of Dr. Strub," I said to Brice.

Brice nodded. "He said it was the least he could do. I mean, they're buddies."

As cheerful as Dr. Markowitz had acted when I first asked him about his wife's cancer, now he looked awful. His face looked like it was slipping down his skull. On two separate days he showed up with bits of tissue paper glued by blood to his chin. "He's starting to look like his mother," Dr. Strub confided, "and I always thought she looked ancient."

∾

When Jesse first started working, back in March, he never missed a day. But now that he was almost done with high school, he started to get sick. Once a week or so he missed an afternoon in the office. Nothing serious, Al said. A sore throat, a headache, back pain. "Jess, you're only seventeen years old," she said she told him. "What's going to happen when you're fifty?"

Dr. Strub said, "It's just senioritis, that's all. Don't bother him."

"I hope he's okay for London. This is a big prepaid trip, we can't cancel if his stomach hurts."

Alicia talked about the trip every day. Patients poked their heads in my window to suggest to her sights and restaurants. She read biographies of Princess Di; bought a tea ball and a box of loose Earl Grey; found a library book that translated British English. "Did you know an elevator's a lift? That makes sense, doesn't it?" I'd never been to England, but I couldn't imagine approaching it with Alicia's gee-whiz zest. I found her excitement touching: it reminded me of the poverty of her experience, how marrying Dr. Strub had been a coup for her. At Target, I saw T-shirts decorated with a Union Jack, and I bought three for Dr. Strub, Jesse, and Alicia.

Brice's mother was back home from the care center. He had a new name for her, Krazy Kat. Beyond that nothing had changed. One morning he came in with a wrinkled shirt and a lock of hair plastered to his forehead. It took me a moment to realize he was in the same clothes he'd been wearing the day before. I felt a little sick, wondering what adventure he'd been out on.

"What happened to you?" I said.

"Oh, Krazy Kat had her claws out. Because I saw a movie."

"What movie?"

"*Coffee and Cigarettes*. You probably haven't heard of it. It's arty."

I had heard of it, in fact. "Did you like it?"

"We did."

We. "Jesse?" I asked and Brice nodded. "So"—I indicated his clothes—"are you trying to look like someone in the movie, or what?"

He gave me an intense look. "Krazy Kat locked me out. I started keeping the key in a can in the garage"—he'd complained to me before about the key, an old-fashioned one maybe three inches long, and how his mother refused to modernize the lock—"and Krazy Kat moved it. Dr. Marcus told her if I was living with her, I had to follow her rules."

"Dr. Marcus really told her that?"

"Supposedly. I mean, who knows what she told Dr. Marcus."

I shook my head. "Your mother doesn't want you to see movies now?"

"No movies out. No nights away. She doesn't feel safe if I'm not there. Meow."

"I think Dr. Marcus is doing you a favor," I said. "You need to buy her a decent lock and get out of that house." *Exhortation*, I thought. But Brice was special, I reminded myself. I allowed myself to exhort him.

Brice stared at me. "Yeah," he said.

"So do it," I said. "You have an income."

"Yeah," he said.

He wouldn't do it. There were men like Brice who in a sudden rage shot their parents, burned down their houses, disappeared. He could be a new century's Lizzie Borden. But no, I thought. Brice would never have the guts to hurt his mother.

He turned toward his office, tossing out his leg like a goose step, *striding*, and it was the parting glimpse of his pants caught on his Achilles tendon that unnerved me. That rubbery cord in his posterior ankle, that cord that could be snapped—I didn't know, I realized then, what Brice would never do.

Jesse never came to work that day. Stomach flu, his mother said.

HAP MARKOWITZ

"You've got to be kidding," Janis said to Dr. Noverkian. "A transplant? Save the livers for the thirty-year-olds."

Dr. Noverkian said, "It's up to you. I'm happy to put your name in." He looked at me; I clutched at the side of the chair and didn't say anything. *You say you're pro-life!* I wanted to scream at Larry Noverkian. *How dare you let my wife say she wants to die?*

But I wasn't going to argue with my wife in Larry Noverkian's exam room. I'd talk to her later.

Janis's face was hard and set. We drove home in silence. Outside our front door, Janis pointed at a tulip with sagging and broken petals.

"See? It's had its big life."

You *didn't have a big life!* I thought. *You had this house and this garden and me!* Instead I said, desperate to sway her, "Get on the transplant list for me. You may not even get a liver, but at least, at least, at least get on the list. Please. Do it for me."

There was the tiniest waver in her gaze, and for a moment I was sure that I'd convinced her. Odd the competitive exultation I felt, like I'd just plunked down a ninety-point word in Scrabble. But Janis looked at the tulip again, shook her head. "I can't do things for other people anymore," she said.

Like all my tiles had been swept off the table. Like my opponent was standing up and screaming that they'd never wanted to play with me at all.

What had she done for my sake? Had I ever tried to control her? Were there things she dreamed of doing that she'd never done? We didn't talk, we'd never talked. Each day we made our own way through the world, approaching each other in the evening to huddle, a pair of barnyard animals sharing the same stall.

We should talk more, I thought. Should we talk more? I turned my head to confront Janis's profile, her eyes narrowed, her lips pressed together. We each had only so much strength. I remembered that night in the car when Janis told me about Zuni. I didn't want to go again through that unpeeling, and neither did she. We were on our own front stoop now, facing our front door. She shrugged, I smiled faintly and touched her shoulder, and it was a mutual, unspoken decision that made me turn the key in the lock and go inside. If anyone ever accused me of giving up on her, I'd tell them that we made the choice together. Our final collusion, as it were.

"I wonder if I'm getting arthritis," she said as I pushed the door closed. She peered at her hand as she clawed it. "My ring finger kind of hurts. Oh well, it doesn't matter."

∼

"Go," I told Will. "Janis and I want you to. Go." Their trip was ten days in early June, leaving the day after Jesse's high school graduation. They'd go through the Tower of London, take a dinner cruise on the Thames, climb to the top of St. Paul's, ride the underground. They'd scheduled a fourteen-hour bus trip to take them to Stonehenge, Bath, and Cambridge. Other than Mexico on her honeymoon, Alicia had never traveled farther than Illinois.

"Are you excited?" I asked Jesse.

"Oh, yeah," he said. "Can't wait to get away."

∼

Most medical problems weren't tragic. Pesky, irritating, exhausting, embarrassing—not tragic. I'd always known this. I tried to cajole my patients into knowing it too. A tragic view of illness only made your problems bigger. Even if it gave you a certain grandeur, it wouldn't help you through the line at the grocery store.

A little Eeyore, me. A little one.

A hepatoma, though: that was tragic. I looked across the table at Janis, I fetched her soy milk from the fridge, her sandals from upstairs, and I hoped that she understood I knew.

She sat outside in a deck chair, going through old *Architectural Digest*s Caroline had passed on. She wasn't wearing sunscreen and didn't intend to. If it got any hotter, she said, she'd go naked.

"I'm sorry about your wife," Pastor Roger said. "Will told me." He scheduled with me every two weeks, despite his lack of new physical complaints.

I was sorry about Cyrinda too—the phone calls and e-mails she refused to answer, the duplex in Columbus Pastor Roger wished she hadn't moved into, owned as it was by an old acquaintance she should know better than to trust.

"Uh," Pastor Roger said, gesturing toward his fly, "barn door." I pulled up my zipper quickly, glad he'd noticed this before Caroline did.

Later, Caroline left a copy of Will's e-mail on my desk. The Globe Theatre, Madame Tussaud's, a mixture of mashed potatoes and cabbage that went by the name of bubble and squeak. He couldn't have sounded more oblivious. *"Go,"* I'd said. "Go, don't worry." I hadn't known he'd take me quite so literally.

"You two should come over for dinner," Will said before he left. "I haven't seen Janis in ages."

In their year of marriage, Will and Alicia had never before mentioned Janis and me having a meal with them. We'd had at least two meals a year with Will and Harriet, our seder in the spring, and a cookout at their house in the summer. This year Janis hadn't had the strength for a seder—we'd joked that our saltines from Tim Hortons were our matzo—and now Janis wouldn't want to go out. She didn't eat, didn't sleep well, rarely walked beyond our backyard. She had a lot of itching. Even tea upset her stomach. Lately, her only consistent intake was water sipped from a plastic bottle. Our silent house was even more silent. My heart would have leapt with joy to hear the clink of a cup on a saucer.

CAROLINE

"You heard from Dr. Strub? What'd he say?" Brice was out of his cave in a flash. "Are they okay? He say anything about Jesse?"

Clearly, Brice himself hadn't heard from Jesse. Clearly, Brice was bothered.

"They're fine." I handed Brice a printout of Dr. Strub's e-mail. "He sent it from an Internet café." Brice's eyes were already halfway down the paper. "I bet he went there on his own," I said. "I bet Alicia and Jesse weren't even with him."

Brice's shoulders slumped. He dropped the e-mail on my desk, turned away. "They're really busy!" I called. "Look at all they've seen!" And, under my breath, because Kirby-the-His-Way-pusher had just come through the front door with his big wave and hello, "Jesus, would it kill you to be subtle?"

∼

I was calling people with their lab reports one evening after office hours when I noticed Dr. Markowitz in the lobby looking out to the street through the small window in the front door. "I know you want them to find something," I was saying to Mrs. Fish, whose daughter was scheduled for exploratory abdominal surgery the next week. "Whatever it is, it's just better to know."

"I'll be glad when Will's back," Dr. Markowitz said once I hung up. I stood and poked my head through the opening to the lobby to be sure he was speaking to me. It had rained early in the afternoon, then cleared up, and the shadow of our office on the front grass was unusually strong and clear. "We all want something, right?" Dr. Markowitz said, turning. "We all yearn, desire things that we can't have."

"That's life, I guess," I said, surprised to hear my voice sound so sad.

Dr. Markowitz came around the partition and into my office, took a seat in the chair beside my desk. "I want her to die in peace, that's all."

"You can call in hospice when you need to, right? You can get pain meds."

He nodded, but I felt like I'd disappointed him. "Not that it solves anything," I said quickly.

"It helps." Dr. Markowitz stared at nothing a moment, then stood. "You can't give peace to other people. You can give comfort, but not peace."

"Comfort is good."

He looked at my eyes like he was peering into a lake, trying to make out the floor. "I guess so," he said.

~

"Anything from Dr. Strub?" Brice said the next morning. He read the e-mail on my computer screen over my shoulder: a description of a pub in Cambridge, how windy it had been at Stonehenge.

"Shit!" Brice slammed his hand on my desk. "They're blocking his e-mail, I know they're blocking his e-mail."

"What are you talking about? Whose e-mail?" Although I knew.

"Goddamn Christians. I've sent Jesse all kinds of stuff and nothing gets through. Stuff he'd answer. Stuff, you know, with little jokes in it he'd want to answer."

I shook my head. "I'm sorry."

"I feel like I'm a bug and someone's tearing my wings off."

"Brice. You're not a bug."

"That's what I feel like!" In that moment, I understood why Jesse wanted to be free of him. I understood that Brice was his mother's son.

HAP MARKOWITZ

"Unbelievable," Jesse had said at the Internet café, hurriedly clicking the window of his e-mail closed. *Hi Again, Foucault You, How's London???*—those were the titles Will saw.

Maybe twenty e-mails from Brice, Will said. The titles filled up the whole screen. If Jesse had scrolled down the page, Will was sure he would have seen more.

"You don't want to read anything?" Will asked Jesse.

"Forget e-mail," Jesse said. "We're on holiday."

"Yes, yes, me boy," Will had answered.

Will said to me: Remember Joni Krummel? A dialysis unit nurse during our residency, when Will was just getting started with Harriet. Remember when Joni's parents whisked her off to Australia? She sent Will three letters a day. You were nice to someone and they grabbed you like a life raft. A lonely person thought about you ten thousand times a day more than you thought about them. After a while Will didn't open Joni's letters. Desperately boring, kind of like Joni herself. And why go to Australia to spend your time writing home? "I don't think she saw a kangaroo," Will said to me.

"Did you get my letters?" Joni asked when she got back.

"I threw them out," Will said. By then Joni was a joke between him and Harriet. Not that Joni was a bad person, just . . .

"That Brice," he'd said to Jesse in London. "He's kind of a lonely guy, isn't he?" He'd told Jesse about Joni Krummel. "And I warned him, I'm not sure Brice is a normal male. I don't think he's had real girlfriends, and he might want things from you that you don't want to give." Will frowned and looked my way. "What do you think, should we find Jesse another job?"

I thrust out my lips and considered, remembering suddenly that Janis used to find this gesture endearing. I wondered if she still did. "Not a bad idea," I said.

Will nodded. "That's what I thought." He brightened. "Hey, how's Janis?"

CAROLINE

"You know, it's funny," Alicia said, twisting her chair around to face me, "you go off and it's great, but when you come back you realize what you have here. We wanted to go to church in London but there was nothing, there were all these Anglican places but that's like Catholic, and the only church that looked Bible-based the concierge said was, I don't know, Jamaican. So we didn't go. And this Sunday we were jet-lagged but we got up, and when we walked back into Zion Bible we felt . . ."

The church mattered to her now, I realized as Alicia kept talking. And not just Mrs. Frampton, who was back to services for the first time after breaking her hip, not just Casey Watkins, whose husband had left her despite the triplets, but the music, the scripture, Pastor Roger's message: ". . . and Jonah really didn't want to do what the Lord needed him to do, he was stubborn about it, and after he got out of the whale he ended up sitting under a tree for shade and you know what? The tree died." She was a new Alicia, I realized, attached more to her religion than to our office or even her husband.

When had this happened? How had this happened?

"How's Jesse?" I said when she had finished.

She glanced toward the wall around Brice's office, dropped her voice. "He's relieved not to come back here. Brice was getting a little . . ." She twisted her right hand back and forth as if trying to loosen a lightbulb, and I wondered what the gesture was supposed to mean. "You don't need that, I told him. You have your own life."

I nodded.

"He can get a job at Subway with better pay and more flexible hours. He's got a friend that works there, says he can get him in."

I nodded again. Alicia bent closer, dropped her voice more. "You know Hap's wife isn't leaving the house? That's what Hap told Will. I swear, we wouldn't have gone off if we knew." Alicia's brow wrinkled. "She just found out six weeks ago. It's scary, isn't it? I'm going to take her some chocolate chip cookies."

All that day, Brice periodically emerged from his office, hands in his pockets, shoulders slumped, casting reproachful glances at Alicia and me. "Jesse was sick all spring, Brice, you know that," Alicia said at one point. "And when he was with us in England he was fine."

"How's he going to live?" Brice said. "How's he going to pay his bills?" He turned his back on us, disappeared into his cave once more.

"Not your problem," Alicia called after him. "Not your problem at all."

HAP MARKOWITZ

Every morning when I woke up I could feel, very definitely, my teeth in my mouth. There was a toxin in certain fish that made people think their teeth were about to fall out (a dental-school fascinoma, one could imagine); my teeth felt, in contrast, as if they'd been hammered further in, their very roots wedged and aching. The dentist could find nothing wrong. Still, every morning I felt this, and it hit me the sensation might be less from my teeth than from the bones underneath, and what were bones but a reminder we must die? It was the skeleton, classically, whose teeth clattered. It wasn't that I ever forgot death (me?), but every morning, after I rested my hand for a moment on Janis's chest to be sure she was breathing, it was the first thing that I noticed: two U's, one atop the other, discomfort increasing to actual pain when I clenched my jaw. This sensation lasted for several minutes, even after I'd crept out of bed (I wanted her to sleep as long as she needed) and gone to the upstairs bathroom and brushed and swished. I never mentioned this to Janis. I never would.

Lately I'd been thinking about my residency, the three years after med school when I worked for the hospital and learned how to be an internist. We residents worked hard: every fourth night overnight when we covered the wards, every third night overnight in the ICU. Will and I went through the program together, even shared an apartment our first year, until he met Harriet and moved in with her. Janis and I got married. Looking back, those were a strange three years, both Will and I young and mating and surrounded by death. It was a kind of sickness to want to do a residency in internal medicine. The surgical people rarely had a patient die. If the ob-gyns or the orthopodic residents had a death on their service, they made it a crisis. The family practice residents were quick to transfer their dying people to us, giving them more time for their younger, less complicated patients. People called us internists fleas, "the last ones off a dying dog." It was true. Some weeks as many of our patients died as we sent home. Pale deaths, bloody vomit deaths, yellow-man deaths; quiet deaths, angry deaths, relief deaths; wheezing, panting, gasping deaths. Deaths on the respirator when the heart stopped and you turned off the mechanical breathing and let silence flood the room. Code deaths where old ladies' ribs snapped beneath your pumping hands. Deaths where the smell of feces was the first thing that you noticed. Once I was leaning over a bed with my stethoscope, watching a louse crawl through the hairs on my patient's chest, when I said, "Another breath," and nothing happened. He was gone.

What kind of life was that for a young person? It wasn't really dramatic, not like on TV. It was simply hectic—wearying, too bright or too dark, like living in a room with a rheostat that cycled wildly. I dragged Will into that life, Will who was unsuited, who should have been a dermatologist or maybe not a doctor at all, maybe a salesman, Will who, at the door of the room of demented Mrs. Loblolly, whispered, "Jesus, Hap, you think I really have to tap her?"

"You have to rule out meningitis," I said, because she had a fever and no clear source of infection, and the attendings at morning report would jump all over Will if the spinal tap wasn't done.

"It seems mean," he said.

"It's thorough."

"Maybe I'll say she refused it."

I made a face and looked from Will to the patient, who was staring into space with her mouth open and her tongue flopped out of her mouth. "The Q sign," we used to call that. "FUO," I warned. Fever of unknown origin. Meaning: our bosses want a tap.

"I know, I know," Will repeated, sighing, already untaping the spinal tap tray. "You're right."

"We can go into practice together," I kept telling him. "We'll complement each other." Meaning: You'll be the face and I'll be the brains. Meaning: I can't do this on my own.

I told him: "Office practice isn't like this. What we're seeing is office practice failures." What I didn't tell him—what I didn't myself realize—was that the office practice failures we'd see later would be worse, since they would be our own.

Mrs. Nugent with inoperable aortic stenosis filled up with fluid and died. Lenny Hopkins, who was stroked out in the nursing home, grunted at me as I walked in. Kathy Bocovici's lymphoma blossomed in her armpits and her groin.

In the cineplex of death, I was the usher. I carried the flashlight and pointed people toward the better seats. I warned them to avoid the sticky spots. I said, "Don't forget the handy cup holder." I said, "Sooner or later, everyone sees this movie." No one left; all the people clutched their tickets, they were committed. The lights went down and they were transported; the lights came up and I checked the floors and between the seats, I reported to the people outside how calm things had been, how contented everybody seemed. The cineplex of death was open twenty-four hours a day. I was a good worker, people said. They could trust me.

CAROLINE

The next few weeks, Dr. Markowitz buried himself. He added office hours on Wednesday afternoons, and saw patients until six on his other days. I always left the office before he did. There was plenty of business for him: follow-up visits, acute calls, new patients. When he had a cancellation he asked me to fit in another patient. Where before if someone had phoned in with a cough Dr. Markowitz might call in an antibiotic, now he made the patient come in for an office visit. To me, this seemed less like patient care and more like billing. He told patients to try His Way. The new patients from Zion Bible had heard that

Pastor Roger saw Dr. Markowitz, so they were as happy to see him as Dr. Strub. In July, Brice was elated because Dr. Markowitz's billing for June was up twenty percent from the year before.

"Don't you think that's weird?" I said. "His wife's dying."

Brice looked shocked. "That's not what he said to Hildy Kahn. She said he said his wife was fine."

"He doesn't want us to realize. People with hepatomas don't do fine."

"Are you a doctor now?"

"Have you seen her?" I had, in the line at the local drugstore. Her face was gaunt and her abdomen protuberant; I'd wondered if she'd had to buy maternity pants. "Mrs. Markowitz!" I called, and she seemed flustered, as if she didn't want to be seen. She didn't answer me, just waved and returned her attention to the bottle of antacids in her hand. By the time I'd finished my shopping, she was gone.

Have you called in hospice yet? I wanted to ask Dr. Markowitz. *Isn't it time?* But his bustling way repelled any questions.

"Maybe it's hard for him to be with her," Brice said. I was surprised by the compassion in his voice. He was unhappy those days—rejected and mournful and overwhelmed—but in many ways he was improved. When Alicia was in the bathroom and he had to go to the lobby for Mrs. Marinelli, he presented her with his arm to help her up. I had never seen him offer himself so gallantly. I wondered if he imagined Jesse watching him from somewhere in the ether. A broken heart, I realized, might be as improving as cancer.

CAROLINE

Kirby had on a purple shirt and a purple tie, like the host of *Who Wants to Be a Millionaire*—the show for old people and dreamers. He was sitting in the chair to the right of my desk. "I'm looking at losing my house," he said. "Do you care? You don't care. You don't care about anything, do you? You're Lady Madonna."

Hazel Jenkins handed me her billing sheet. I tore off the top page and handed the receipt back to her. Hazel rolled her eyes in Kirby's direction and wrinkled her nose; I smiled and lifted my hand in a good-bye.

"I banked everything on it. I bought two hundred thousand dollars of product."

"His Way? Why?"

"It was a deal! Haven't you heard of a deal? The market value's two-point-four million, but I can't get it to market. I depend on people like you and your docs for that and, no offense, but . . . people like you let me down."

"Three weeks," Jerry Krebs said.

"You want a Thursday again?"

"That'd be fine." I typed in Jerry's appointment and filled out a card for him.

Kirby leaned forward, propped his arm on my desk, and looked at me conspiratorially. "Two patients."

I shot him an inquiring glance.

"Two patients just walked out of here and you didn't talk to them about His Way. Two missed opportunities! Two lost sales!"

I wanted to slug him.

"There! There!" Kirby was almost bouncing in his chair. "I saw that look! You do have passion, you do!" His eyes narrowed lasciviously. "I bet you—"

"Stop," I said, knowing where this was going. Kirby giggled.

~

Jesse liked a girl at church, Alicia said. Jesse had asked her to go putt-putt golfing with him on Saturday.

A girl? I thought, confused. But I said: "What's her name?"

"Mallory."

Mallory, a honking name, a sound that carried. Brice must have heard every Mallory that Alicia said. The date was really fun, Jesse was going to ask to take her out again. Soon Mallory was coming over to their house, and almost every day Alicia had news. Mallory had tickets to . . . Mallory's parents were . . . The four of them—Will, Alicia, Jesse, and Mallory— cooked out hamburgers Saturday night, then watched the DVD of *Sleepless in Seattle,* which was fun, but why did they have to imply that Meg Ryan and Tom Hanks slept together? Didn't anyone wait for marriage anymore? You didn't want to watch those things with your kids.

Of course, Jesse was going off to Tecumseh University in two months, and Mallory was still in high school, but Tecumseh wasn't all that far away, and Mallory's parents said they'd bring her to Tecumseh for the football games if she wanted.

I wondered if it was sexual, Jesse and that girl. I wondered if Brice knew, or what he assumed. I wished I could forget about all of them: Brice, Jesse, Alicia. There were moments I recalled the boat ride in Costa Rica, wanted more than anything that day back.

"Okay today?" I'd ask Brice every morning.

And his ritual answer: "I'm alive."

"What did you watch last night?"

He was revisiting his old favorites: *The Maltese Falcon, Sunset Boulevard, Singin' in the Rain.* Nothing too recent or fast.

"Is Brice upset about something?" Alicia asked. "He's been gloomy lately. Between him and Dr. Markowitz . . ." She made a sad-sack face, then abruptly changed it, as if a wave of guilt had slapped her. "Not that Dr. Markowitz doesn't have a reason."

~

One day in July, the back door creaked in the early afternoon. I looked up, and there was Jesse, a short and curly-haired redhead behind him. She wore red shorts, a white-and-blue-striped T-shirt, and canvas shoes. "Jesse?" I said, sounding as puzzled as I felt. Why was he there, was he being cruel, was he playing with Brice's head?

"Jesse!" Alicia jumped to her feet. "Mallory!"

Jesse hugged Alicia, Mallory hugged Alicia.

Brice was in his doorway. "Hi, Brice!" Jesse said heartily, not looking at either Brice or me. "I wanted you to meet Mallory." Brice held out his hand, but Mallory didn't seem to see it.

"Hello, Mallory," I said. She looked about fifteen. She was wearing earrings shaped like hearts and a cross around her neck.

"Are you Miss Caroline?" she said.

There was an awkward moment of silence. Brice looked my way.

Had I noticed? he asked later. Her whole body was an irony-free zone.

He'd started watching horror, he told me. He'd never watched horror. He loved horror.

"I don't blame you," I said.

HAP MARKOWITZ

Listen, you start your career in hope and end it in fear. I knew what I did those last weeks was crazy. I could imagine how I appeared to Caroline: my billing—mine!—like a kid clutching a toy. I knew I missed valuable time with Janis. And yet, and yet . . . I don't think I could have done it differently. I had to push through that time.

Too many days I walked up to my desk and stood there frozen, forgetting why I'd come into my office.

A lot of staring into space. Air that felt so thick I could punch a hole in it. A constant noise like white noise in my head.

When I was home, I tried to make it up to her. Janis couldn't get up the stairs, so we'd rented a hospital bed and put it in the dining room. I couldn't abandon her by sleeping upstairs alone. I tried sleeping on the sofa in the living room—no good. Ultimately we arranged ourselves in her hospital bed in the conformation we'd slept in for years. There wasn't a lot of room for motion, but I put my back against the railing and we fit. I usually didn't get home till after seven. I stuck a cut-off broom handle in the hole in the headboard meant for the IV pole and hung one of Janis's fabric L. L. Bean bags over it. I put my cell phone, pen and paper, and a flashlight in the bag and clipped my beeper to its side. When I got paged I could take care of things with almost no movement. I stopped going to the hospital at night to see my newly admitted patients; I had one of the critical care people cover me until morning. My patients seemed to understand. Janis took long-acting morphine and a sleeping pill, notched her ankle between her toes, and generally slept well. There was a purring sort of snore she made (she never snored before) that I found reassuring.

Sometimes I took one of Janis's morphines too. Not every night, just the evenings when I couldn't turn off my brain.

As time passed Janis had the occasional accident and developed an odor, a half-sweet, half-rotten smell I'd noticed before in people with cancer. Every morning I took a hot shower and scrubbed myself with Irish Spring soap and Herbal Essence shampoo, strong scents I hoped would lift me into the realm of the socially acceptable. I thought of wearing cologne but never resorted to it—rarely, during the day, I caught on myself a whiff of Janis, and that was not, to my mind, a possibility I wanted to deny.

CAROLINE

Kirby called wanting a meeting with Dr. Strub. "What should I tell him it's about?" I asked over the phone.

"You guys get to sell more His Way!" he said. "I just found you a couple outlets, beauty shops that'll let us put up His Way displays in their lobby. How about that?"

"Who's 'us'?"

"'Us' is you! People buy the product, they make their checks out to you."

"What about the beauty shop people?" I waved at Mrs. Hopshire standing at my window.

"They're happy to offer His Way as a service."

A service to whom? I should have asked. What's in it for the beauty shop people? But that was the doctors' business, not mine, and Mrs. Hopshire's billing sheet said *Referral to Dr. Wynn: Bright red blood per rectum* and Dr. Wynn's office was always a pain to call.

After office hours on the day of his meeting with Kirby, Dr. Strub walked into Brice's office and shut the door. Alicia and I sat back to back at our own desks, each knowing that the other one was listening.

There was the low rumble of Dr. Strub speaking, the higher-pitched, bit-off notes of Brice's response. The rumble got a little louder, an occasional word thrown out like a hunk of magma. Expectation, contribution, records (Dr. Strub); no direction, taking advantage, inundated (Brice). "You never even thank me," Brice said.

Alicia's chair creaked. "Jesse might lose that scholarship," she said quietly. "There's another debater who all of a sudden wants to go to Tecumseh, and he was number three at the national championship last year."

Surprised, I turned around to look at her. Her face was puffy and red. "I think I'll go stock the exam rooms," she said, standing.

It felt indecent to keep listening after she left. I went to the lobby, started arranging the products on their shelves. Out there I couldn't make out Brice's or Dr. Strub's words. One of the Child's Garden bottles didn't rattle when I shook it. The foil top was peeled off and the bottle was empty. Who in the world . . . ? I didn't expect that sort of thing from people in our waiting room. The discovery made me feel unbalanced, as if my prosthesis had been replaced by one made out of Styrofoam and paper.

A bottle of Eve's Elixir was wedged under the cabinet. I went back to my desk for a ruler to fish it out. Through the wall I heard a low mumble that sounded like collusion. Maybe I heard the name Markowitz.

Sure enough, by the next week we were getting envelopes from beauty shops. One return address said *Konni's Kurls* in pink and swirly script. Another had a salon name printed on the blades of a pair of scissors. "Put those straight on my desk," Brice had told me. "Don't even slit them open."

~

One night Dr. Strub hung around after office hours and asked me if we could talk. He sat himself in the chair beside my desk. "You're a reasonable person," he started.

Uh-oh, I thought, wondering both what he wanted to talk me into and how long he planned to take doing it. It was Fred's VA volunteering day but he should be at his house now, and I was supposed to go there and grab a bite to eat before we headed to a free jazz concert.

What if a court, Dr. Strub said, thought that writing a check to our practice implied that our doctors had endorsed *a particular product for a particular person*, and what if the beauty ladies were selling something we didn't even know about—say, diet pills? Diet pills were on Dr. Strub's mind because Irv Sabol, one of the local gynecologists, had just been sued by one of his patients because she'd had a heart attack while she was taking some herbal weight-loss pill Irv told her was okay. Irv didn't even sell the thing, just approved it. His Way had a weight-loss product—Kirby loved it—but Dr. Strub had put his foot down about carrying it, because poor Hap would go crazy if he saw diet aids in our lobby. Practically every other day he was yelling down the hall reminding some poor lady not to take ephedra—the main ingredient in His Way to Slimness.

Hadn't ephedra just been banned? I thought. Well, something had been banned, but I couldn't remember what.

"Here's the thing," Dr. Strub said, giving me a quick glance from under his eyebrows. "You may not understand this part. Al says you don't really go to church."

"No," I said. "Not really."

He'd told me before: a cut of all our office's His Way sales went to Zion Bible. Almost every week when Pastor Roger shook Dr. Strub's hand after services, he added in a low voice, "And thank you. Our Reclaiming Zion account . . ." and gave Dr. Strub a thumbs-up.

If someone else sold His Way from the beauty shops, the cut would go to their own charity, and Pastor Roger would be . . . Dr. Strub slumped his shoulders and drooped his head like some sad-sack cartoon character. Just as quickly, he straightened. "And those gals are performing! The last two weeks they're selling more than we are!"

I was confused. What was I the jury about? What was the crime? And I wasn't surprised the ladies were selling more than we were: my enthusiasm for His Way was zero, and even Dr. Strub didn't seem to be recommending it as vigorously as he used to. Sales fatigue, I called it in my mind.

I said, "You want me to say that it's okay that we're getting money from beauty shops maybe selling His Way diet pills?"

"Basically, yes."

Since when was I the arbiter? Since when was I the office conscience? But in an odd way I saw that I indeed was, and that Dr. Strub was right to ask me.

"Well," I said, "you don't know for sure if they're selling diet pills?"

Dr. Strub shook his head.

"And you want to keep selling there because it's money for us and money for your church?"

Dr. Strub nodded.

"I think you should go to the beauty shops and check out their product line."

He looked disappointed for only a moment. "Think about Dr. Markowitz," he said. "What if, with his wife being sick, what if he has to take off?"

I felt my brow twitch.

"That changes things, doesn't it?" Dr. Strub said.

It did change things. But what would Dr. Markowitz want? I thought as I lay in bed that evening. It seemed wrong to keep him in the dark about the beauty shops, if a primary goal of that business was bringing in money to help him. Although Dr. Markowitz was acting lately as if all that mattered was profit. When I got up to use the toilet, I hit my stump on the bathroom door. Some nights I was wobblier than others.

HAP MARKOWITZ

There were two main nurses hospice sent to our house: Mary, a cheerfully efficient, broad-shouldered woman of late middle age who managed to make coffee and pick up downstairs while she was caring for Janis; and Kaitlin, a wispy thing in her mid-twenties with big eyes and a cringing attitude. I thought Mary was a wonder, but to my surprise Janis liked the cringer. It took me several evenings of listening to Janis's stories of Kaitlin's pets and cruel parents and disappointing boyfriends to understand why. To Mary, my wife was the newest sausage in the hospice pan, an item to be watched for scorching and rolled over. To Kaitlin, my wife was an advisor, an appreciator, even a friend. Kaitlin often stayed past her allotted time, sitting in the upholstered chair we'd moved from the living room into the dining room next to the hospital bed. On the dining room table—which I'd pushed against the wall—Kaitlin spread out the paperwork for all her patients, filling in check marks as she talked to Janis. "Such a sweet person," Janis said. "I hope things work out for her."

Janis spent almost all her time in bed, although Mary could sometimes bully her into the upholstered chair that Kaitlin sat in. Bedsores were a worry. By the middle of August, I was coming home at lunch to turn her, and we brought in a special mattress and a lambskin. She would still eat soup from Tim Hortons, although she refused any soup from a can. I tried to buy a whole pot of soup at our local franchise, but the manager was not helpful. I think he didn't want me to realize that his staff didn't make the stuff from scratch. The hell I cared about scratch. I couldn't get him to understand this.

I no longer prayed for Janis to be healed. It was nothing she wanted, and it didn't feel right to pester God solely for the sake of my desires.

CAROLINE

I never visited Mrs. Markowitz, not once. A thousand times I thought of visiting, but I didn't. I always had a good excuse—but what is an excuse but a wink and nod to your own weakness?

Alicia saw her twice, once in June when Janis—that's what Alicia called her—greeted her at the front door in bare feet and pajamas, and once in August when Janis was in her bed in the dining room, curled up away from the door, her vertebrae making a staircase of her back. Terrible how thin she'd gotten, Alicia said.

The second visit, a bug-eyed nurse let Alicia in. "I'm Kaitlin, Janis's head nurse," she said. Head nurse? Alicia had thought. Kaitlin was a hospice nurse at a patient's house—what did she mean, "head nurse"?

Janis's head looked like a lollipop on a stick. The whites of her eyes were as yellow as egg yolks. "How are you feeling?" Alicia asked Janis, but before Janis could answer, Kaitlin cut in to talk about the ear of corn she'd hung outside the window for squirrels and the special chocolates Kaitlin bought for her that Janis liked.

A worn-looking Oriental rug in blues and reds sat under the bed. A starburst chandelier threw wedge-shaped blocks of light onto Janis's face. The wallpaper was golden and printed with pink flowers and vertical shoots of bamboo. "The smell!" Alicia said, wrinkling her nose.

The first time Alicia visited Janis, in June—she told me now—she had walked around the garden while Janis went upstairs to change. It was a beautiful clear day. Al had never seen plants placed with such obvious care—delicate plants tucked under plants with big flat leaves, plants that looked like they were reaching out their arms and plants that dug their fingers in the earth, glossy plants nestled next to furry ones. It was even nicer than the gardens they'd seen in England. So much beauty and variety in the world, Al thought, and soon she was stumbling without thinking up steps, down paths, as if large hands wearing something like oven mitts—God's hands—were moving her about. When she finally knocked on the back door, Janis let her in. She had changed into a pair of sweatpants and a man's flannel shirt unbuttoned at the bottom. Her belly bulged like a pear.

"You all right?" Janis said, pouring Alicia a cup of coffee.

"I'm fine." Alicia took a seat in a kitchen chair, exhausted and restored.

They didn't talk about her cancer once. Janis didn't need to talk about her cancer. Alicia listened without hearing as Janis told her of her plants. When Alicia left that time, back in June, she and Janis had hugged with real affection. They'd each gotten from the other what they needed.

"Here, honey, let me fix your pillow," Kaitlin said on Alicia's second visit, bustling in an exaggerated way. Janis's eyes slid to the side as Kaitlin lifted her. "Oh, Janny Jan," Kaitlin said, stroking Janis's temple. "Janny Jan's taught me so much."

Alicia said, "Are you an RN?"

Kaitlin was. But no nursing degree. The usual lame excuse about being busy.

"She's not a child." Alicia looked from Kaitlin to Janis. "Lawdy."

Eternal vigilance, the cost of everything. *I'll get Will to warn Hap,* Alicia thought, watching Kaitlin put a straw to Janis's lips. And Will had tried, but Hap hadn't wanted to listen. Janis loved Kaitlin, Hap said. Kaitlin relied on her.

"I don't understand why he's here all the time," I said. "These days won't come back."

"He goes home at lunch now."

"Well. For half an hour."

Alicia and I swiveled our chairs and looked at each other, united in our unspoken questions. Had Dr. and Mrs. Markowitz been unhappy all these years? Did their marriage have a central hole in it, like an apple that a worm had cored out?

"I hope Will would stay home for me," Alicia said.

"I don't want anybody talking to me in baby talk," I said.

HAP MARKOWITZ

Mary the wonder nurse called me at the office to say that the only thing that sounded good that afternoon to Janis was breakfast, specifically pancakes. I could make a decent pancake with Bisquick, Mary said, and advised me to pick up some real maple syrup too. I headed for the grocery store right after my last patient, on the way thinking that if Janis wanted breakfast for dinner, I could scramble her an egg for protein. The list on the car tray beside me said *Bisquick, milk, yogurt*, and when I stopped at a red light I pulled a pen from my shirt pocket and scribbled *egg* before the light changed, but as I turned right onto Canasta it bothered me that I left off the *s*—ridiculous to care about, and anyway I couldn't buy a single egg if I begged the grocery people to let me—but *egg* on a shopping list just wasn't right, I couldn't stand it, and even though Canasta Street was four lanes wide and at this time of day fairly crowded, even though I'd already moved into the inside lane in preparation for my left turn two blocks away, I still felt compelled to fish for the pen on the tray beside me—got it!—and turn it in my right hand so the tip was down, and glance—glance, it was quick—at the paper beside me and find the offending word to add a squiggly—

A horn sounded and I looked up—headlights coming at me on the left, Jesus—and I dropped the pen and swerved and there was another horn and a white rectangle whizzing past me on the right. I thought: Hap, you could have gotten yourself killed. Killed for the *s* in *eggs*; no one would believe it. Worse, they'd run a tox screen on my corpse and find morphine. What an embarrassment for Janis. And although I saw, in equal measure, the humor and the implausibility of this scenario, it was enough to make me swear off Janis's soothing capsules forever. What was I thinking? What was wrong with me? There were things a person had to face naked, and one of them was death. I should have known that.

~

I cried on Will that week. I was telling him about Janis's pain meds, just a normal conversation, and Will said, "Wow, does she ever feel comfortable?" and I started flat-out crying. Crying and crying. I couldn't stop. All the years I'd known him, he'd never seen me cry.

I felt like one of those cartoon characters a bomb had been tossed through, someone walking around with a hole the size of a bowling ball in his middle. Air seemed to be blowing right through me. I was useless to my wife, to anyone. I wanted to be dead.

Will put an arm around me, sat me in the patient chair in my office, went down the hall, and returned with one of Caroline's Diet Cokes from the fridge. "Have a drink," he said, lifting the can dangerously high and arcing its stream into the mug in front of him, and since I'd said and done the exact same thing for him a few years before (the day after Harriet left), there were layers of comfort, for both of us, in that gesture. I calmed down. I sipped the pop and talked about Janis. Will sat and listened, occasionally wincing. He cared.

A friend was something like a blanket. Something like clothes.

～

Janis died in her sleep, in my arms. I got a page about one a.m. I reached the phone, dialed, and was waiting for the ER to answer when I realized that I didn't feel her breathing.

I asked the ER doctor to call the critical care people directly, to not even tell me the patient's story. "I've got my hands full here," I said, but I didn't explain why.

I lay there with her for some time, until she stiffened and went cool.

Kaitlin seemed to think she knew my wife better than I did. Maybe she did. The funeral home asked me to bring in clothes, which I did, and then I got a call that Kaitlin had appeared there with a different dress for Janis. I had forgotten that Kaitlin had the key to our house. "I'm Jewish," I apologized to the funeral director over the phone from my office. "I didn't grow up with open caskets."

"Well, this woman was very helpful." The funeral director spoke in a cajoling way. "Said your wife and she had discussed it."

"That's possible, sure. They were together a lot."

"Women, you know. It's a very lovely dress, blue with white flowers."

"Maybe she got it special. That doesn't ring a bell."

"Oh, Dr. Markowitz"—he was very good, only an inoffensive trace of amusement in his voice—"you'll recognize it. Kaitlin said your wife wore it in your twenty-fifth-anniversary picture."

Caroline knocked at my door, slipped an open chart in front of me. Jessica Warner had burning when she urinated. Would I call something in?

The funeral director was talking about flowers. I put my hand over the receiver. "I'll see her. Add her on at five."

Caroline's eyes widened, but she nodded and left.

". . . maybe a blanket of white roses, very beautiful," the funeral director said.

"What did Kaitlin think?"

"We didn't actually discuss the flowers. I do have her number, I can—"

"No, no, don't ask her. A carpet of roses sounds fine."

"A blanket, yes." He sounded so nice, God knew what he was actually thinking. "And I've arranged a very nonsectarian minister, a Unitarian Universalist, lovely man. You'll be pleased."

But I was not pleased. There was nothing about the funeral that pleased me, not one thing at all. Maybe the worst thing was before the visitation finding Janis in the coffin on her back, hands folded like she was praying, a way I never, ever saw her lie. I wanted to reach under the apron of the coffin and tuck her ankle and foot together. I had my hand poised in the air above her waist, ready to reach in, when the funeral director tapped me on the arm.

CAROLINE

"Now, I didn't send flowers," Fred said. "Dr. Markowitz doesn't need flowers, but I've got a pan of baked beans in the cooler and I made him some trail mix too. Think that's okay? I wanted something easy he could pick on."

"Perfect," I said, wondering why I hadn't thought of food myself. I'd sent flowers.

~

Jesse was at the graveside service with that girl Mallory. Her eyes welled and she clutched a handkerchief through the entire service, although she had never met either Dr. Markowitz or his wife.

It was terribly hot. We clustered together under the awning just to get a piece of shade.

"The good thing is, death is final," Brice said as we walked from the grave. "If you're dead, you don't have to see the person you love holding hands with someone awful."

What possible response was there to that? I didn't take it as a threat: I took it as a big harrumph. "How's your mom?" I asked, wondering if he'd make the connection between her self-absorption and his.

"The same."

"I'm sorry."

Fred gave my hand a squeeze. "Gosh, I bet the M&M's in that trail mix are melting. I should've put it in the cooler too."

Looking back, I see that I was cruel to Brice. It was a rough day for him, and all he needed were some crumbs of mercy. He'd want more, of course. But he could have lived on crumbs.

"What're you two doing now?" Brice said.

I glanced at Fred.

"Go back to my house, watch TV, maybe grill up some chicken," Fred said. "Want to come?"

I almost jabbed Fred in the side. Brice glanced at me, and I wrinkled my lips together quickly, an unwelcoming twitch.

"That's okay," Brice said. "I'll go home."

HAP MARKOWITZ

Will came to the house the evening after the funeral. When I opened the front door for him, heat and the odor of roses hit me like a washcloth drenched in ether.

I took him to the living room, pointed at a chair. I sat on the sofa.

"You got any lights in this place, Hap?"

I switched on a lamp.

"Hap, you eating okay? You, like, showering?"

I didn't want to shower. It seemed like too much work to adjust the knobs for the proper temperature. Also, I didn't want to be completely naked. Socks and briefs and shirt off all at once: too much. "I can't shower," I said. "It's a Jewish thing," thinking Will wouldn't dare to contradict me.

Will was looking around the room. "You missed that one," he says, pointing at the mirror beside the fireplace. "Want to tell me where a towel or something is and I can cover it?"

"You know about covering mirrors?" Not a single mirror in the house was covered.

"I talked to Rabbi Kerchner, he told me all about Jewish burial customs. Are you doing a shiva, Hap? You got anybody coming with food?"

Uh-oh. I snorted in amusement, and Will gave me a strange look. "I have some baked beans and trail mix," I said. "My patient Fred, Caroline's buddy."

Will nodded; we sat in silence.

"It was peaceful," I said after a bit. "Maybe twenty-four hours of Cheyne-Stoking, then a decrescendo at the end." I was describing a pattern of breathing: Cheyne-Stoke breathing consisted of shallow, quick breaths followed by deep, very slow ones.

Will didn't say anything.

"Decrescendo," I repeated, lifting my hand and letting it glide down through the air. That was beautiful, that word. Like the dying resurrection lilies outside with their hanging petals, giving them a wanton, iris look: decrescendo.

I hoped it had been like that. It probably was like that. She had done nothing to wake me.

I saw Janis on her red stool digging holes for the tulip bulbs. I wondered if the bulbs she'd planted last fall would bloom again next spring. Tulips were unreliable, Janis said. She used to dig the bulbs up and replant them in the fall, but that would be more work than I could even imagine.

"We should be used to it, you know," I said. "Death."

"I'm glad it was calm."

"I'm good at death. Good usher. I thought I'd give Kaitlin her jewelry. The nurse. Unless Alicia wants some."

"No, that's okay."

"Alicia visited Janis twice. You should take her something. Maybe earrings."

"Al doesn't have pierced ears, Hap."

I forgot what we said next. Eventually I took Will across the hall to see where Janis stayed.

I pushed open the double doors into the dining room and the right-side door made its usual thud as it hit the wall.

"We used to eat in here, remember?" Will said. "Your seders." Although we didn't eat matzo all through Passover, Janis always liked hosting Passover seders. She wasn't a dedicated cook, but having to leave out leavening made a fun challenge out of preparing a big meal. We'd have Will and Harriet and the girls for the ceremony and food. Once I had a brainstorm and duct-taped the *afikomen*—the matzo wrapped up in a napkin—to the bottom of the dining room table. Added excitement in the girls' search that year. Chloe found it, won the silver dollar.

Will said, "Remember? Janis used to spread the matzo with Nutella for the girls."

The bed looked messy—sheets stirred, pillow bunched up—and the dining table was stacked with Janis's clothes. The long mirror over the buffet was certainly not covered.

"Hap," Will said, "you're not . . ." He stopped. "You're sleeping in here, hunh?"

There was a styrofoam Tim Hortons bowl on the table, a white plastic spoon beside it. Got to throw that out, I thought. "She'd eat soup," I said, noticing Will's glance. "Hearty vegetable."

"She loved this room," I said. "Loved the light." This reminded me that it was dark, and I switched the light on.

In the corner of the room I noticed the portable commode draped with a blue towel. For a second I thought of snatching up the towel to cover the mirror, but I didn't want Will to spot the toilet. I needed to call the medical supply company about retrieving it—but that would mean picking up the bed too.

I didn't want to lose the bed. The bed with her scent still in it, her scent mingled with mine. "People should shower in the morning," my mother used to say, "get the bed smell off"—which was really, I realized when I grew up, the smell of sex. Not that Janis's and my bed had that smell. But it had her smell, mixed with the tang of the peach-mango body lotion Kaitlin rubbed into her legs and arms each day. I made my way to the bed now, leaned forward, opened my nostrils.

"Hapster," Will said, suddenly beside me, "you need to shower."

He rolled his eyes in my direction, his eyebrows twitching into a frown.

"And get this bed out of here. This is a sickbed. You need to sleep in a well bed." He pointed at the ceiling. "In your bedroom. Upstairs."

"Okay." Little faint sound.

"Okay? Good. I'll come back Thursday to be sure. When are you coming back to the office, a week from tomorrow? I think a week from tomorrow would be good."

I nodded.

"Rabbi Kerchner said after a week you should leave your house. I'll have Caroline schedule you half the day Wednesday and Thursday, how's that sound? Friday you can be full. And I'll do call that first weekend, then we'll go back to every other."

"Okay." Maybe a bit louder.

"What did you say?" Will cupped a hand behind his ear. "I'm going deaf here."

I felt a spasm of irritation. "I said *okay*."

Will smiled, patted me on the shoulder. "Good boy," he said.

~

In the Jewish tradition—Will could have told me this—the close relatives of a deceased person said the Kaddish prayer in their loved one's memory every day for a year. It was three or four days after Janis's death that I thought of saying Kaddish, and, oddly, the prayer came to me while I was on the treadmill in our basement. Janis had bought the treadmill for me several years before, and was chronically nagging me to use it. She got enough exercise outside, she said. After she died, I took off the tablecloths that had been draped for storage on the tread- mill's rails and dusted the display with the side of my hand and cranked the thing up in Janis's memory. Once I'd said the Kaddish on the treadmill, that was where I said it every day. I couldn't miss my exercise because I couldn't miss saying Kaddish.

Goofy, really. Maybe even sacrilegious. But Janis wanted me to exercise, and Janis would have smiled.

HAP MARKOWITZ

A couple of weeks after Jesse had confided to Will that he was thinking about splitting up with Mallory, Will had a dream in which Jesse was drowning. This was just after Janis died. Mallory was great, Jesse said. He loved Mallory. It just wasn't fair to keep her hanging, because he didn't think she was a person he could marry, and he wanted to set her free before he went off to college.

In Will's dream of Jesse's drowning, a man was clutching Jesse from behind in the water. At first Will thought the guy was rescuing Jesse, but then Will realized that the guy had eight arms like an octopus, and he was the thing pulling Jesse down.

"What do you think?" Will said.

"What happened next?"

"I woke up. I'll tell you what I think: I think that dream was almost embarrassing it's so simple. Maybe the Lord knows I need things spelled out."

Several of the BIC guys had battled through homosexual urges. One had even lived with another guy for several years. Now he was married with a baby—amazing, Will said, what the Lord could do for people who had faith.

"You think the dream was telling you Jesse's"—I didn't want to say the word "gay"; that might offend Will—"not heterosexual?"

Will shook his head quickly. "He's not gay. But maybe he has some . . . homosexual urges."

"Urges," I repeated, wondering when urges shaded into actual homosexuality. Will nodded. "Uncontrollable itching," I said.

"It's not uncontrollable!" Will burst out. "Look at me. I can use myself as an example for him, come the time."

I could have argued, but there were things then that I couldn't make myself think mattered. I let it go. Was Jesse gay? I almost hoped he was. Show our more intolerant patients that a young gay man could be a normal person, someone they couldn't help liking. Of course, Brice was probably gay, too, but he wasn't as endearing as Jesse.

Ned Fanconi's potassium was 5.6, a smidgen elevated but not deadly, and he was a diabetic with mild renal failure, and high potassium was a thing he got. I wrote *OK* on the lab sheet paperclipped to his chart and stuck it on Caroline's desk for her to notify him. Before I knew it Alicia was rapping on my door frame, saying "Dr. Markowitz?"

I was looking out the window.

"Dr. Markowitz, Ned Fanconi had a potassium of 5.6. I don't know if you saw it."

Disingenuous bitch. "Did I write on it?"

"Well, you wrote *OK,* but, generally, I mean in the past you—"

"If I wrote *OK,* it's okay."

"It was 5.6."

"As his kidney function gets worse, his potassium is going to go up. Five-point-six isn't going to kill him. Six-point-six wouldn't kill him. Seven-point-six, well"—I shifted, looked out the window again—"seven-point-six might matter." I have a crummy view, I was thinking. Will at least looked across our parking lot to a patch of honeysuckle. I looked at nothing, I looked across the Hallersville–Kenston pike to our fair city's commercial palace, the Midburg Mall.

I could hear Alicia's indecision behind me, her half-step forward, half-step back. I could read her little mind. *But what if Ned Fanconi keels over dead and a lawyer comes and grabs our charts and . . . ?* "I'll just leave this on your desk, then," she said, and I turned to see her thrusting the chart on top of my central pile and skittering away. Normal potassium, read the lab report sheet: 3.5–5.5. As if a deviation of point-one mattered. A little mind wanted strict limits to its normal. A little mind craved the tyranny of normal.

"You've got to talk with him," I heard Alicia telling Will in the front office. "He's not right and he's going to get you in trouble."

"I think he's okay," Caroline said. "Under the circumstances, I think he's fine."

Part of me was saying, "Yippee, Caroline!" Part of me was mortified she felt the need to defend me at all. Part of me said: " *'Under the circumstances?'* Caroline, is that the best you can do?"

The practice was losing money that August. Every day's billing was important. Every His Way sale helped. Fortunately, there was a nasty respiratory virus that seemed to require two office visits to get over. Fortunately, the war in Iraq was making everybody anxious. Within a month or so, I was sure, my billing would be back within Alicia's limits.

I was *normal,* go to hell.

I was *normal,* screw the world.

Brice was the only person in the office when I left that evening. I stuck my head in his door. "You aren't normal, are you?"

A flash of alarm filled his face. Then he saw my grin. "I guess not," he said, looking sheepish.

"Good," I said. "Stay that way." And I left.

CAROLINE

In the middle of the night, standing in the bathroom looking in the mirror, I realized that my hair was the wrong color. Overall, I was paler than I used to be. My face was fading like a cloth left in the sun. The skin under my eyebrows was chalky. My eyebrows were studded with red-brown streaks, but my hair was the same dark brown—I think they call it "chestnut"—that it had been before it fell out with the chemo. God knows what color it really was: Kim at Utopia had been coloring it for years.

"Your hair's fine," Fred said later, chuckling. "Nice brown hair." There might be ego in this, I realized: if my hair was grayer, people might not assume that I was his daughter.

"It's not too dark," Kim at Utopia said in a startled tone. "It keeps you looking young!"

I looked at her in the mirror, realizing that Kim's hair was chestnut too.

A moon-shaped face leaned in through my window. "Hello, Pastor Roger," I said. "All set for your trip?" He was traveling with a group of ministers to Israel for twenty days. His divorce was final and I'd just mailed Cyrinda's records to a nurse practitioner in Taos, New Mexico.

"Two weeks from tomorrow," Pastor Roger said with a little laugh. "Journey to the center of the universe."

I glanced up and there was Jesse at my side. He must have come in the back door. "Where's Mom?" he said.

"Taking back patients."

He had to have passed Brice's open door, and I looked behind him to see Brice standing outside his doorway, his figure tense and his fingers tapping his thighs. At least this time Jesse hadn't brought Mallory with him.

"Good to see you, Jesse," Pastor Roger said.

"Yeah, you too."

I handed Pastor Roger his receipt and waved him good-bye. "Be safe!"

"Hey, Brice," Jesse said, turning and nodding a little stiffly. "Seen anything good lately?"

Brice shrugged.

"Any winners, in the parlance of our time?"

That had to be a quote from something. A private joke, a nod to their shared past.

"No," Brice said.

Jesse looked flustered, glanced toward the photos his mother had taped to the wall over her desk. Jesse's senior picture, Jesse and Dr. Strub at the Tower of London, Jesse with his arm around Alicia on their backyard patio. "You're so into cinema, I thought I should ask you if there's something Mallory and I should see." Talking to the photos, not to Brice.

"You and Mallory."

"Yeah." Eyes still fixed on the photos.

"You're still with her."

"Yeah, sure. She's a nice person." Jesse looked toward me nervously and erupted in a grin, as if he were trying to enlist me on his side.

Brice said, "Rent *40 Days and 40 Nights*. You'll like it. It's about abstinence."

Jesse's face went slack in dismay.

"Theory is an easy grader," I remember Leslie Solganik saying once, about what I couldn't recall. "Reality, she grades hard."

The door to Brice's office clicked closed. Alicia bounded in from the hall behind the lobby, almost crashing into her son.

"Whoa," Jesse said. And then: "I heard."

"From Tecumseh? And?"

"It's no problem. I've got the scholarship."

She did the dance again, the head-back, whooping dance of joy she had performed when Jesse won his debate tournament, and once again I felt touched and envious and totally left out. She was loud; several people in the lobby turned to look and smile. God knows what Brice thought.

~

Pastor Roger told Dr. Markowitz he should come with him to Israel. "He seemed serious," Dr. Markowitz said, shaking his head. "Said he'd get me a free ticket."

It was too odd, too urgent, too *needy*. Dr. Markowitz was fond of the guy, but it struck him that the Prozac capsules Pastor Roger had been taking for the last month could be making him a little manic. That happened sometimes. Pastor Roger didn't see it: he felt great, he'd found a perfect place for Cyrinda to live, his trip to Israel would be blessed, his fellow travelers were God's people.

Dr. Markowitz was sitting to the left of my desk in what I came to think of as the Chair of Confession, where Dr. Strub had sat when he asked for my opinion about selling *His Way* in the beauty shops.

Toward the end, everybody sat there, even Alicia, who had her own chair right behind me. Everybody except Brice, who stayed in his cave.

Dr. Markowitz had never really wanted to visit Israel. He knew people who'd gone there and loved it, but it was a trip that required some desire to make—unlike one of those mindless vacations (a Caribbean cruise, a week in San Francisco) any schlump could simply roll into.

"I guess there's nothing I want that much," Dr. Markowitz said. He fell silent, tapped his fingers on my desk, knitted his brow. Maybe to see Janis alive again. Just a glimpse. He'd look out the kitchen window, spot her sitting in the garden on her little red stool. He wouldn't need to see her face, her back would be enough.

"Not too greedy, hunh?" He Laughed. "All I want is the dead brought back."

He'd said to Pastor Roger, "Listen, I'm thinking you should stop the Prozac. Sometimes it can make you a little . . ." Dr. Markowitz had raised his hand in the air, palm down, and made a jittering motion.

Pastor Roger said he felt wonderful. For the first time since Cyrinda left him, he felt alive.

That got him, Dr. Markowitz said. His wife, his Bosc pear (his Bosc pear?—I didn't ask and Dr. Markowitz didn't explain it), had disappeared, and for the first time he felt like living since that loss. That was a blessing, Dr. Markowitz said. Even if Pastor Roger only felt it for a minute, that was a blessing.

"Maybe I need Prozac myself," Dr. Markowitz said.

But he didn't want Prozac. He'd been thinking about grief. What was grief but desire in reverse? But desire had a seed of hope in it, which gave it both its cruelty and its joy. Grief was a robin's skull, an empty space that once contained a birdy world. All you could do was treasure it, keep it in the top drawer of your bedroom bureau. Or hide it in a special pants pocket, safe from the bashing of coins or keys, where you could stroke it with a finger for reassurance.

I loved Dr. Markowitz at that moment. If he had said, "Move in with me," I would have split with Fred and done it.

"You got Prozac samples to get me through my trip?" Pastor Roger asked, and Dr. Markowitz was already bustling down the hall, thinking, *Yes, yes, I do.*

HAP MARKOWITZ

The next weekend, Will went out of town for a conference. Apparently I'd passed his test: I was normal enough that he could leave me without backup. I assumed he was attending a medical update meeting, but at the last minute he let slip that he was going to a "Saved by Love" conference, part of a national movement teaching evangelicals how to deal with loved ones "caught up in the homosexual lifestyle."

"You mean gay relatives?" I said.

Alicia was clearly irritated he was going. "It's a whole day and a half and three hundred miles."

Will said, "It's like I was meant to go. I got on their website, and kaboom, there's a conference this weekend. I told Alicia it might help me with some of my patients."

I wondered if Alicia, running through Will's patients in her mind, would think the same thing I did: not likely. But Will believed that the direction of Jesse's urges had never crossed Alicia's mind.

Jesse was at Tecumseh for a week before the quarter started, practicing with the coaches and other students on the debate team. The equivalent of summer football training, Alicia said. "The only debate scholarship!" Alicia kept telling the patients she brought to the exam rooms. "No other freshman has a scholarship!"

What Will learned at his conference were the many reasons for the sexual identity confusion rampant in the United States today: absent fathers, overwhelming maternal attention, loss of faith-based values and teachings, the insidious effects of media outlets and schools and organizations where homosexuals, under the banner of tolerance, actively promoted their agenda. No wonder, Will said, that people didn't know what they wanted. In an ideal world, a physician could de-confuse them.

"Not this physician," I said.

~

About a month after Janis's death, her younger niece stopped by the office with her son to take me out to dinner. Janis's nieces were good to me. One of them came to the house weekly bringing vitamins and flowers, stocking my freezer with single-serve entrées they bought through their children's schools. That day Marissa had her six-year-old with her, the fertility clinic wonder. They'd just been at the mall shopping for items for Caleb's new grown-up bedroom, and in his hand Caleb held several paint chips. "Will you watch him for a minute?" Marissa said. "I've got to use the bathroom."

Caleb eyed me soberly from the chair across from my desk. I found him a little unnerving. He had dark eyes and hair and an exuberant fringe of eyelashes. When Marissa's school system wouldn't let Caleb skip kindergarten, she briefly talked about a lawsuit. Marissa's big sister, with her four children, thought Marissa was insane, and it was true that Clara's crew, for all their noise and squabbling, were somehow easier to deal with than Caleb.

"How was school today?"

"Adequate," Caleb said in his little voice. He clutched the paint chips so tightly I wondered if a sliver of paint might break off, and what would happen if I told Marissa that her son had eaten it.

"Why don't we go see Caroline?" I said.

Caroline was calling in refills. I glanced into Brice's office and was relieved to see it was dark, because sometimes when I talked with Caroline I had the feeling that Brice was listening in. Brice seemed rattled lately. He'd lost weight. I'd told him to get his blood checked for hyperthyroidism, but I'd never seen the results. Caroline set down the phone and extended her hand. "How's Mr. Caleb today?"

I left them alone for a moment as I went back to my office to fetch my jacket, and when I returned, Caroline was holding up for Caleb a blue chip, then a green. "What about three green walls and one blue one?" she said. "Then you'd have three happy walls and a calm one." She glanced at me and smiled. "Caleb says the colors have emotions."

Janis's niece emerged from the bathroom. "Mommy," Caleb shouted, "we're going to have two colors!" and Marissa halted with her mouth open and gave me a skeptical look.

I roused myself. "Think about it," I said, trying to sound jovial. "Go a little wild." I met Caroline's eyes, and—this was thrilling, this felt like a tuning fork abuzz in my brain—the globes of her eyes became mirrors of my own thoughts. Caleb would benefit from Caroline. I should ask her to marry me, I thought, and instantly my mind blossomed with images of my life with her: Caroline at the zoo, holding Caleb's hand as we watched the gorillas; Caroline in my kitchen pulling a turkey from the oven; Caroline beside me in the car reading a map. It hit me almost instantaneously that these fantasies were less about Caroline than *the things that she could do for me,* and I felt remorseful, as if I'd blasphemed her in my mind, because what was Caroline but calm and happiness—blue and green herself—and who was I to make her a thing of use? Her simple presence in my life would be a blessing. Her simple presence in my life would raise me up.

She felt as I did, I realized, and it seemed for a moment that our future together—whenever it might come—was already assured. Our eyes meeting felt like a promise made by God.

God? I was a believer now? I noticed my hands were shaking, I was damp in the palms. Maybe this was lust, not belief. Oh, great, I thought, turning away, remembering Alicia and Will in their early days: another outbreak of chaos in the office.

"We should get going," Marissa said. "I need Caleb in bed no later than eight."

"See you tomorrow, Dr. Markowitz."

"I'll look forward to it, Caroline."

It was too early, I thought as I flossed that night. There was a quivering agitation in my chest, and I leaned against the edge of the sink and took my pulse: 84 and regular, normal. Janis had said once I should marry again, and wasn't getting remarried quickly a sign of a good prior marriage? (That's what my aunt Myrna always said, and she did it several times.) I looked at the ceiling, said "Forgive me, Janis," and felt stupid for looking at the ceiling (an implicit acknowledgment of heaven), and then I felt bad that I was denying Janis heaven, because God knew she deserved it (God knew??), and then I decided I was hopeless and I could hear Janis's low-pitched laugh. I reminded myself to think of that laugh every day, to keep her memory fresh with use: there were certain of my deceased patients, people of whom I was very fond, whose voices had disappeared to me forever. Not Janis, never Janis. I went into my closet and picked out a blue-striped shirt and a paisley tie. Then I went to the laundry room and plugged in the iron.

Toward the end, the purple below Janis's eyes made it look as though someone had hit her. The last few weeks there had been a chill coming off her, as if she were a hunk of ice the caterer had left melting on a table. Unclear if the carver would show up to make sense of it. Unclear, looking back, if the carver ever did.

CAROLINE

Fred's old Army buddy, Paul, came through town and spent a Friday night at Fred's. I met the two of them at an Italian place after work, and Paul was pretty liquored up by the time I got there.

"Just ignore him if he starts in on his jokes," Fred said before he headed to the bathroom.

But Paul was in a sentimental mood, not a joking one. Did I know about the time Fred saved his life?

"Whole platoon got hit. Just me and Fred and a guy named Lou left, and I had this torn-up leg. Open from my thigh almost to my ankle. Looked like a flank steak. That's when Fred took off his shoelaces and laced me up."

I wasn't sure I understood. "Tied up your leg? With shoelaces?"

"Used his penknife to make holes on either side." Paul made jabbing motions with his shaky hand. "Yeah, he laced that wound up, and him and Lou carried me out. Want to see the scar?" With some effort he rolled up his pants leg, revealing a scar as wide as a ruler. "Goes up to here." Paul pointed at his upper thigh.

"Paul, what the heck you doing?" Fred said, retaking his chair. "I leave for two minutes and I come back and you're undressing for my girlfriend."

Fred had a fussy house, but that had been his wife's style, and in the seven years since she'd died he hadn't changed it. Hummel figurines everywhere. It surprised me that he never put these away. In fact, he regularly picked them up and dusted them.

Sunday he was sitting on the left end of the sofa where he always sat, behind the morning paper.

"You never told me about rescuing Paul," I said, taking a seat at the other end of the sofa.

The paper didn't move. "You mean in Vietnam?"

I nodded. I wondered if there were other times he'd rescued Paul, from other, more amorphous dangers.

"He told you about that?" Fred dropped the paper. "Well, see, he had a wound and Lou and I had shoelaces, and it just seemed like we could put those things together."

"You're amazing."

"That knife was real easy to make holes with it, no worse than stabbing bacon. That was lucky, having that knife. It wasn't regulation issue, I only had it on me because this guy at camp used to hunt wild boar with his dad in Arkansas, and one day he . . ."

By then he had set down the paper. On and on he went, deflected. He could wear red Ohio State sweatpants, he could eat potato salad for breakfast—it didn't matter. I would be his as long as he wanted me, warm and bathed within the radiance of his soul.

～

"Why would Jesse think such a thing?" Alicia asked. Why, she would never know. They were halfway through watching that year's version of *Survivor*, Will was at Lowe's getting pipe to fix the downstairs bathroom sink, when Jesse said, "Mom, there's something I should tell you before I head off to college for good. I'm gay."

Alicia thought she was dreaming. She'd fallen asleep in the chair and this wasn't real. Or maybe an alien had taken over Jesse's body and was talking through his mouth. She just couldn't get her mind around what he was saying. It made no sense. He'd just split up with Mallory—with

Mallory. He was just back from debate practice at Tecumseh where he had a scholarship. A *scholarship.*

"What are you talking about?" she said.

What did she mean what was he talking about? Don't tell him she didn't know what he was talking about.

"It's a phase he's going through," Alicia said. "I know him. I knew him before he was born."

That was absurd, Jesse said. She couldn't read his mind.

Your father's just been to a conference, she said, suddenly wondering just why Will had gone. She knew how confused someone Jesse's age could . . .

Jesse closed his eyes. It's not my age, Mom.

She said: I was married to your bio-dad at that age! You think that was rational?

She said: I'm surprised people's pets aren't gay. I'm surprised people have babies anymore. You listen to the mainstream media, you'd think the only sex people have these days is sodomy!

He didn't look gay! Alicia told him. He wasn't all . . . She stood up and swished in front of me.

I said, "You didn't do that for him, did you?"

"Of course I did! He isn't like that; he doesn't do that!"

Jesse was almost out the door, car keys in his hand. Alicia flung herself at him, grabbed the back of his T-shirt. The fabric stretched and twisted. "Get off me!" he snapped, twirling so quickly Alicia fell and hit her arm against the counter.

"Here," she said, pushing up her sleeve to show me the bruise.

"Ouch," I said, because it did look nasty. The day's first five patients were all sitting in the lobby, reading magazines with suspicious intensity.

"That wasn't Jesse, Caroline," Alicia said. "The boy who pushed me over wasn't Jesse." Her eyes were wide and red. "It's like there's a demon inside him. And he hasn't come home yet, and Will made me come to work, and I want to talk to Pastor Roger but he's in Israel, and I can't live through this, I can't."

"Brice?" I tapped on his door frame. "Can you take the patients back? We're getting a pileup and Al's . . ." I gestured with my head in her direction.

"He's fine," Brice whispered. "Don't worry."

Shocked, I pulled Brice's door closed behind me. "You've seen him? You should at least tell Alicia. You hear her. She's desperate."

"I don't need to tell her anything."

"You know where Jesse is?" My voice was low and urgent.

"Maybe." A smirking smile. I hated Brice at that moment.

"Does he know how upset his mother is? Would he want to punish her like this?"

Brice wrinkled his nose. "Mothers—how tedious."

"I'm telling Dr. Strub." I reached for the doorknob.

The threat seemed to knock out Brice's cockiness. "I didn't tell you so you could tattle to Dr. Strub," he hissed.

"What?" I said. "Afraid you'll lose your job? I'd fire you if I knew you knew where Jesse was and didn't tell."

Brice glared.

"Okay, here's the deal," I whispered. "You get hold of Jesse and tell him to call Dr. Strub. I'll give you one hour." I checked my watch. "If Jesse hasn't called Dr. Strub by then, I'll go to Strub and tell him everything. Everything. I know what you two were up to in the basement."

He didn't say *You don't know anything*. He didn't tell me I was wrong.

"Now, you've got five minutes to get hold of Jesse and then you come out and move these patients. Got it?"

I'd never done something like this, and it was disturbingly exciting. Maybe that's why people harrumphed, I thought: being a threat was fun.

HAP MARKOWITZ

The morning after Jesse disappeared, he phoned the office and told Will he was okay, he needed some time to think, he'd be home in a few days. Will regretted for the first time not having caller ID on the office phone.

"How'd you do it?" Will asked. "When Janis was sick, how'd you keep coming here?" Until Jesse actually got home, Will hated being at work. He could hardly stand listening to people sob about their bowel movements. On the other hand, people with real problems terrified him. Each exam room he walked into, he got a vision of Kevin Peterson at the end of the exam table with his hands over his face, talking about his son hanging from the shower rod. *Help us, God,* Will said in his mind a million times a day, and then: *Don't let us lose him.* At night Will prayed so hard his ribs hurt, and it was a bolt of pure gratitude that paralyzed him when he saw Jesse that Saturday morning, getting out of his car outside Will and Al's house with a leather jacket (whose?) slung over his arm, looking none the worse for wear.

"Al!" Will shouted. "Al!!" Then he phoned me.

CAROLINE

Did Alicia look different? she asked. She had to look different. She felt weighted down with grief, like some chimp with its knuckles dragging.

He used to wear a harlequin snow hat, reach for Alicia's hand with his little fingers.

"Who are you?" she'd ask.

"I Jesse." He would nod, pointing at himself.

"Isn't that a girl's name?" some idiot woman once said.

Jesse James. Jesse, father of David, king of Israel.

Better if he was a drug dealer. Better if he was living with some slut. Better anything. There used to be, for Alicia, a thick curtain between what was impossible and what was. Now the curtain had gotten so thin, she could see straight through it.

HAP MARKOWITZ

We heard all about Will and Al's uproar, their "tragedy," as Alicia called it. Caroline glanced at Brice and Brice disappeared inside his office. I smiled at Brice whenever I spotted him, to show him I approved of him no matter what his sexual orientation. With Will and Alicia, I listened, but, like Caroline, I was studiously impartial. Poor Jesse: one simple fact threw his mother and stepdad into conniptions.

Caroline and I discussed it whenever we could. Our conversations were private, little rooms that only the two of us entered. "Light in his loafers," my mother used to say. "Not the marrying kind." No more judgmental than that. I loved my mother. People's flaws, to her, were part of the whole package. Herbie Watkins swore; Jerry Evans (poor Gladys) had a wandering eye. "Pleasant sort of guy," she said when she met Will. "Friendly. Not stuck-up like some." In certain ways my mother had low expectations. I was brainy, my head always stuck in a book, like my father's uncle Davey, the full professor at Swarthmore. My mother never simply said he taught at Swarthmore: she always used the phrase "the full professor." Uncle Davey never married. I wondered.

At any rate, I told Caroline, it seemed to me that being gay was nothing to fret about. It was inconsequential. Promiscuity was something, because that carried the risk of diseases, but gayness itself was, well, like having red hair. In this view I supposed I was liberal for my age and gender. Good. Certain gay drug reps might leave our office extra samples if they knew.

Caroline and I conjectured about which drug reps.

When you thought about it, I told Caroline, what did a society need? Food; shelter; a steady pool of young people; jobs; social order. Look at infant and child mortality throughout most of mankind's history: there had to be an emphasis on mating and fertility. But now that we as a species were outstripping our resources, maybe gay people would become the new ideal: productive community members who, by and large, didn't create more members. Like Janis and me! And gay marriage, like any marriage, sounded wonderfully stabilizing.

"I'm not married," Caroline said. "Does that make me destabilizing?"

"You? You're a pillar of society! You're the center of our office!"

Caroline snorted.

I couldn't talk like this to Will, of course. And certainly not to Alicia. But what hit me as I rolled over in bed that evening was the pleasure not just of talking to Caroline but of my own logical and mildly subversive thoughts. Worry, I realized, had squeezed me like one of my aunt Rose's corsets. The mind unfettered was a glorious instrument. I'd missed it.

~

Jesse went off to Tecumseh—they moved him into a freshman dorm with a roommate from Bopkins who'd probably never laid eyes on a gay person—and for a while Will was seduced (his word) by the thought that Jesse's homosexual urges weren't a problem. Really, there was nothing mincing about Jesse. When he shook Will's hand before they left, Will grabbed him around the shoulders and wrapped his stepson in a hug, reminding both of them that he would always be sweet Jesse, Will's honorary son.

"I don't know," Will told me he said at the next BIC meeting. "I'm wondering if it's really that big a deal."

A wave that might be fear or disgust went through the room, as if Will had yanked a corner of the floor and made everything ripple. Will wondered if he could have dared to say what he had if Pastor Roger had been at the meeting and not off in Israel.

Bob Reasoner, the retired banker with the thick, wavy white hair all the women called beautiful, spoke first. Usually, he said, it was women who were tolerant of male homosexuals. For a man, generally, hearing about male homosexuals was disturbing, because, let's be frank, the mechanics were disgusting.

"Maybe it's not a threat to Will," Joe the contractor announced in a stalwart way. No one else spoke up, and Will understood that his bit of acceptance would fester like a sliver caught in the group's collective finger.

"We can't forget that sodomy is a sin," someone said. "Love the sinner, hate the sin."

Will couldn't stop himself from wondering about this. What actual harm did gay people do? he asked aloud. The few gay patients he'd seen through the years—and some of them he admitted he was guessing at—seemed regular enough. Maybe in general they were fussier than normal guys, but not predictably so. Engineers were the fussiest guys of all, and Will didn't know a single gay one. "Heck"—he laughed—"most engineers are lucky to have sex at all!"

No, he would not have said that if Pastor Roger were there. No, the joke did not go over.

I offered Will my theories about society, my mother's relaxed view of human folly. His response disappointed me.

"It's more complicated than that, Hap. It's tough. You're logical, but I'm trying to figure things out with God."

With the BIC guys he argued. With me he argued. I supposed that he was arguing with himself.

He thought he knew what Pastor Roger would say: that no one should want to understand gay people. It would be like walking into a swamp without boots or sunscreen or a gun, having blind faith that the snakes and alligators wouldn't get you.

"I don't want Jesse in a swamp, Hap," Will said.

He and Alicia had sent several e-mails about Jesse to Pastor Roger, but Pastor Roger hadn't responded to a single one. Will understood it, in a way: Pastor Roger was probably so wrapped up being with God in God's land that he couldn't even think about computers. Alicia was in despair. They trusted Pastor Roger, she said, and he was making the choice not to help them. They were like little hungry dogs he was kicking away. When he came back, she didn't even want to see him. When he came back, she wanted another church.

∽

Something hit me on a day in the middle of September, the Monday between Rosh Hashanah and Yom Kippur (even though I, unlike Pastor Roger in Israel, would not observe either holiday), which was therefore one of the eight Days of Awe. Will was carrying the practice beeper that night and the air was soft and the light was golden and something, something—I couldn't say what—called me to get away.

"See you sometime, Caroline," I said, cruising out the front door just after five, delighting in the flash of puzzlement in her face.

My walk was almost sprightly. I got into my car, opened the sunroof, pulled out of the parking lot, and pointed myself toward the highway.

How long since I'd gone nowhere? How long since I'd driven freely?

I slipped *The Best of David Bowie* from its case, and here I was above the world with Major Tom, flying in my tin can (in my case, a 1999 Accord), and I was more than ready to shoot off into space, never to be heard from again. By the second go-through of the tape, it was dark and I was at the outskirts of Indianapolis. I stopped for gas, used the restroom, and bought of pack of Marlboros. It'd been thirty years since I smoked. I was almost on the highway, unlit cig hanging from my mouth, when I realized my car didn't have a lighter. Betrayer! I pulled back into the gas station, went in and waited in line for matches, got back in my car. By now David Bowie was singing "Ch-ch-ch-changes," and I lit the cigarette in tribute to Janis, a small act of recklessness like hers, a reminder that the world was big and my mind was big and no one, no one, no one was going to box me in again. I could wander where I damn well pleased, not just Caroline's Relax Inn or Will and Alicia's Mall of Jesus or Brice's Plaza of Good Management. Where I damn well pleased.

West of Indianapolis I took some state route north until it was good and dark and farm-y. Indiana was flat and covered with corn. At midnight I parked my car on the berm, got out, and looked up at the sky. An ungodly number of stars up there—hundreds, thousands, more than I could count. How was it possible that light had enough energy to travel for millions of miles over millions of years, and what was light, anyway, and why couldn't I remember any of this from my physics class in college, and if I could would it explain the problem? If I ever learned a thing about light, I'm sure I didn't understand it, just wrote down some formula to spit back on a test. I was a dutiful student.

Days of Awe. We Jews were clever with labels. Even an ordinary fall day became special once you called it a Day of Awe.

My neck started to hurt from looking up, so I laid myself down on one of the rows between the stubs of corn in the harvested field next to the road. This wasn't at all uncomfortable, it was sort of glorious, the great glittery dome above me and the high-pitched *tiki-tiki-tiki* of some insect beside me and the smell of dirt enveloping me. Always good weather on the High Holidays, my mother used to say. Above me there was a shooting star, which I thought I must have imagined, but no, there was another one—they were remarkably fast, like crickets hopping. I was tingling with hyperalertness, and the next thing I knew I was floating above the field, in space myself. It was odd because I was totally alone and unfindable—I was lying in a harvested cornfield in Indiana, for crying out loud—and yet I felt as if my package of skin had become permeable. I was floating in a bath of life, isotonic to the universe. I bobbled in the current. I was warm and relaxed and perfectly at peace.

Maybe this was a religious experience, I didn't know.

When I got up I felt dazed and pure, as if I'd been rinsed in some celestial ionizing stream (ironic, since I smelled of dirt). I got in the car and shut the door with a space-capsule clang, but before I started the car I turned off the tape, because any extra noise might jar me out of this moment, disturb my sense of slipping like a shooting star through the night, heading for home.

I felt my heartbeat, like someone in the basement rapping on the door.

Death. Death. But also its gorgeous converse: I'm alive I'm alive I'm alive.

CAROLINE

Of course Pastor Roger didn't answer, Alicia said. All summer, she said, his sermons had been the same. Blah-blah-blah God's anger—at the Israelites for worshipping idols, at Jonah for not going to Nineveh, at Saul for not wiping out the Amalekites. In God's covenant with Israel, God had taken Israel as his bride. And his bride over and over had betrayed him. Again and again, God had been forced to forgive.

"He's divorced now, right?" I asked.

Alicia sighed. "She wasn't perfect, but you know what? He's not, either."

With Pastor Roger gone, one of the associate pastors got to lead the services. Pastor Owen was no dummy. He seemed to know the congregation was desperate for something hopeful. Maybe God Himself was telling Pastor Owen to deliver Pastor Roger a message.

Pastor Owen talked about mercy. He led with the story of Abraham, who before the angel of God stopped him had walked up the hill to the altar to sacrifice Isaac, his own blood.

"Blood, he said," Alicia said. "That hit me. Jesse's my blood."

I'm not a nice person, Alicia said. She admitted she said nasty things, she judged people. She'd called Thomasina Phillips's son a serial marrier. She'd moaned, "Haven't you had your ten minutes of fame yet?" when Kit Marin showed up again at a church potluck with her Famous Party Mold.

Jesse had never been mean. "What animal are you most like?" the guide at the fifth-grade zoo trip asked. "A golden marmoset!" Jesse shouted.

She herself, Alicia said, was more a hyena or a vulture, a predator, someone who took advantage. Or maybe she was an armadillo, armored all over, skittish, ready to curl into a ball and hide if anything threatened her. And, like an armadillo, she had a soft spot. Her soft spot was Jesse. Pastor Roger liked to say—or he'd used to say, back before his wife left him—that God never gave a person more than he or she could handle, and if that was true, God would never ask her to give up Jesse. She remembered the day last summer in Janis's garden, walking around feeling guided by God's hands. Only now she was curled up in bed and over her was God with his oven mitts, reaching in to touch her in her soft spot. God loved her, she could feel it. God loved her even more than she loved Jesse.

It didn't all make sense—marmosets and blood and God with oven mitts—and it took quite a while for her to get it out—I was late turning off the answering machine that morning—but I was listening not to judge but to absorb, and something in Alicia's face and voice and metaphors made me happy.

"Good for you, Al," I said, startled at the catch in my voice. "Good for you."

HAP MARKOWITZ

I saw two patients in a row with hooplas coming up: Trishna Venketesh, whose daughter was having a Hindu wedding complete with the groom on horseback, and Irene Krupski, who was working on a needlepoint to commemorate her grandson's first communion. What hit me, walking down the hall to get my tuna sandwich and apple from the fridge, was the staggering particularity of belief. The god with six arms; the God with a secret name that could not be spoken; the God who presented the Book of Mormon inscribed on golden tablets in a strange language to a young man named Joseph Smith. It seemed that specifics got tossed in to make the whole thing more believable.

How absurd. Beliefs in glorious detail pulled out of thin air. How about this: There were forces beyond us we couldn't understand, couldn't see or touch, couldn't even comprehend. Wouldn't that be enough? Apparently not. It was as if we had a God mold in our mind, ready for the ball of clay we felt compelled to stuff into its farthest corners. *Now take out the clay and let it dry and add more details,* the instructor said. And each person took out his little paintbrush and added his touches, until the molded face of God became his very own. The button nose, the curvy lips, the round all-seeing eyes. There. That's my deity. And my God said the usual: "I am above all others," "Love your neighbors," "Honor the life force," "You're all right." And sometimes my God was intolerant, said things like "My way alone" or "Kill the infidels." And when I'd finished with my God, I'd stick it in my pocket and carry it around the playground. When I needed reassurance, I'd touch it. When I needed help, I'd take it out.

I looked down at my hand, surprised to find my sandwich and apple gone. I didn't remember eating them.

The indefinability of God. Another topic to discuss with Caroline.

∽

It was windy, leaves were raining from the trees. It was only late September, but that day you knew that winter was approaching.

It was probably too easy, Will told me, his getting saved. He ran into that sign, he met Pastor Roger, he found his church, he gave up looking at his websites—not that hard to do, really. Everything improved when he got saved. It wasn't difficult like some convert in China who got thrown into jail or some African who had to give up two of his three wives or some Jewish kid whose family said the prayer for the dead for him. Even Will's BIC friend Bruce had almost lost his marriage, because his wife was Catholic. In contrast, Will's getting saved was cheap.

"See?" Will said, giving me a hopeful look. "Giving up Jesse could be my payment."

Give up Jesse? What was he saying? "But Jesse loves you," I said. "You're a dad to him."

What upset the BIC guys most, Pastor Roger told Will, sitting him down in his office the day after his return from Israel (and Pastor Roger hadn't checked his e-mail in Israel; God had wanted him totally *present* in God's chosen country), was Will's abdicating his position as head of the family. A family shouldn't be like the Hebrews in the time of Judges, when there was no king in Israel and every man did what was right in his own eyes. A man was called to tie his family to God, Pastor Roger said. If Will said, "Oh, Jesse's a homosexual, and that's fine," then Will wasn't being the leader that he should be.

"Then he kind of gave Al a way out," Will said. "He didn't give me a way out."

It was Alicia's place to love Jesse totally, Will said, no matter what Jesse did. Will was the same with his daughters. Really, stepchildren weren't the same. You wanted them to be, but the distance between you and them showed up at funny times. When the phone rang with a stepchild's bad news, you didn't get the same spasm in your gut.

The Bible said that homosexual actions were wrong, period. And Will could reject Jesse when Alicia couldn't. Al and he, together, could be good cop/bad cop. They could use their disagreement to bring Jesse in and book him.

Here was the deal: After this college quarter (it ended the first week of December), Jesse would have to get his own job, find his own apartment, pay his own tuition if he insisted on the gay lifestyle. If he repented, Will and Alicia would pay full tuition and room and board at a Christian college.

"But he's got that scholarship at Tecumseh," I said.

"He doesn't change, we'll get it revoked. We'll tell his coach what he's doing. Moral turpitude."

"I don't think the coach will care."

"I'll go there and talk to the administration! I'll get it cut off. I'll take Pastor Roger with me."

I couldn't believe it. I said, "You want Jesse to say, Oops, my mistake, I'm not gay at all? That seems illogical." But "illogical" was too generous a word: it seemed mean. I told Will this.

No, no. Will and Alicia would be doing the Christian thing, the right thing, in forcing Jesse to give up the homosexual lifestyle. Was it love to let a person walk into a burning building?

"And Alicia's going to go for this?" I said.

She felt a little responsible, Will said. All through Jesse's growing-up years, she'd been thinking only of herself, forgetting that a son needed a father.

"She never thought of herself!" I said, remembering the mornings she took off to meet with teachers. "She was always thinking about Jesse."

That was a problem too, Will said. Too much maternal influence.

I felt as disturbed by Will as I had ever been. I felt as if I'd walked into a barn and found him whipping a horse that was cowering in its stall.

"I really see this as making our marriage stronger. Facing up to Jesse, even on opposite sides, Al and I will be a team."

Will gave me examples. "He's still my son," Alicia might say, or, "If I just knew he had a single partner."

And Will: "In terms of disease I suppose that's better, but in terms of morality . . ."

"I wish you liked him more!" Alicia might say.

"But I *do* like him," Will would answer. "I *love* him. That's why I want him to change."

"Where did this come from?" I said to Will. "When did you get this cruel streak?"

He didn't seem to hear me. It had hit him, he said, that he and Al were truly married. Between them, they were rebalancing their boat.

"That's something I admired about you and Janis," Will said. "Between the two of you, you always kept things steady." For a second, astounded by the compliment, I had to blink back tears. What was he thinking of? Specific examples? Was it true?

It could be true. Certainly, Janis and I colluded. But what I thought at that moment was how fortunate we were to have had no one to disturb our balance, no passenger hopping from the backseat to the front or swimming up from the side and grabbing on.

"We didn't have kids. It's"—I almost said easier, but that wasn't right, precisely—"less uncertain." Yes, that's what I meant.

And poor Jesse. Poor Jesse who Will and Alicia were handing the rope to, basically, so he could pull the boat with both of them as he swam.

Out of loyalty to Will, I didn't say more.

Wait a minute, was it loyalty? It was fear. As disappointing a man as he was turning out to be, I still needed him as my friend.

CAROLINE

I should have paid attention to how Brice kept easing shut the door to his office, little by little, over weeks, until it was completely closed and you had to turn the knob to open it. Before, he had left it open and called to me out the door. Before, he had watched for Jesse coming out of the basement. Now his voice was muffled even if he shouted. I could go all morning without seeing him at all.

"Uncollectibles," he said one day, laying a computer printout on my desk. "I'm writing them a letter that we can't see them."

I nodded, wondering vaguely if that was legal. Marjorie Bodil was on the list, and I liked Marjorie. Then I saw the other names and thought: let them go.

"I saw a great movie last night," Brice said. He glanced toward Al's empty desk; she was off with the watering can in the doctors' offices.

"What did you see?"

"*Y Tu Mamá También*. The film club at Tecumseh was showing it."

"Is that the sexy Mexican one?"

Brice's hand gave a twitch. "Is my friend?" He laughed uneasily. "It's a pretty erotic movie. Let me put it this way: *mi mamá* would not approve."

A pause. "Your mother let you go?" He didn't answer. "Were you visiting Jesse there? At Tecumseh?"

Brice didn't answer, but his mouth made a conceding twitch.

"What's your relationship with him, exactly?"

"What, you want to know what we *do* together?"

"Is it physical?"

"It's everything," Brice said. He seemed immediately to hear the peevishness of his tone, and he repeated the words softly, almost achingly: "It's everything."

I was afraid for him. "Your mother still seeing Dr. Marcus?" I asked. For weeks at a time I forgot about Brice's mother. She was a storm system who'd moved through our office to become a stationary front over somewhere east of us (yes, she still saw Dr. Marcus). For Brice, the storm of his mother never left. For Brice it must have been constant clouds and a mildewed basement and an endless thrum on the roof.

"I talked to Dr. Marcus on the phone, and she told me she'd tell my mother she shouldn't be a dictator. She'd tell my mother that she had to let me out *sometimes*."

I could hardly stand to look at Brice's hands. Once they had looked elegant to me, but now they looked like waterlogged appendages, white with puckered fingers. If I had had the strength or the compassion I would have grabbed them up to warm under my arms or between my thighs. Our physical relationship had been a disaster, but that didn't mean I had no feelings.

"Tell your mom I said hi," I said.

"Be careful, Brice," I said. He shrugged and left, shutting his door.

CAROLINE

What I remember most about the month after Jesse went off to Tecumseh was that Alicia was busy, busy, busy. Suddenly, she was counseling patients about osteoporosis; she was bringing stacks of charts from the basement to take home to thin; she was on the phone arranging pick-up times to take the elderly of Zion Bible to church functions.

She never really noticed Brice. Except to ask him work-related questions, she didn't seem aware of him at all. They had been friends, once. Now it would be an exaggeration to call them coworkers. They were two people who worked five feet from each other, separated by a wall.

I knocked on Brice's door and pushed it open, slipped into the chair in front of his desk, and closed the door behind me. "Are you okay?"

"We were buddies once, right?" Brice said, not turning from his computer screen.

"Until I screwed it up."

"Screwed, yes. 'Screwed' is the operative word."

I took a big breath. "How's Jesse?"

Brice considered the screen another moment, then swiveled and faced my way. "Okay," he said. "Are you ready for the gory details?"

"Please."

The night before, Brice drove out to Tecumseh after work and spent an hour circling the block of Jesse's dorm. When Jesse wasn't home by nine, Brice parked on the street and hovered around the dorm's front entrance until a student in a hoodie held the door open to let him in. Brice knew that Jesse's room was on the fourth floor in the front, but he didn't know which one, and he had to walk down the hallway trying to look casual as he read the names on the doors.

Jesse and Brian's door was closed, and no one answered when Brice knocked. Brian: odd Jesse was assigned a roommate with a name so close to Brice. Jesse's room number was 410, and Brice's birthday was 4/11. Brice left a message on the wipe board tacked to the door. He sat in the dorm lobby behind a newspaper. Finally he drove around for a while longer, then went home. By the time he'd gotten back to Midburg there was an e-mail from Jesse saying not to come to Tecumseh again.

"Is that crazy?" Brice said. "That's crazy. We had our regular weekend three days ago."

Their regular weekend, it turned out (they'd had two), was Brice picking up Jesse at Tecumseh late Saturday afternoon (at a new pickup spot the second time, not in front of Jesse's dorm but at a laundromat on the edge of town) and taking him back to Krazy Kat's basement, where they ate pizza and watched movies and spent the night together on the plaid sofa. Then Brice drove Jesse back to

Tecumseh Sunday morning. Brice's mother was oblivious to Jesse's presence; she just liked knowing Brice was home.

"Did Jesse seem different Sunday?"

"Just the laundromat thing. And, you know, he always has debate work and he has to study."

"He's in college now, Brice. He probably wants his independence."

"He sees me fifteen hours a week! That's not much. Half that time we're asleep. And I let him do debate stuff while we're watching movies."

I let him: the hair on my neck stood on end. "Brice," I said, "if you want to keep Jesse as your friend—and he's a nice guy, I don't blame you for wanting to—you're going to have to let him go a bit."

Brice's eyes flashed. "What do you know about passion?"

I snorted in astonishment. "Brice, you don't want him to think you're a stalker, do you? Don't go out there again, okay? Listen to what Jesse's telling you and don't go to Tecumseh again."

But of course Brice did, that very evening, and he spotted Jesse walking toward his dorm between two other guys. Brice screeched into a handicapped parking spot and hopped out.

"Brice?" Jesse said. "What're you doing here?"

"Hi, Jesse. I was driving by and I thought you might want to . . ." Brice held up the DVD he'd been keeping in his car. "It's supposed to be good."

A funny look on Jesse's face. "What does that mean?"

"The reviews are good. Rotten Tomatoes gives it four fresh tomatoes."

Jesse shook his head like he was shaking off water.

"This is Mick and Dave," he said, pointing to his companions. "They debate with me."

Not *Do you want to join us?* Not *This is my friend Brice.* Not *This is my good friend Brice.* Not *This is the movie expert I've been talking about.*

The humiliation of it. The puzzled sneers on Mick's and Dave's faces. How inappropriate Brice's tie and cuffs seemed on the sidewalk. How he felt like a spider scampering away.

Brice said, "I want him not to be rude to me in public."

Brice said, "I want to be extravagantly loved. Is that too much to ask?"

∽

In our office, fall was a hectic time. People who wanted to be seen before the holidays, people who were heading south for the winter, people who wanted tests and specialists before the calendar year ended, people who were calling about flu shots, people who got depressed when it got dark earlier at night.

"You've got to go," Pastor Roger told me for the third time, appearing again at my window.

An emergency visit for a cough he'd caught in Israel; I'd slotted him between an ear cleaning and a follow-up for diverticulitis. "God's fingerprints are all over that land. God's fingerprints! Did you know— if I had an aerial map here I'd show you—did you know the Hebrew name for God is written in the hills north of Jerusalem?"

"How interesting," I said, reaching for line one. "Why don't you sit down?" I suggested to Pastor Roger. "Alicia will take you back as soon as an exam room opens."

It was Kirby on the phone. "What's your situation there?" he said. "Dr. Strub have time for me after office hours today? How's the skin line selling? You finally talking to people? Think dryness. With the cold out and the heat going on, people will be suffering dryness."

I put Kirby on hold, said I'd check with Dr. Strub.

"What's your background?" Pastor Roger said, not noticing my exasperated sigh. "A lot of Christians don't realize that they're really members of the House of Israel in disguise. Those 'lost' tribes you hear about? Those tribes moved across the Mediterranean into Europe."

"Excuse me," I said to Pastor Roger. "I need to get to . . ." and I gestured toward the gray-haired woman behind him.

"Good morning, Helen," I said, and it wasn't until I spoke that I saw the wild look in her eyes.

"I want my records and I want them now. I know my rights. I want you to hand my chart to me and I'm walking it out the door."

This was Helen Cliffdorfer? She looked possessed.

"All right. Is there"—this wasn't the time for simple absorption, I had to ask a question—"a problem?"

Helen Cliffdorfer's niece was Marjorie Bodil, and Marjorie Bodil had gotten an unbelievably rude letter kicking her out of the practice. ". . . and you know she's been Dr. Markowitz's patient for sixteen years, and she sends in twenty dollars every month and skips her . . ."

"See, this lady's a Dane!" Pastor Roger said over Helen's shoulder, pointing at someone in the lobby I couldn't see. "And Dan was the second son of Jacob whose name was changed to Israel by God, and where do you think the word 'Dane' comes from?"

"Let me have you talk to our billing person," I said to Helen. "He sent out those letters, and he certainly didn't want . . ."

Brice's door was closed. I knocked and turned the doorknob, but the doorknob didn't move. It took me a moment to grasp this: I didn't know it was possible to lock our doors.

"Brice?" I said, knocking louder. "Brice?"

Line one with Kirby was still flashing. Line two lit up.

Alicia was calling Pastor Roger to take him off to an exam room, and I scurried to the window to catch her before she got away. "Alicia," I called across the lobby—and this was unprofessional, really, but I had no choice—"can Dr. Strub see Kirby after office hours? I've got him on the phone."

"How about you?" Pastor Roger asked me, walking backward in Alicia's direction, almost stepping on the feet of several waiting patients. "Are you Danish too?"

"English."

"Did you know the Druid priests were really Hebrews? Did you know that some people believe the prophet Jeremiah traveled to Ireland?" Alicia made a face over his shoulder. "You have a cough?" she said loudly, touching him on the arm to guide him safely past the door frame.

I looked up at Helen Cliffdorfer. Her resolve seemed to have slipped; I could see she felt sorry for me. "Our billing manager must be on the phone," I lied. "Why don't you take a seat and when he finishes I'll have you talk with him?"

HAP MARKOWITZ

"How's Jesse?" Alicia said. That's all Pastor Roger needed to ask. Some acknowledgment that she was human too. He knew about Jesse not coming home on visits, about Alicia taking the weekend job at the nursing home to help cover his future college costs, about Will no longer referring to him as "my stepson" but as "my wife's son." Pastor Roger was a *pastor*, someone with a flock, someone supposed to care about lost sheep, and instead he was talking about his ancestors who had come to Saxony from Palestine, as anyone would have to realize from their name: SAX-ons, I-SAAC. As he talked, Al felt like some befogging mist was spreading over her mind. She would have liked to argue but the mist made her too sleepy.

"*How's Jesse?*" Simple as that.

"She had a good point," I told Caroline. I wondered why Alicia had come to me with it, possibly because Pastor Roger was my patient. Maybe she suspected something off about him. Maybe she was trying to warn me.

At the time, in my exam room with Pastor Roger, I asked him the usual respiratory questions: cough, temperature, shortness of breath, chest pain. It took a while to get through these, and when he launched into the saga of Phoenician sailing vessels, my mind wandered. He was the midpoint of my afternoon. Ten patients down, ten patients left to go. "Let me listen to your lungs," I said, when he hesitated a moment to catch his breath.

Pastor Roger gave a surprised frown, as if he'd forgotten where he was. He pulled up his shirt in the back.

He was wheezing. I ordered a chest X-ray and put him on oral steroids and an antibiotic.

~

A day or so later I was checking Rupert Newsock's feet—he was diabetic—when I heard a knock on the exam room door.

"It's someone from the newspaper on the phone," Caroline said. "Want me to get their number and you can call back?"

"It's okay, I'm just finishing up." I wrote Rupert some refills, ordered blood tests for his diabetes, and handed him the form.

"I'll look forward to your words of wisdom in the paper," Rupert said.

I'd talked to the *Midburg Daily Ledger* health reporter on several occasions, providing him with such pearls as "Dr. Markowitz recommends all his hypertensive patients get exercise."

"This is Dr. Markowitz," I said into the phone.

It was a young-sounding woman, Nancy Wu. I felt a spasm of pleasure, sure that she would ask better questions than a flabby, middle-aged white male.

She got right to the point. Was I aware that the dietary supplement ephedra, used for weight loss, had been banned by the FDA because of deaths it caused?

"Last spring," I said eagerly. "April, I think." I was happy to see that happen, I told her. I didn't know how many patients I'd advised against taking it. It never should have been on the market at all, but the health food lobby used their—

"I've just been talking with a woman named Marilyn Kramer," Nancy Wu said, "and she's only thirty-six, and a couple weeks ago she had a stroke that left her whole right side weak, and her hospital doctor thinks it was caused by ephedra driving up her blood pressure."

"That's very possible," I said. "People think that natural substances are harmless, but—"

"And she had been taking an over-the-counter weight-loss aid that she bought at her hairdresser's, and I spoke to the owner of the salon, and she said she got her supply of the pills from your office."

It had to be a mistake. That was one thing I'd checked in our lobby: His Way didn't have a weight-loss product. Maybe the hairdresser was covering up for some other doctor. Maybe the hairdresser had given Marilyn Kramer His Way vitamins she'd bought in our lobby, told her they might help her lose weight. I said, "What's the owner's name?"

A second of hesitation. "Her first name is Konni." She spelled it. I didn't know anyone with that name.

"I went to her salon," Nancy Wu said. "She showed me receipts for checks she made out to your office. Checks from Konni's Kurls."

"We're Drs. Strub and Markowitz," I said. "We're South Midburg Internists."

"South Midburg Internists, yes—that's exactly who the checks are made out to. I have copies of the receipts. Could I stop by your office and show you?"

∼

Later that day, I walked down the hall to Will's office. He was just sitting there—not going through charts, not reading an article in a medical journal, not on the phone. I told him about my visit from Nancy Wu, about my call to Konni's Kurls, about the unanswered messages I'd left on Kirby's cell phone.

"What else?" I was bellowing. "What else?" I knew I was too loud but I was talking not just to Will but to anyone who'd kept secrets from me. I was bellowing, I suppose, at the dead.

Will's face crumpled. There was more, I thought in fierce exultation. My breathing got as loud as some giant rotating fan. "Let's hear it," I growled.

"I . . . I . . ." Will was barely able to squeak out that simple word. "I still go on some of those websites."

It took me a moment to grasp what he was saying. *Some of those websites?* Then I remembered the fake prostitute and the sign and his meeting Pastor Roger.

"That's it?" I sank into one of his patient chairs, deflated. "For crying out loud, I don't care about that."

"I care."

"I do it myself sometimes, you know? Late at night, home alone." Since Janis's death, that was true, although the experience each time had left me feeling more foolish than excited.

Will's head was in his hands, and he looked across the desk at me like a little boy peering through his fingers. Will was a child, I realized. An absolute child: impetuous and self-absorbed and afraid of disapproval. All those years I'd thought that I was childless, and here I had a youngster all along.

CAROLINE

"I can't believe Kirby," Alicia kept saying. "What a lying bastard." Konni of Konni's Kurls, it turned out, was Kirby's sister; his wife owned the other salon that sold "our" His Way products. Alicia had already drafted a letter to the *Daily Ledger* explaining why the ephedra wasn't our office's fault, and it drove her crazy that Dr. Strub insisted the lawyer assigned to the case by our malpractice insurance—who had already had several long phone chats with both him and Dr. Markowitz—wanted to approve its text. "What is it that they say," she said, "'No good deed goes unpunished'?"

I wasn't sure to what ostensible good deed she was referring, unless it was her husband's helping Kirby get rid of his product, which seemed like a questionable cause to me.

A few patients cancelled after the article was published on Thursday morning (front page), but the ones who came to the office trailed Alicia to the exam rooms meek as ducklings. Dr. Strub and Dr. Markowitz said they didn't get a single question.

At the end of office hours Friday, Brice toted a black plastic garbage bag to the lobby and heaved into it the bottles and tubes of His Way.

"Good-bye, good-bye," he sang. "Good-bye, skin care. Good-bye, pep. Good-bye, health."

The last two days he couldn't have cared less about the office scandal or Marilyn Kramer with the stroke or the doctors hurrying past us without speaking or Alicia's anger. I knew why he was happy. Wednesday evening on the phone Jesse had agreed to being picked up Friday, not Saturday, to spend the whole weekend with Brice in his basement. Brice's presentation of Jesse's reasons didn't sound very promising to me—a fair chance, hash things out, no distractions—but Brice acted as if he'd received a once-in-a-lifetime phone call: *Yes, we are going to film your screenplay!* or *The Nobel Committee was looking for a man like you!* "Thirty-nine hours!" Brice kept saying. "He'll be with me thirty-nine hours!"

In her furor, for two days Alicia had been barreling around the office running into trash cans and knocking papers off flat surfaces. She had almost pushed Mrs. Pierce and her walker into the wall. Now she climbed up on my desk on her knees and leaned through the window to observe Brice. I watched her in fascination, trying to read the brand name on the soles of her white shoes. "Did someone tell you to do that?" she demanded of Brice.

Brice said, "Your dear husband, milady."

"You're throwing it away?"

"I'm putting it in storage in the basement. Cold storage for cold cream. Good-bye, Eve's Elixir, sleep tight with your little friends."

Alicia clambered down from my desk with her eyes wide and her lips pursed, giving me an infuriated look. "I hate him," she said. "I hate him!"

I almost said, "Which him?" before she muttered the name Kirby.

CAROLINE

On Monday, Brice came in, hung his jacket on the hook on the back wall, and closed his door. I was sure his weekend hadn't gone well: on our two days out of the office I'd been so preoccupied worrying about him that Fred asked me several times if I had the flu. Finally I had told him about Brice and Jesse. He didn't say much. "You know," he said, "people aren't logical."

Monday morning I booted up my computer, emptied the refill line, checked the answering machine for cancellations and requests, then knocked on Brice's door.

His shirt was pressed, his tie was nicely knotted, his hair was in its usual fashionable tousle. Someone who didn't know him would have thought that he looked fine. I took a seat in the chair across from him and waited.

"I like you," Jesse had told him, Saturday morning on the sofa, after all they'd done the night before. "I really like you, and you're a good person, and you've always been nice to me, and . . ."

"You know what I thought," Brice said, interrupting himself, making an imaginary slash across his throat.

"... all you do is watch movies, but it's like you bathe in them, it's movie soup, you don't talk about the characters or the story lines or even technical things like lighting or camera angles. It's mindless, what you do. And you're not stupid, Brice, you're a smart guy and you're wasting ..."

"Don't you ever think *why* does a film make you feel that? Don't you think, What's the motive of this thing? Maybe it's something interesting, something the people who made it don't recognize themselves."

"I only watch good movies," Brice said he told Jesse. "I don't watch Hollywood dreck."

"You watch movies that get good reviews! You don't rent a movie unless someone's told you it's okay. Try some independent judgment! You're capable of that, Brice. You're capable but it takes work."

"God," Brice said to Jesse, "why don't you just shoot me? Why don't you take out a knife and split me open like a dead deer?"

"Brice," Jesse said, "that's a typically defensive and melodramatic comment. That sort of reaction lessens you. I want you to be *more*."

And later: "I don't want to live my life at that Hollywood level. I want to go deeper."

"That's why I'm on the bottom, right?" Brice said. "That's why I'm your *receptacle*. I'm your *woman*."

A flash of interest on Jesse's face, and Brice saw what it was like to bring up a debate point Jesse hadn't thought of. It was flattering, erotic, something Brice wanted to do again.

"See?" Jesse said, and he grabbed the sides of Brice's face with both hands. "You're *capable*." He kissed Brice quickly on the mouth with both hands holding his neck—the Judas kiss—like Michael Corleone in *The Godfather: Part II* kissing his brother Fredo in Havana at midnight at the New Year's Eve party, marking the moment when Michael, aware that his brother has betrayed him, knows that Fredo must be killed.

Brice said, "Jesse knew I'd get the reference."

Brice said, "I remember him spinning around in my chair when he was six years old. Now he's giving me lectures." His jaw set. "I'm not Fredo. I'm not stupid."

Brice said, "It isn't fair! I never betrayed him."

After Jesse finished gutting him Brice drove Jesse back to Tecumseh a full day before they'd planned (drove Jesse to Tecumseh! Can I imagine what that ride was like?), got himself back to Midburg, went to the video store and picked up Julie Taymor's *Titus*, based on *Titus Andronicus* by Shakespeare. "Mediocre reviews, okay?" Brice told me, almost shouting. "Mediocre reviews!" Strange film. The director must have meant it to be set in Everytime: Jessica Lange wore a toga and a bracelet around her upper arm and Anthony Hopkins sported a helmet and armor like Sir Galahad, but people drove cars and smoked cigarettes. Striking colors, Brice said, giving me a *See, I noticed* look.

The worldview was brutal. Anthony killed Jessica's son. In revenge, Jessica's sons raped and tortured Anthony's daughter. Charming people. Jessica captured Anthony's sons, said she'd give them back if Anthony cut off his own hand. Anthony did. Jessica sent back his son's heads. Anthony fed Jessica her sons baked in a pie. "That Shakespeare, I had no idea," Brice said. "In high school I thought *Romeo and Juliet* was boring.

"But don't you think it's insulting," Brice said, "that the only thing someone would cut off their hand for is love for their child? Don't you think that's parent-o-centric? I wonder if Shakespeare and Julie Taymor even noticed."

I said, "That's not a movie I'll be renting."

I absorbed. I absorbed for maybe half an hour early that October morning, until Dr. Strub knocked on Brice's door to tell me there were patients waiting. Alicia sent Dr. Strub to get me, she told me later; Brice might have tried to keep me in there if she knocked, but he couldn't refuse his boss.

After what Brice told me I couldn't eat, couldn't sit still. His agitation was like a parade balloon I'd swallowed uninflated that was filling up with air inside me. Every part of me felt stuffed, even my fingers were aching, and my head felt like it would fly right off. I didn't want Brice's balloon inside me anymore, I wanted it punctured and decompressed, but I couldn't find a needle and if I did I'd have to get the thing aimed right and I didn't know how.

I signed people in and out, called in prescriptions, spent a good fifteen minutes going over the difference between Medicare Part A and Medicare Part B with Mrs. Vickers. I did all this like a Caroline hologram that somehow managed to be taken for the real thing. Amazing what other people didn't notice. If they'd looked, they could have seen right through me. I supposed Brice had a day like that too.

When I got home that evening I phoned Fred. "You can come over and fall asleep next to me," he said, but I knew I couldn't sleep.

There was nothing on TV.

I couldn't read, couldn't settle down to do a crossword.

Sometime after ten I went out driving. Fred's house was indeed dark. I found myself taking the long lane down the golf course past Dr. Markowitz's house, hoping for a downstairs light. No light at all. How old are you? I screamed in my mind at Dr. Markowitz. I had had it with old men. I drove by Evan's parents' house, but in the carport there was only one vehicle, a Buick LeSabre that had to be his parents'. I drove by

Kitty and Brice's, and slivers of light leaked out from the sides of every window—upstairs, downstairs, basement—as if the place itself were a cube of light ensheathed in curtains. How ironic, because really there was no light in there at all. Should I stop and visit, be sure he was okay? No. I couldn't stand to face his monster mother.

About one in the morning I stopped off at an all-night drugstore and bought a box of Benadryl tablets. I took three and got in bed, and the next thing I knew there was music on the radio, and birds singing, and light. My mouth was incredibly dry.

He'll be fine, I remember thinking. *Caro, cut the drama*. Caro, a name I'd forgotten, one my father occasionally used. Not every child-hood memory of mine was painful.

HAP MARKOWITZ

Will and I were going to have to sit down with our accountant, take a long look at our finances. We were going to have to sit down with our lawyers—both the ones we'd already talked to at Ohio Mutual, our malpractice carrier, and the personal lawyers that the Ohio Mutual people had insisted we would need. Liability for Marilyn Kramer's stroke, liability for selling banned merchandise, negligent oversight: we were in a mess. It wouldn't be over soon. It might never be over. It was too early to see a drop in our patient visits, but I wouldn't blame any patient who didn't want to stick with me.

The staff had no idea. No idea. Even Alicia didn't seem to recognize the sharks around us. Will and I sat in our separate offices like great grouchy-looking fish who lurked under rocks, while the staff in the front office and the patients in the lobby swam about merrily, oblivious, striped and spotted and colorful, with skittering movements and flickering fins.

CAROLINE

"Don't talk to me," Brice said on Tuesday. "Don't look at me. I'll be okay if you pretend I'm not here."

I nodded, stepped away from his door. "Close the door," he said. "If you have something for me, give two quick knocks and I'll know it's you." I nodded again. "I'm trying my best to survive this," Brice said. "I just got a message from Jesse threatening legal action if I try to contact him again."

"I'm sorry," I said, feeling almost sorrier for Jesse than for Brice. "Do Jesse's parents know?"

"I don't think so. I guess his roommate's mom is a lawyer." Brice shrugged in a fakely nonchalant way. "Students," he said, the way someone might say, "Women."

Well, it was weird, Alicia said at lunch break, moving herself from her chair to the chair beside my desk. The night before all the BIC guys waited, but by eight o'clock Pastor Roger had still not shown up for the meeting.

"Maybe we should just go on," someone said. Bill Cripes had already mentioned the rough day Pastor Roger had had, with two strange men in suits coming to speak with him in his office for three hours.

"Who were they?"

Bill didn't know. They looked official.

Kenneth McMasters looked up sharply. "You think they were government guys?"

There was a general agreement that they must have been.

"I'm only asking because you know there's a CIA think tank in the old sanitarium on Wilmington," Kenneth said. "The sign says it's the Guffy Foundation, but it's really CIA."

Will wasn't sure about Kenneth, Alicia said. Kenneth had seen a UFO once. Kenneth had felt Jesus tap him on his shoulder.

Max Cooper had another idea. "It wasn't the CIA," Max said in a low voice. "It was the Mossad. That's who Pastor Roger's working with."

Will told Alicia that gave him a thrill, wanting to believe it. Pastor Roger, Israeli agent! Pastor Roger, battling for the preservation of Zion!

Everyone was exchanging glances. *He was just there . . . I heard he met with . . . He said there was a lot of work for . . . He realized his family was really . . .*

"Did the guys have accents?" someone asked.

Max said, "They don't have accents. The Mossad has a whole training program for accent eradication."

Alicia paused, looked at me in a skeptical way. "Do you believe that?"

"No."

"I don't, either."

"People always say crazy things about Jews," I said, feeling a surge of protectiveness for Dr. Markowitz. "And then they excuse themselves by saying it was a compliment."

"Will didn't believe it," Al said staunchly.

"Good. And those two guys in suits who came to Pastor Roger's office? They were probably Mormons."

Alicia and I started giggling. "That's what Will said, it was unreal, the guys were jabbering on like the choir ladies on the old *Andy Griffith Show*, all wound up and excited. So he left."

"Will walked out of a BIC meeting?"

"He said no one noticed." Alicia looked at me confidingly. "He's not right, Pastor Roger. Don't you think he's not right? I want Pastor Owen back."

Brice's door swung open; its doorknob hit the wall and made us jump. He stood stock-still facing Alicia and me; our mouths must have both dropped open. "I know you two have your opinion of me," he said, his voice shaking, "but it's beyond cruel to hear you laugh at me. If you're going to laugh at me, I ask that you take it outside."

We objected, of course, we denied it and talked about Pastor Roger and hopped up and tried to reassure him, but before long we were talking to a locked door.

∿

Fred called them "bar stories," which I took as a military term. He might have called them "grandkid stories" if he had grandkids. I felt bad that he didn't have them. His two children's deaths in their early twenties had left him with no one down the line. I often wondered if he yearned for them. He was helping the guy next door extend his deck, and he would stop his work and stand outside waiting for one of the young daughters to come help hammer nails.

This could be my bar story: I was a receptionist in a doctors' office, and one afternoon I looked up and saw two men with neat haircuts peering through the patient window. I thought they were Mormons, although one of them surprised me with his age. I figured he was a convert who had to put in some required missionary time. I was about to tell the men—in an annoyed way—that this was a medical office, but if they absolutely had to they could leave their literature with me. But they weren't Mormons. They whipped out two badges: IRS.

They talked, individually, and several times, to all five of us who worked there. They were doing what one of my coworkers (Brice) referred to as "the highly traditional practice of following the money."

What seemed to interest the IRS men was that our office was an outlet for the sales of His Way nutriceuticals and dermatologicals.

For months, regular payment for these products had been sent to a distributor named Kirby Meadows. Further regular payment, with the annotation *His Way proceeds*, was sent to the Reclaiming Zion Fund at Zion Bible Church. Brice Kelvin and Dr. William Strub signed the checks.

It was Kirby, we thought at first. Kirby hadn't been paying taxes. Maybe the IRS was going after him for taxes because the federal prosecutors didn't have enough evidence to nail him for his worse crimes. Maybe half the cases of His Way products were filled not with pills but with heroin. Maybe His Way produced steroid products for athletes. Maybe the His Way capsules were filled with sugar, not succinium.

But the agents had as many questions about Pastor Roger as about Kirby. Could the guy from BIC be right? Was Pastor Roger really an Israeli agent? Maybe he used Zion Bible money to obtain state secrets or pay off congressmen. Maybe he was hooked up with someone at the CIA center on Wilmington, or maybe—wait a minute, this was it!— the IRS was after Pastor Roger because the FBI was angry that Pastor Roger was working with the CIA and not with them. The IRS agents were pretty curious about the CIA office, Dr. Strub said. Oh, they tried to seem casual, but they asked him for the address and everything he'd heard.

"I bet Pastor Roger's got a girlfriend stashed somewhere," I said. "He uses money from the church to pay her rent."

Brice said, "I don't think the IRS would care about a girlfriend."

"Maybe she's fifteen."

"Maybe Pastor Roger's got a boyfriend," Brice said. "Maybe *he's* fifteen."

Alicia said, "Caroline! Brice! He's not like that!" But she was grinning.

Sometimes Alicia and Brice and I got so wound up talking about the dire possibilities that patients at the window and phone calls seemed like irritating distractions.

By the end of that week, Brice was hanging out in the front office with Alicia and me, as animated as I'd seen him in years, especially when the doctors were in their exam rooms seeing patients.

We were central. The *Daily Ledger* would move beyond the beauty shops and the nasty natural pills and do a series about His Way corruption.

Soon there'd be a movie of our office. Dr. Strub could be played by Harrison Ford, the actor with no sense of humor. Patricia Neal, Brice said, had to play me.

"Great, I'll be dead."

"We'll get a clone of her. I'm sorry, but you *are* Patricia."

Alicia, Brice said, would be Jennifer Lopez in a surly mood, maybe just after ditching a husband.

"You're crazy," Alicia said, blushing, reaching behind her neck and lifting her hair.

Dr. Markowitz would be Danny DeVito.

"That's insulting," I said.

"Think of a stocky Jewish guy, then," Brice said. "Jerry Stiller?"

"Why bring ethnicity into it?"

"Ethnicity is destiny, darling."

"You sound like a parody, Brice."

"Prejudice? Do I hear prejudice?"

"If you understand our office, you understand the world," Brice said, and then he started blithering about Ajax carting the globe around on his shoulders.

Alicia leaned over my ear and whispered. "Do you think he's on drugs?"

"We can hope."

Al giggled. More fun than she'd had in months, I thought. She and Dr. Strub were skipping church this Sunday. What would they say? How could they look at Pastor Roger without staring? How could they say hello to their friends and not blurt out what they knew? "Do you think Pastor Roger could be the mastermind of something?" Alicia said. "He's really smart."

"I'm part of an investigation!" she said later. "I told Jesse on the phone last night, never in my wildest dreams did I think I'd be part of an investigation."

I glanced at Brice, saw him quail for an instant at the mention of Jesse's name.

HAP MARKOWITZ

"Sending a quarter of the His Way profits to your *church*?" I said to Will. "What was that about?" Will frowned and took a seat in the patient chair and didn't look at me for a moment. He bit his lips together. And I had asked him only half my question. "And ten days ago I asked if there was more I should know and you started talking about dirty pictures on the Internet! What about *this*? Did you really think you shouldn't tell me about giving away our money?"

It took him quite a while to answer. Before he spoke, his mouth widened in an involuntary grimace so full of grief I had to look away. "His Way was basically my thing, Hap. You laughed at it, you didn't have any interest. You threw it at me, remember?"

I closed my eyes, not wanting to remember the afternoon the hurled bottle bounced off Will and disappeared in silence. A lawyer could make a case that in Will's selling of His Way I was ignored and betrayed and bamboozled—and I was—but I could see Will's side too.

I never asked to look at the His Way balance sheets. I never read the literature. I never even figured out what succinium actually was. Yet, every month, in my paycheck, I saw benefit. And when Janis got sick, Will offered to credit me with all the His Way income.

"The money to Zion Bible"—Will was still talking—"it was for the Israel fund, okay? It was for something that would be good for you."

I nodded, seeing his point. A ridiculous point, true, but I had no doubt it was sincere.

"We got the tax deduction, at least," Will said, running his hand through his hair. An amazing head of hair it was, not a hint of male-pattern baldness. I wondered fleetingly what it felt like to have such hair, to rest your head each night on its own pillow. "I was talking to the Zion Bible treasurer, and I guess . . . I think the board's going to ask Pastor Roger to quit tonight. He's been taking money from the church." Will winced again. "Remember his wife, Cyrinda? I guess she had some shady stuff in her past, might even have been a prostitute or something. Anyway, there was this guy she'd been involved with before she got married, some organized-crime guy in Columbus, and Pastor Roger was sending him money to pay him off so he'd stay away from her and keep quiet. Thousands and thousands to this guy. I guess once Cyrinda got her divorce she was maybe heading back to him, so Pastor Roger used the Youth Activity Barn money to get her that house in New Mexico. Wanted her far away."

"He really loved her," I said. "He called her his Bosc pear."

"His what?"

"His treasure."

Will's brow furrowed slightly. "This is just recent; I guess he's been lifting money for years. He's got all these CDs and bonds and stuff. Then this Reclaiming Zion Fund, I guess he took money out of there to make a down payment on an apartment for himself in Jerusalem."

Will's voice broke. "I hate to see him as a thief, Hap. I hate it, but that's what he is."

"Guess that puts our tax deduction in doubt." I snorted, a small and ragged explosion. "Those foreign vacation homes are hell to get deductions for."

"Lot of paperwork," Will said, forcing a smile. "Good thing we have our crackerjack accountant." This was a joke: our accountant was as ordinary as toast. Will sniffed. "I know I was stupid. I should have talked with you before I sent the church anything. It was just . . . I wanted to help Pastor Roger. I thought I was doing something good."

Truthfully, I was relieved to hear what had happened to Zion Bible's money. So many worse things Pastor Roger could have spent it on— drugs, sex, fancy cars, gambling. Investments and a dwelling place at the center of the world: those things I could respect. And the money that had gone to protect Cyrinda: if I could have spent South Midburg Internists' funds to keep at bay my own wife's past, would I have done it? Of course I would have.

I wished, at that moment, that I were harsher. I wished I could get angrier. I wanted to hate Pastor Roger. I wanted to stand up and walk out of the office and away from Will forever. I wasn't sure if it was strength or weakness that I couldn't.

"I'm sorry," Will said. "I'm sorry for everything. I got you into this."

"I know," I said. "It's all right. You didn't mean to."

～

The next morning Will appeared in my office before office hours and shut my door behind him.

A shock: we never talked behind closed doors. Even the evening before, for his confession, he'd left the office door open.

Will sat down in the patient chair and spoke without hesitation. "I'm firing Brice today. It's not up for discussion. Today I fire Brice."

I was surprised at how adult he sounded, resolved and confident and sure.

"Okay," I said cautiously, meaning that word as an acknowledgment, not an acquiescence. "Why?"

"Alicia."

"That's not a reason."

"Listen to me. Do you know Brice is gay? Do you know he and Jesse had a sexual-type relationship? Do you know that Brice is obsessed with Jesse, that he doesn't want to let Jesse go?" Will gave me a meaningful look, straightened in the chair, and crossed his arms in resolution. "It all came out last night. Jesse showed up home and he was terrified. It took a while, but he told Al everything, and of course she told me. He's going to stay with us all weekend. He's afraid of Brice coming after him at Tecumseh."

"He's afraid of Brice?" Brice was neat and tidy and quiet. Brice was totally unscary. Someone might as well be afraid of me.

"They started some relationship this summer when Jesse worked here, they . . . did things in the basement. Right here! Right under us. I know Jesse's saying he's gay now, but maybe Brice . . . We think of Jesse as mature, but Brice is fifteen years older and I guess in college he . . . had some homosexual experience. At any rate, Jesse tried to do the right thing and split it off and get out of that lifestyle, but Brice went nuts, Brice sends him fifty e-mails a day and shows up outside his classes and leaves messages on his cell phone and . . . Would you want your son stalked like that? Think about Alicia. Think about her. Brice is . . . almost a rapist, almost a pedophile, and he's working with his victim's mother! That's not right. Even you, Hap, and I know you're a liberal and you love gay people and want them to get married and adopt children and sleep in tents with Boy Scouts—even you have to admit that that's not normal."

I did admit that.

"I'll do it, I'll talk with him," Will said. "You don't have to get your hands dirty."

I chose to ignore the insult in this comment. "Have we got cause for firing him independent of Jesse? In case he comes after us legally?"

Will's face darkened. "Listen," he said, pulling from his pocket one of those handheld recorders we dictated notes into. He pressed play and I leaned forward to listen.

It was someone singing, sort of. It was Brice singing.

I have my Cam-era
I have my View
I have my Fea-ture
Made Just for You!

"That's what he left on Jesse's cell phone yesterday," Will said, clicking the tape off. "That's what drove Jesse home. Want to hear it again?"

"What does it mean?" I felt nauseated. I had said hello to Brice behind his desk that morning. He was wearing a shirt with crisply creased sleeves and a red patterned tie.

"Jesse thinks it's some movie reference. It's spooky, isn't it?"

I nodded. "Maybe you should call the police."

"I don't think I can deal with any more crazy people," Will said. He sounded exhausted. "They fired Pastor Roger last night. They've got church people taking turns staying at his house, kind of a suicide watch. Now, don't get mad, Hap, but I've been thinking about this. Brice comes after us for firing him, I go after him for Jesse. I can do that, Hap. Don't forget, I've got Bernie Esposito."

"You're kidding!" I almost started laughing. How B-movie. Will's patient, Bernie Esposito, was our local mobster, whether or not the threat he represented was real. When Bernie was in the hospital with a blood clot, half the Four East staff threatened to call in sick, while the other half jockeyed for reasons to enter his room.

"I'm not kidding. Bernie likes me. He always says, 'Doc, if there's anything I can do for you . . .' "

I felt even queasier. Midburg wasn't paradise: a couple months before there had been a body found shackled to the backseat of a burned-out car. "Okay," I said, for Brice's sake, "go ahead and let him go. But tell him if he needs a reference, I can give it."

"Are you going to vouch for Pastor Roger too?" Will said as he stood. He strode to the door, opened it, slammed it behind him as he left. That was the price Will paid, I supposed, for having me forgive him: he had to see me forgive people he thought were worse.

I hadn't realized the door to my office was so flimsy. I felt almost ashamed of the hollow sound it made when it was slammed.

CAROLINE

"It's okay," Brice said once Dr. Strub left his office. "Don't sleep with the boss's son, cardinal rule. Especially if you're a he." Alicia wasn't there that morning: she had a toothache, Dr. Strub said, and she had to make an emergency visit to her dentist. "I'll be fine. I have other things to do. Plenty of other things to do. It's like this was meant to be."

He was talking faster than I was used to, tossing things from his desk drawers into two paper grocery store bags on top of his desk.

"Take it easy for a few days, Brice, okay? You want to have dinner with Fred and me tonight? He made chili."

"I'm not going to have a lot of time to eat, Caroline."

What was he going to do that would leave him without time to eat? It made no sense. "You need to eat, Brice. You're already thin. Listen, I'll write down Fred's address and phone number and you think about coming by. We'll plan on you. It's two minutes from Meijer, off Hoeppel. If you get lost, just call." I handed him the sheet of paper. He tossed it in the bag, followed by a stapler and his wall clock. The stapler technically belonged to the office, but I didn't want to point that out. Whatever small reparations Brice was taking were certainly deserved. I unplugged his desk phone from the wall and put that in his bag too.

"Take care of yourself, Brice," I said when he had both his paper bags loaded. "Be safe."

"Oh, I will!" I held open the back door for him, stayed to wave him off when he drove away.

There was a line at my window and both phone lines were lit up. "Somebody get canned?" said a woman I didn't recognize, before I had a chance to sit down.

I ignored her.

"I think it was that money guy you never see," said George Llewellyn from farther back in line.

"Oh, is he the one who handled the checks from those . . . ?"

A hubbub started, words and phrases flying at me like rotten tomatoes: . . . *no wonder . . . Channel 7 . . . had the lady sued yet? . . . doctors didn't even know, the salon woman . . . frankly, I was nervous about coming here, but . . .*

Our office, our wonderful office. We were the ABCs.

Alicia's chair was empty behind me, scooted far under her desk. Brice's office was bare except for an overflowing wastebasket and scattered paper clips on the floor. I had maybe five patients to check in and obtain vitals on. Line two stopped flashing, then line one. I couldn't move. I stood there looking at the gossiping patients and found myself in tears.

"You get his key?" Dr. Strub said later.

That jarred me. For years Brice brought in bagels on Fridays and chopped the ice off the back stoop and started the coffeepot every morning. The little extra things he did, things that weren't in any job description: those things should have bought him a key. Or, more accurately: those things should have bought our faith that he wouldn't use it.

"I just locked it in my desk drawer," I lied. "Can I get it for you tomorrow?"

That night, I copied my own key to give to Dr. Strub the next morning. The head was different from the real key's, but Dr. Strub would never notice the difference.

HAP MARKOWITZ

That Monday there was a police car in the front of the office main door, two police cars in the back, and, at the side of the building, a rescue vehicle with two EMTs sitting on the back bumper. It was the EMTs just sitting there who scared me.

I couldn't take any more bad news, I thought as I got out of my car. Will's car was already in the lot, parked in its usual spot. Will? I had a moment of panic, but inside his car there was a cup of coffee in the cup holder and this morning's *USA Today* on the passenger's seat, two things that bespoke a normal morning. Maybe a patient had come in early and arrested and died in the waiting room: that had happened years before to another internist in town.

I was blocked inside the back door to the office by a large man in dark blue pants and a lighter blue shirt carrying a gun. I glanced at his name tag: LT. UTNEY. Behind him, I could make out Caroline's legs in front of her chair in the main office, and I thanked God that she was okay. "You got an office?" Lieutenant Utney said, and I realized there were strange voices coming from the basement. Why would a patient be in the basement? Maybe it was a robbery, Kirby come to steal the His Way products, and the rescue vehicle got dispatched by mistake.

Caroline leaned around Utney and gave me a bleak look. "Brice," she mouthed. "Suicide."

"We'll talk in your office," the policeman said, touching my shoulder in a shepherding way.

I heard Caroline's voice. "Don't worry about downstairs, Dr. Markowitz. Everything's taken care of."

"He didn't hurt anybody, did he?" I said urgently, desperate at that moment to glimpse Caroline's face—but Utney was large and I couldn't see around him, and at the same time I was thinking, No, Brice wouldn't hurt anybody. Brice didn't have the anger for it.

What did his song say? Something about frames and features?

Utney was still trying to turn me around and head me toward my office, but I was on my toes, I wanted to get past him and back to Caroline. "He hung himself and he cut off his left hand," Utney said in what sounded like irritation, and the letters on his name tag became curves and lines, things that no longer made sense.

"All the way?" I said, thinking of the bones and the ligaments and the incredible *durableness*—there was no other way to think of it—of a hand.

He nodded. "Used an ax"—and the word "ax" put everything into place, everything impossible seemed plausible. I believed it right away.

I couldn't believe it, people would say. Couldn't believe it!

I believed it. I accepted it in a microsecond, yet I missed it coming. This wasn't a minor failure. This was a spectacular failure, the sort of thing that made me think I shouldn't be trusted with a hamster, much less with people's lives. The sort of thing that made me think that Janis was better off dead and free than tied to the likes of me.

I'd missed Pastor Roger, I'd missed Brice. I'd missed everything.

I stopped resisting, turned around, and headed meekly to my office. Lieutenant Utney was talking behind me. "This sort of thing is hard to take, it's a natural reaction to wonder what . . ."

We were large browsing animals. Buffalo or elk or moose in a field, and behind us the ground was rising and smoking and rumbling, and our noses and eyes were so focused on our little clumps of grass that we missed the volcanoes.

"No," I interrupted, and I realized my right hand was gripping my left wrist. "It makes sense." Brice and Pastor Roger, our office failed them both. I turned my head and saw the policeman's swinging arm hesitate in quick alarm—Did I know something? Was I a cause?—and all I wanted was to push past him to Caroline in the front office, to someone who would understand. We failed him! I would shout. We should have known! I turned to do it, ready to fight Lieutenant Utney if he resisted, but at that moment Caroline pressed past him from behind. She had her arms out for me, and we embraced there in the back hall behind the waiting room, and suddenly there were two new arms around us—what odd behavior for a police officer—and then I realized the arms were Will's.

"You're here," I said.

"I found him," said Will.

He smelled it, that was the thing. He came in early to dictate his weekend calls and unlocked the back door and saw the basement light on and at the same time he recognized the rawness in the air and he knew. Medical people recognized the smell of blood.

"Did you think it was Brice?"

Will nodded. "For a second I got scared about Jesse. But we took him back to Tecumseh yesterday."

Will figured Brice had shot himself. When he walked down the steps and saw the blood on the floor he wasn't surprised.

What did surprise him was the video recorder on the tripod, aimed at the unfinished end of the room. What did surprise him was the light clamped to the tripod, illuminating the dark vertical of Brice's body. Brice was hanging by a belt around his neck. Will said, "Remember those post-hanging patients we'd sometimes get in the ICU?"—ones who'd been cut down in time for family conferences and brain-death EEGs. They looked awful—faces distorted and blue-purple, raw streaks around their necks. I remembered one woman running from the ICU screaming, "That's not Bobby!"

What had shocked Will—what absolutely flummoxed him, for an instant—was the clawed piece of tissue in the pool of blood on the floor. He had had to bend over and look before he realized it was a hand. Near it on the floor, set at an almost jaunty diagonal, was the ice ax. Will lifted his eyes to Brice's body, saw the left cuff dangling and drenched red. The same outfit Brice was wearing on Friday. There was a chair Brice must have knocked out from under him and, between Brice's body and the tripod, the card table that Jesse had once used as a desk. The card table top was dented and bloodied, its fabric split. "Brice must have rested his hand on that thing and . . ." Will made a whacking gesture.

The will that took, my God. I was frozen for a moment by the will.

"There has to be a Devil, make a person do that," Will said.

Will had walked back toward the steps to upstairs, punched the button that opened the video recorder. The spine of the tape, printed in Brice's neat block letters, said MY LIFE IN RED.

A title, Will realized. Brice had made a movie. "And you know, I looked around for a machine to play it on before I thought, What am I thinking?"

He heard Caroline upstairs. He turned to see her feet and legs coming down the steps. The fake leg under her pants was a little thinner than the real one—had I noticed? Will never had—and it hit him that Caroline could handle the hanging and the blood, but he didn't want her to have to see the hand. But it was too late: she moved quickly.

She didn't scream, Will knew she wouldn't scream.

CAROLINE

"Is everything okay?" I said, holding the railing, because as good as my prosthesis was, I was still more cautious than bipeds on the stairs. Dr. Strub, still in his overcoat, was looking up at my legs, and as I descended he backed up until he hit the basement wall. In retrospect, his face might have surprised me: there wasn't anguish in it, or horror, or even bafflement—it was more a sorrowful understanding, the face of a man (I've thought about this often) who really did believe in The Fall. I respected him for that look—really respected him, maybe for the first time—because when I got to the bottom step I could see past the carpeting under the chart racks to the blood on the blue-painted floor. Above the blood hung Brice, and in the blood was something awful, something wrong.

He cut his heart out, I thought. Then, once I got closer and recognized the object: *He could have lived without that hand.* Both thoughts being illogical but deeply sensible, as first thoughts often are.

That hand was not essential to him. But he chose instead for it to be a vehicle of his death.

Q: If you're dying in the dining room, what do you do?
A: Chop off your hand.

Bzzzt, wrong answer.

Of course, I knew what he was thinking. *To prove how much I love you, I will chop off my own hand.* Evidence that he loved Jesse more than Jesse's mother did. Proof of the superiority—or at least equivalency—of erotic to parental love. I wondered if he'd told Jesse about the Shakespeare movie.

Insanity.

The day Brice was fired, the day he stomped around throwing things into the paper bags on his desk: I should have insisted he eat dinner with Fred and me.

Come on, Brice, get in the car. I'm not taking no for an answer. Brice, get in the car.

Hard to believe someone would voluntarily cut part of themselves off and toss it away. I looked down toward my prosthesis beyond my real thigh and thought: knee and calf and my own foot, I'm sorry. I only let you go because I had to.

He looked so little. His drooping head was almost level with mine; his feet were maybe two inches from the floor. I was sorry about Brice, but in my center, in my core of cores (and this was the thought that was shocking, the one people rarely voice), I didn't care. He was the dead one, not me.

The hand was totally disgusting.

I noticed the camera on the tripod, its red ON light glowing.

"It's a movie," Dr. Strub said, and I gave a small shiver.

I walked back to the stairs, stood in front of Dr. Strub and looked at Brice. Upstairs there was my window and the lobby furniture and the pile of papers at the right upper corner of my desk; upstairs there was the phone and 911. "I don't care," I said out loud. The words emerged with an eerie force, angry and tragic and defiant. I took several steps up the stairs. "I don't care!" I screamed.

Silence. Silence.

Dr. Strub and I looked at each other. I knew he'd never repeat what I'd just said.

There was a difference, if you listened, between the slap of my right foot and the clunk of my left not-foot on the stairs.

~

Everyone has their story, Dr. Markowitz and I agreed later. Brice's mother was born to suffer. Dr. Strub had wasted his life until he got saved. Brice had to die to prove his love to Jesse. I survived my cancer, and then I *knew.*

But maybe I didn't know. Maybe what I thought was wisdom was no more than resignation. Maybe my denying Brice my exhortations was just another way of abandoning him, of getting him off the radar of my worry. Because, really, how can anyone *know?*

Fred over the phone was strangely consoling. "He just must have been crazy," he said. "He hadn't done this, he would've done something else. You got one of those cleanup crews coming? They got special cleanup crews for things like that."

"I know," I said. "They're here."

Fred said, "First thing, I'd get rid of that ax."

HAP MARKOWITZ

It was maybe three-thirty in the afternoon. Caroline was gone, the cleaning crew was done. Al never came in: Will had called and warned her away. Caroline managed to reach all but two patients to cancel, each of whom was too self-absorbed to notice anything strange about our empty lobby or my mood. Will was in his office, I was in mine. The office had never been this quiet on a normal weekday afternoon. The heater kicked on with a thump and a whir.

Because it was a clear suicide, Lieutenant Utney had said, we didn't need to worry about the paper. The *Daily Ledger* was good about suicides: the publisher had had some family experience. An obituary if the family wanted, that was all. Lieutenant Utney's partner had informed the mother; she said her son hadn't been home all weekend. She asked if he had any insurance.

Will had one request: Jesse should never know about the movie or the hand. "No problem," Lieutenant Utney said. "Only way he'd find out is from you people."

I walked down the hall. Will was behind his desk with no lamp on, his back to the window. The blinds on his window sliced the light into blurred, vaguely horizontal rays.

"You okay?" I said.

He shook his head, not looking up. "It's like a dream, these last eighteen months. One minute I'm in the exam room looking at Al's ass and the next I'm sitting here staring at dust in the air. It's like: Where am I? What happened? Is any of this real?"

"It's real."

"I went down there and tasted the blood. Spot the cleaning service missed, size of a sesame seed. Still sticky. I wet my finger, rubbed it off . . . Salty. Like anybody's blood, really."

Will did this? Will Strub? It shocked me. Did I know this person? For a moment I was stunned into silence. He didn't look at me. "How's Alicia?" I said at last.

"Hysterical. Thinks it's her fault."

"*Her* fault?"

"Because I fired him for her. Because she hated him."

I sighed and took a seat. "Did you tell Jesse?"

Will closed his eyes. "I called him at school—he knows. I didn't tell him about the hand. I won't. When I told Alicia about the hand she started screaming." He squinched his eyes tighter. "It's not Jesse's fault. He was the vehicle, is all. The Devil's vehicle."

The Devil. This really was how he was going to make sense of it. He could be right, I thought. It was as good a story as any. "Well," I said, standing, "I'm heading out."

"I'll sit here for a while. I'll lock up."

I hesitated at the door. "I guess we'll have to think about the future. It'll be a regular day tomorrow."

"There is no tomorrow in this office," Will said. "A month, six weeks, to close things down . . . that's it for me."

"You're sure?"

He nodded, his eyes still tightly closed. "I tasted the blood, remember?"

~

A few days after Brice's death Caroline went to the police station. Just like at our office, there was a woman at the front counter behind a window. Caroline explained who she was and how she had seen Brice's body. ". . . and I know he made a tape, and I figure there must have been a reason for it, something he wanted to communicate. Not many people knew him, really, and he said once I knew him better than anyone. So it's not that I want to see it, it's that I think he'd . . ."

The woman behind the window frowned, stood up, and disappeared. Caroline wondered if she thought Caroline was crazy; looking up, Caroline saw a camera trained on the space where she was standing.

The woman returned with someone who looked like the guy they called when there was trouble. He stationed himself behind the window, leaned forward with his hands on the counter, and said, "You don't want to see it."

"He'd want me to. I . . . absorb things for him."

The word "absorb" seemed to throw him. His mouth set in a peculiar alertness, as if, behind his still eyes, he was running through a list of aberrant behaviors that might be related to absorption. After a long moment, he gave up. The eyes flickered. "You really his friend?"

"Yes. We worked together for years. We talked."

The man took a big breath. "If you're really a friend, he wouldn't want you to see it."

"He would. He wanted to make a movie, he put his favorite title on it, I think he meant it as an artistic sort of . . ."

The man's body straightened. "Lady, he offed himself. Let it be."

"But I feel like it's my duty to him, I—"

"Let it be."

For the first time Caroline really *saw* the guy, beyond his posture and size. Flat eyes, sagging mouth, flared nostrils: she was looking at a face that had probably absorbed too much. *Choose life,* the voice in her head said. Her mantra, she called it. She glanced down at her handbag, caught the glint of the keys to her car. "Okay," she said, backing away, shooting a look toward the camera. "Thank you anyway. Okay."

"So what's your story?" she asked me, on one of those tender final days. "If everybody has a story, what's yours?"

I thought a moment. "I'm someone who's lost without a mate."

"You'll find one," she said, leaning forward, laying her hand briefly on my wrist. I can still feel the warmth of her fingers.

CAROLINE

Alicia, after Brice's death, never came back to the office. Will emptied out her desk later that week. "Love the sinner, hate the sin, that's what they say," he said. "Al thinks she hated both."

Avoidance, that was one way to handle guilt. I felt a little envious of Alicia being married to the boss: I wished that I could disappear like she did.

Looking back, I could trace the events that brought Brice to our basement: his mother's sickness, getting fired, that crazy Shakespeare movie he rented, Jesse's cracks about his intellect. Like a trail of crumbs Brice followed through the forest to the house where the dreadful deeds were done.

Could I have stopped him? Maybe. It would have taken encouragement—*Brice, get in the car; Brice, you'll stay and watch TV with us tonight; Brice, here's a gun to shoot your mother*—that I was too chicken to give. Encouragement was just that—en-couragement—and there might be a fine line, yes, between it and exhortation, but it was a line I should have crossed. What kept me from crossing it? Only pride. I didn't want to hear myself as an exhorter. I thought exhortation was beneath me.

I made myself a rule—*no exhortation*—and I didn't have the strength to break it.

It was funny: I had no regret at all about cutting off my own family, but cutting off Brice . . . He needed me. I should have believed that when he told me.

In our last few weeks in the office, Dr. Markowitz and I spoke as much with our silence as with our words. Once I was unrolling fresh paper to cover the top of an exam table when Dr. Markowitz appeared in the door. "His mother would never kill herself," I said.

"Probably not," he agreed, and we looked at each other a moment before he wandered off.

Another time I was on hold with a cardiology office when Dr. Markowitz appeared beside my desk. "Who's ever seen that movie?" he said. "Who's ever read that play? Why didn't he pick something more iconic?" I shook my head and rolled my eyes his way, not moving my mouth from the receiver. Our aching look cemented our understanding: that the obscurity of Brice's reference only made his death hurt more.

Jesse had an appointment with Dr. Markowitz about nausea and pain in his abdomen. "Can you talk to Jesse after Hap sees him, Caroline?" Dr. Strub asked. "He's having a rough time." His voice dropped. "Just don't mention the hand."

I nodded. Brice's suicide had ended up a private joke with nobody to hear it. The person it was aimed for would never know—could never know—the elaborate work that had gone into its performance.

"He thinks he did too much," Dr. Markowitz said, setting Jesse's chart on my desk as Jesse made his way from the exam room. "I told him you felt like you did too little."

Jesse sat in the chair beside my desk. "I don't think I'll ever get over it," he said.

The hairs on Jesse's upper lip were downy, the raw spot on the knuckle of his thumb looked suspiciously like a suck mark. He was eighteen. Part of me wanted to mourn that he should have to face Brice's death so young, but at his age I was cured of cancer, of bodily wholeness, of my childlike belief in the value and normalcy of my own family. If I could get through that, then Jesse could make it through his trauma. He didn't need coddling. I said, "You can't be perfect, no one's perfect."

"I almost think he killed himself to impress me," Jesse said. "He wanted to make a statement beyond intellectual reproof. He wasn't stupid, but . . ." Jesse stopped, sniffed, gave the bottom of his nose a quick rub. "I thought he could think more systematically, more clearly, and I kept pushing him to do it. But he couldn't, really. I mean, that mother . . ." Jesse brought the back of his hand in front of his eyes as if a flashbulb had gone off inches from his face. "Brice had his limits," Jesse said. "You can't blame him."

I watched him. I absorbed.

"It's like my mom," Jesse said. "She always wants me better—at least, her view of better—but you can ask too much of people." Jesse's voice had gone as thin and squeaky as an old man's. "You can ask people to do what they can't do."

"Jesse," I said, "I'm twice your age and I have no idea what we should have done for Brice." Not totally true: I had ideas, I just wasn't sure they would have worked.

A stab of fear in Jesse's eyes. "Something," he said.

"Something," I agreed quickly. This was what you said to a young person: We could have changed things, we could have made a happy ending.

HAP MARKOWITZ

A year goes by before Will and I get together for breakfast. Our practice has been sold—complete with supplies and furniture—to an Indian doc just out of residency, our corporation dissolved. It's almost winter again, the year wheeling around in its merciless, merciful way. We talk about our new jobs (I am full-time in the medical clinic at the VA, Will is working part-time at a doc-in-the-box), our former houses, the new condos we've bought on opposite sides of Midburg. My condo actually has more square feet than Will's and Alicia's. Alicia doesn't want a second floor. She's gotten involved in a life-with-less Christian movement that encourages buying shoes from Goodwill and growing your own food. She'd live in one room if Will would let her. Before she and Will moved she held a huge garage sale and donated the proceeds to Habitat for Humanity. The best moment, Will says, was seeing Harriet's old furniture heading off in the back of a battered pickup.

Will and I are co-defendants in two lawsuits, and the IRS is auditing our former office. South Midburg Internists still has loose ends to tie.

It may take years, our lawyers tell us, but Will and I don't talk about this at breakfast.

It takes us two cups of coffee to get to Brice. "Were you surprised?" Will says. "The hand surprised me."

I shake my head. "I missed it." I never saw either Brice's body or his hand, an omission that feels to me now like weakness. I should have gone down those stairs. I should have faced it.

Al's busy, Will says. She's doing nursing part-time and three days a week she delivers church meals-on-wheels, with Brice's mother as one of her customers. Brice's mother mentions Brice, Alicia says, only to say how mad she is that he abandoned her. Alicia's in a women's prayer group at her and Will's new church, which Pastor Owen moved to as an associate after Zion Bible fell apart. She gets up fifteen minutes early to read a daily devotional. "She's like a saint now, I'll tell you," Will says.

"Is she happy?" I wonder what has possessed her, if her fervor is a sort of competitive goodness or something deeper, something real.

Will wrinkles his brow and considers. "Happier," he says. "She sure keeps me in line."

Our young waitress approaches with the pot of coffee, and Will puts his hand over his cup. "Are you torturing me?" he says. "Are you trying to make my hands shake?" The girl backs away in confusion. "Doesn't know what to make of me," Will says, smiling.

He asks me if there are any docs or former patients I run into.

I don't see anyone, I tell him. Just a bunch of vets.

He says, "You hear Jim and Kathy McNally are splitting up?" A cardiologist and a pediatrician.

"Someone else?"

"He says no, but it looks like he got hair plugs."

We both laugh.

"How about Caroline?" I say. "You ever talk to her?"

"No. You?"

It takes me a second to answer—less than a second—but Will senses my hesitation. I see his eyebrows rise: *Hap and Caroline, hunh?* He glances at my hands as if he's thinking of them doing something surprising. "A few times," I say. "I ran into her about a month ago at the mall. We had a cup of coffee at Starbucks."

"She okay?"

"Yeah, she is. She's working for Irv Tatum now, replaced that Vicki he had at his front desk." I'm looking down at the table, suddenly shy.

"She's still seeing that old guy of yours, right? I saw them together a few months ago at Kroger. He was holding up this zucchini and they were laughing. . . ."

I shift in my seat. I do not for the life of me see the appeal of Fred Langford. "They're not . . . married or anything. It's companionship, that's all. You know he had a total prostate. He's twenty years older than I am! He could be her grandpa." Could he? I'm trying to figure out the math of this when I see Will's mouth twist into a smile above his coffee cup. "He'll be dead in ten years anyway," I say, surprised at the ferocity of my tone.

Will almost spits out his coffee. "You're wishing him dead? He's your patient!"

"Was. Was my patient."

We have a long cleansing laugh over that one.

I say, "I kind of wish Caroline worked for Ken Struble." Will knows what I'm saying: Ken Struble is a doc I could visit as a patient. Her new employer is a gynecologist.

Will says, "Maybe she'll move."

"Maybe." I grin.

"You should recruit her for the VA."

I grin more. "Government benefits!"

We don't say much else. We don't talk more about Brice, or our old office, or our former patients. We briefly mention Pastor Roger, who is selling cars at Brightstar Motors after a lengthy psychiatric hospitalization precipitated by a suicide attempt with scissors. (One of my VA patients who was a Zion Bible member told me this.) *What a waste,* I think whenever Pastor Roger crosses my mind. There were things he said in my exam room that I know will never leave me. Bosc pear, for one.

"What a shyster," Will spits about his old pastor.

The word stings me: "shyster," "Shylock." I wonder if there's a connection. "But he was an innocent shyster," I say. "He used some money to protect his wife, and some to buy an apartment in a holy city."

"You know what places cost in Jerusalem? Las Vegas would've been cheaper." Will shakes his head. "Loser. Prick."

It's not that simple, I almost say, but I realize this comment would be useless. I say instead, "You still going to church?"

"When I can. Al goes enough for both of us."

"You see Jesse at all?"

A hesitation. "Maybe someday. Al sees him."

"Good," I say. I think, *The pacemaker is settling in.*

Another way to put it: Will's finding Jesus was like falling off a boat in a storm and slapping, with his flailing hand, an inner tube the second he went under. He had no choice but to grab it and hold on. Now the waters have calmed and he doesn't have to grip the thing so tightly. He can let go and paddle around. On clear days, he can see the shore. He can wonder about swimming there alone.

CAROLINE

I ran into Alicia in the nut store, of all places. I was buying Christmas baskets for the docs in my new office and Alicia was picking up a cashew order for a wedding reception at her new church. She was one of the kitchen volunteers there, she said. They did meals-on-wheels and church events and a dinner every other week for the homeless. "It's very organized," she said. "We have a paid HMC who used to manage a Holiday Inn."

"HMC?"

"Hospitality mission coordinator. That's one of three major missions in our church, hospitality. Hospitality, family values, and biblical truth. Everything our church does has to fit in with one of those missions. We're very accountable."

She spoke at me, not to me, her chin lifted, as if she'd just stepped up to a microphone and was establishing her credentials. Her hair was cut short and she'd gained some weight, but there was still the same tension in her voice, the same quick speech.

"Are you working?" I asked. "I mean, besides all your volunteer stuff."

She put in twenty hours a week at a doc-in-the-box—not at the same site as Will, but under the same management.

"You two sit around at night and complain about your bosses, hunh?" I said, and Alicia shot me a frankly hostile look. I wondered if I'd offended her by reminding her that now her husband had a boss.

"How's Jesse?" I said.

For the first time, she softened. "He's great! Getting straight A's at Tecumseh. And he's gotten very active with student government."

The way she said this—the slight change in intonation for the words "student government"—tipped me off that what Jesse was involved with was nothing as straightforward as student council. Gay and Lesbian Alliance, maybe. "Good," I said.

She said, "He wants to go to law school."

"Perfect!" I said, and this word from my lips surprised me, it was not a concept I normally believed in. But Alicia now was beaming like any proud parent, and I thought how for all her status-seeking and self-righteousness and crazy machinations, she had always, always struck me as a good mother.

~

I glanced up and there was Fred at the other side of the counter, a big smile on his face. "Hello, pumpkin," he said. He held out a sheaf of paper printed off the Internet. "Guess what I just did."

"What?"

"Bought a house in Costa Rica."

The conversation of either side of me (Etta the scheduler, Audrey the nurse) stopped.

"Want to move there with me?" Fred said. "I'd like you to."

"Is this a proposal?" Audrey asked. She and Fred had known each other forever—she'd been babysat by his wife, who always referred to her as the Jenkins brat.

Fred gave her a startled glance. "I guess it is. I mean, I guess it should be, it's a Catholic country, they might not like us living there together without . . ." He tapped his left ring finger.

"I accept."

"And it'd be easier for you to inherit the place when I'm gone," Fred said, not seeming to hear me.

"I said I accept."

"You wouldn't have to work. Life of ease and all."

"Did you hear her? She accepted." Audrey stood up and leaned forward. "Are you deaf, old man?"

Fred started laughing. "Poor old soul," he said. He looked at me. "Really? You accept?"

"Of course."

"Okay. When can you quit? Tomorrow?"

"Two weeks' notice."

"For crying out loud, she's a professional, Fred. Two weeks' notice."

He looked adorably sheepish.

"Aren't you going to kiss her?" Audrey said. "Aren't you going to say you love her and all that?"

Fred waved his hand dismissively. "Oh, she knows that."

"Frederick J. Langford!" I said. "Really! You come here!"

~

As a courtesy, I telephoned my parents' house before I moved away. My mother answered. She didn't seem surprised to hear from me, just rushed because she had a hair appointment. We talked for maybe five minutes. "Is he marrying you so he'll have a nurse, is that it?" she said about Fred. And: "Are you going to let your house sit empty? Have you thought about your brother? He could use a place to live."

Maybe she said other, kinder things, but those are the things I remember.

"You're a hard person," my mother's sister said to me once—not an approving comment. What if I was? I remember thinking. You think an amputee has a choice?

~

Brice creeps back in. *My mother was drinking my blood again last night. . . . I want to be extravagantly loved. Is that too much to ask?* The dark hairs in front of his ears that curled in an almost pubic way. I spotted his hands once on a waiter in a restaurant in San Jose.

Tiny tiny tiny, the things that you remember of your love. Tiny and particular and true. I wonder what Jesse remembers of Brice, how he remembers it (tenderly? angrily? with resignation?), but this is something I will never know.

For a while—almost three years, actually, before I stumbled into my job with the doctors—I cleaned people's houses. This was boring, so I played a little game. Everyone has some disgustingly grimy object or area that they don't notice—a makeup mirror studded with dried toothpaste, the inside door of a fridge streaked with chocolate. I'd wipe this thing off, but leave a tiny part unclean. My test. Almost always, on the next visit the object would be spotless. *Look, she missed a bit*, I imagined my clients saying, cleaning up the offensive area with quiet satisfaction. Most of the time, if you clean up for someone, they take the hint and clean up for themselves. But some people aren't suggestible. Some people are doomed to dirtiness and disarray.

Like Brice. Despite his cuff links and carefully rumpled hair and the meticulous way, even with a very rough instrument, he removed ice from the back steps, his inner life was impossibly messy. His inner life was a room a person might walk into and say, "Can he even walk in here?"

At least, that's what I tell myself. At least, that's what I tell myself on my good days.

~

So here I am, seven months later. Señora Langford de Costa Rica, eager for the rainy season to end.

Dr. Markowitz-Hap, as I now call him, is my e-mail buddy. I searched him out, got his address from Dr. Tatum, whom I briefly worked for. Dr. Markowitz-Hap's an amusing writer: *Contrary to widely published reports that may even have reached Costa Rica, there is nothing new in Midburg. . . . Apparently Alicia is attempting to scale new heights of saintliness and has invited Brice's mother for dinner—*

holy Moses! Maybe he's trying too hard. I can picture him sitting alone in his kitchen at dinner, pondering lines he's going to type for me, reaching for a glass of water as a piece of chicken tumbles down his shirt. I wonder who cleans him up now. Maybe (probably) he has a crush on me. How funny, after all those years we spent together in that office, never seeing each other as a sexual being at all. I get to the Internet café in the village maybe once a week, and when I see there's one message from Hap I feel a tiny jerk of joy. Two messages, I wince. One week there were three, and I was tempted to click their boxes and delete them. A report on Jesse (he's fine, working in a law office for the summer), an emendation to the report (don't think Hap's not mentioning anyone Jesse is dating is in any way a judgment, Hap's a big supporter of gay rights, always has been, although he knows Will and Alicia aren't), an apology for not asking about me, accompanied by a tedious list of questions. There's an art to flirting that Hap clearly hasn't mastered. In a way that makes me like him more.

But why do I care about Hap's e-mails, why do I even welcome them at all? I'm married to a man I love, living with him in a cozy cottage in a steamy, lazy land. Eight months ago I couldn't wait to be here. Desire has a way of stealing from the present moment. I'd like to be fully attentive to the life I'm leading, but perhaps I never will be. Is Fred? I hope so. I like to think that on the road to wisdom he's several steps beyond me.

It's not paradise here. There are break-ins blamed on Nicaraguans. Things are routinely stolen from the mail. The woman who cleans our house strenuously denies poisoning the kitten I adopted, although before I found it stiff and dead under the sofa she referred to it as a *brujita*—little witch—and abruptly left any room it wandered into. Fred has turned his technical powers from my orgasms to our rickety house, and, to put it as the old Alicia might, these days I don't get much. My Bali pads disintegrate in the heat and humidity and, after multiple trips to the Internet café negotiating dial-up connections to bra purchase and shipment, the package arrives at our house slit and empty.

I miss English. Oh, I hear it all the time from Fred, I speak it myself, but what I miss is serpentine sentences, dependent clauses, startling adjective-noun combinations, ironic pauses, alliteration. I miss, when I think about it, Dr. Markowitz—Hap's—English. ("I wouldn't object to Hap," he told me when I ran into him last summer buying gas. "I might even find it flattering.") Missing this is a surprise. I thought Fred's flat declarations would be enough for me. I remember almost all of my high school Spanish. Actually, I speak Fred-level Spanish, which means I can make a straight line from subject to desire. I get what I need. But sometimes, what I want is more complex.

One evening, reaching under the bed for a dropped pencil, I catch a glimpse of something glinting. "What is this?" I say, pulling out what appears to be a pistol.

Fred gives me an incredulous look. "I picked it up in San Isidro," he says—the closest city, where he drives to buy building supplies.

"You know how to use it? It's loaded?" Fred's look turns to frank amazement. He may even be angry. Twenty-five years in the Army— yes, I guess he knows how to use it. I slide the thing back under the bed, nudge it to his side.

He doesn't talk about his wars, not ever. He was in the infantry in Vietnam. There's nothing swaggering about him, but he's surely seen things. Done things. "You ever feel guilty about anything?" I asked once. "Yes," he said, and no more, and I knew enough not to ask, "Tell me what you're *really* thinking."

Fred turns out the light. We lie together in the dark, and soon I start creeping over him like an anaconda. I mount his thigh and rub myself against him. I tell myself that this is rational. I'm a one-legged woman living in a country not my own: of course I want a man with a gun. But probably what I'm feeling is more primal.

He does his technical things. I respond.

He's too old for me. We both know this. It's borrowed time we're on, stolen time, and there will come a day when our threats are not burglars and wild pigs but diabetes and dementia and frail, snappish bones. Sooner or later, I will be our protector.

Dr. Markowitz, Hap, I think as I drift off to sleep. Hap I can't see with a gun. On the other hand, he's probably not impotent. On the other hand, he could trap me in his gossamer net of words. Hap could be my wonderful second husband, once my wonderful first one is gone.

HAP MARKOWITZ

At the VA, I end up with a clinic patient named Charlie Rutherford, who has been seen and dumped by every doctor there. Hindus, Muslims, Sikhs, Buddhists, me—we docs are a polyglot bunch. Charlie Rutherford is not happy with any of us. Charlie Rutherford carries pamphlets showing Jesus hunched under a *big* cross, sweating red drops of blood that fall unevenly inside black teardrop-shaped lines. At least you're a Jew, Charlie says. Those other docs are like heathens.

Charlie has ulcers and a leaky heart valve but he doesn't come here to talk about his health, not at all. "I mean, Albert Einstein could say there was no scientific proof of Jesus, and you know what? I wouldn't care."

I'm not arguing with him. I can't. What I call truth means nothing to a true believer.

True believers: they change the world. They volunteer more hours than they sleep; they blow themselves up at checkpoints; they hold up a Bible for protection when the hit man raises his gun. In song and story and eulogy, they're heroes. Lately, Will has been calling me once or twice a week to go out to dinner, because Alicia is off working at a mission clinic in Liberia. Liberia! Each Saturday morning, Will waits at home for her phone call from Africa. If it weren't for Jesse, Will thinks, Alicia might not come back. How did this happen? Who would have thought that, of all of us, Alicia would end up the true believer?

Last summer, I ran into Caroline at a gas station. The credit card reader at my pump was broken and I had to go inside to pay for gas. When I came out, I spotted, at the deck closest to the road, Caroline putting the nozzle in her tank. I was too self-conscious to yell but I scampered toward her (up and over my island, I must have looked ridiculous) and when she saw me her face melted from surprise to happiness—real happiness, joyous and welcoming—as if I were the very thing she'd hoped to see. I'm sure my face looked the same. At our ages, faces don't lie.

Caroline and I talked maybe five minutes. Our new jobs, the living room set I bought for my condo, the gas mileage of our respective cars. "You take care!" she said as we parted. "You too!" I said back. Once I'd seen her every day. Every day. We'd talked about absorbency and exhortation and why people wanted religion.

"Well, this has been very interesting," I say after ten minutes with Charlie Rutherford. I stand and gesture toward the door, although it will take a cajoling nurse and several more minutes to actually get him out of my exam room. My next patient is a huge relief. "Think you finally found the right combo of pills for me, Doc," he says.

At the gas station, I waved Caroline's car in front of me to the street. She was turning left, I'd go right. Just as she pulled out, she turned her head and glanced back in my direction, more at my car than at me. Then she was gone.

That glance back, what was it? It hit me later that she had wanted me to follow her. Or she'd hoped for me to follow her, but didn't want me pressured by her desire. If I followed her, it had to be my choice. I would have seized that moment if I'd realized. Still, she gave me the chance.

I'm putting a lot on that glance, I know that. But it happened. It meant something.

Caroline's face dissolving into happiness, her glance back: those moments are endless loops for me, always playable in the cinema of my mind.

I'm an average schlump, I'm most people. It's rare that anyone notices me trudging through the world, missing Janis, trying to find the right pills for my patients, enjoying personal praise and a good night's sleep and the bright green of spring grass, yearning for the day when Caroline sees that she and I are meant to be together.